The Affair with Flora

A NOVEL

Cheryle Fisher

This book is a work of fiction. Names, characters, places and incidents either are products of the author's imagination or are used fictitiously. Any resemblance to actual events or locales or persons, living or dead, is entirely coincidental.

Cover photo:
Flora by Tiziano Vecellio, ca. 1515, Galleria degli Uffizi
Florence, Italy.

ISBN-13: 978-1511514637
ISBN-10: 1511514639

Acknowledgements

As always, my love and appreciation to my husband Doug, who always encourages me and offers much-needed advice. His efforts in giving me an outline of the plot as it pertained to the art theft was a great help.

With that said, I used the Galleria degli Uffizi as a backdrop for this story because of my great admiration for that gallery and the priceless treasures of art it houses and protects. This story is fiction and in no way do I intend to suggest that the staff or security are anything less than exceptional. I have been privileged to enjoy this gallery more than once and it is out my great love of the art in it, that I use it in this novel.

To Morgan Richter, my sincere thanks again. Your willingness to guide me through publishing is much appreciated.

To my many friends and family who listen to me go on and on about my stories, thank you! You all know who you are!

"Three things will last forever --- faith, hope and love --- and the greatest of these is love."
1 Corinthians 13:1

To My Best Friend "Fancy Girl,"

For the friendship, joy and laughter

you've brought into my life.

ଊ

Chapter 1

HE WAS WATCHING her and had been for almost half an hour. She was young and definitely inexperienced…not someone who should be on her own with people like him around, but that wasn't going to stop him. She looked to be about twenty-six or so. The younger ones were the easiest to handle, especially for him. He was good-looking and never had any trouble getting the attention of women of any age. She would be the next in a long line of innocent tourists who would supply him with a momentary thrill.

He could see she had money by the designer shoes she wore and the ruby ring on her right hand. Her large leather handbag alone probably cost her well over five hundred euro. He'd seen similar ones on Via Roma, a street that was crammed with shops of all kinds that hungered for the tourist money that flooded Florence at this time of year. Hers though, might have been purchased in Rome.

He had already checked her left hand for a wedding ring. It wouldn't do to take her and then have a husband appear out of nowhere. That had happened once and he'd spent thirty days in jail for that mistake.

She was carrying a typical tourist map and he noticed her checking it often. She was looking for something…a certain store or art gallery perhaps? Stepping out of the tangle of people clogging the narrow street, she had stopped and was leaning against a storefront. Now was his best chance.

"Excuse me, *Signorina*," he said as he approached her, applying a little more accent for her and keeping his voice deeper and more seductive than normal. She was very pretty and for a moment he considered not taking her wallet, but perhaps seducing her instead. But he couldn't do both. He'd tried that once before and it had not turned out well either and he'd had to spend time in jail again.

"You are lost, yes?" he inquired. He stood close to her, but not close enough to scare her off. She didn't say anything, the shyness evident in her face, but just nodded her young pretty head.

"Tell me what you are looking for and I will show you how to get there," he offered. He noticed the clean scent of her perfume; it was designer too.

"I'm looking for the Pitti Palace, but I can't tell from this map where I am now," she replied.

She held the map out to him and he got a good look at the ring on her finger. The rubies were surrounded by small diamonds. He was counting the euro in his head as he approached closer, positioning himself on her left side. He took the map in his left hand as she held the right side. He looked at it for several seconds, inhaling the scent of her perfume and saw her blush, the heat spreading across her nose and cheeks making them pink up. He reminded himself how good he was at playing this game and moved closer to her.

"Signorina, I hope you would not be offended if I told you how beautiful you are."

She said nothing, her embarrassment mixed with her interest and so he decided to see how far he could go with her. He moved close enough to feel her body heat, knowing this one would be so aroused, she wouldn't be aware of what was happening. His right hand slipped effortlessly into the opening of the handbag hanging over her left shoulder.

"If you follow this street, it will take you there. I could escort you, if you wish. It is not a very long walk and it would be my honor to do that for such a beautiful woman." He winked at her, showing off perfect teeth behind his best smile as he lifted her wallet and tucked it behind his back and under his shirt, securing it snugly under his belt.

"Thank you for your help. I think I can find it on my own. I'm meeting my parents there." With that, she smiled, folded her map and walked away as DamianoTravani said good-bye to the ring and retrieved her wallet.

☙

Giulio's feet hurt today, but he wasn't going to complain. Part of the believability of what he did was absolute conformity to the clothing, including the sandals. It was busy outside the Galleria degli Uffizi today and he felt every one of his sixty-six years.

He'd been a street performer for the last ten years, occupying a space directly under the stone statue of Michelangelo Buonarroti. Each column outside the gallery boasted a statue honoring a famous Italian of the Renaissance and he was told his resemblance to the statue of Michelangelo was perfect, even down to the properly curled beard. The beard though, was false. He hated real beards and refused to grow one, knowing it would never look like the one on the statue he was imitating.

His facial features were remarkably like the marble Michelangelo: large forehead, square face, firmly set jaw. Fortunately he still had most of his hair and styled it to look exactly like that of the statue. He wore the same belted tunic and long cloak and the uncomfortable sandals. The defining look was accomplished with face and body paint, the clothing also painted; everything was gray.

It was an easy job except for the sore feet: stand absolutely still and pretend to be made of stone. He would move only if an interested tourist looked like they would pay a euro or two to have their photo taken with him. Then he would pose for the camera, hoping to fill his dish.

After his wife died, he gave up his job working as a bus driver. Carlotta never liked the idea of his being a street performer even though he told her he could make more money than his driving job paid. Carlotta was a good woman and a good wife, but insecure and he understood that about her. Now though, he'd perfected his performance and made a better living posing for photos with tourists than he ever did driving a bus.

As he got older it was getting harder to stand on his feet for so many hours, but he liked what he did. He liked seeing the faces of the people as they marveled at his makeup and clothing. He looked exactly like the stone statue in the niche above him and that made Giulio proud. He considered himself an artist too, just like Michelangelo.

A crowd was gathering now and watching him. He stood perfectly still. He saw a heavy set woman step forward as her husband positioned the camera. Giulio's left hand, which was usually clasped on the edge of the cloak, dropped toward the woman as he placed his arm on her shoulder and she smiled for the camera. They were generous, these two: the husband dropped five euro into the dish and Giulio bowed deeply by way of a 'thank you.'

When no one was looking, he quickly glanced down, trying to estimate the total in his dish. Today it was filling nicely. It was a good day to work the Uffizi and he was happy as he assumed the marble pose of Michelangelo once again.

Chapter 2

"ITALIAN MEN ARE so hot! How could you not want to go to Italy?"

"I don't know. Traveling just doesn't seem to be as much fun as it used to be." Noreen stared into her mocha latte while she fingered the rim of the cup and considered the twelve-plus hour flight to Aeroporto di Firenze-Peretola from Washington Dulles International Airport. Even the layover in Paris didn't boost her mood and she loved Paris.

"Do you own a thermometer?" Rachel asked. "I really think I should take your temperature! You've got to be sick! You have the most fascinating, exciting job any woman could want. You get to travel all over the world, meet interesting people including gorgeous men, you make good money and to top it off, you're smart *and* beautiful and you're not having fun? Girl, there's something seriously wrong with you!"

Rachel sipped her hot cocoa and wished she would have ordered herbal tea. She needed to lose a few more pounds to be able to fit into the 'skinny' dress she'd found at the thrift store. "I'm sorry," she added. "I just don't get it."

Noreen didn't 'get it' either. She was thirty-five, well-educated, came from a good family, had men drooling over her and had just been promoted on a very high-profile case. She was now Special Agent in Charge Noreen Issenlowe, a lead investigator in the FBI's Art Crime Team. It was up to her to trace the person or persons who had stolen a famous painting on loan from the Uffizi Gallery in Florence, Italy, to the Merckle-Westenroth Museum in Seattle, Washington. The original was supposed to have left the Uffizi, but when the crate was unpacked at Merckle-Westenroth and the painting examined, it was determined that the Seattle museum was in possession of a forgery.

"...amazing the food is. Noreen, are you listening to me?" Rachel was going on and on as usual and had tapped Noreen's arm, bringing her out of her trance.

"I'm sorry, Rachel. No I wasn't, to be honest. I drifted a little there. What were you saying?" She deliberately made eye contact, feeling bad that she had ignored her best friend.

They hardly ever had time to get a coffee or share lunch anymore. The hours she worked were bad enough when she was just a field agent, but were even tighter now that she was lead investigator. Her friend's work hours weren't any better. Rachel was a nurse in the ER at Fairfax Hospital in Falls Church, Virginia where they both lived. They had agreed to meet for lunch at a small café called Angie's Place.

Noreen had known Rachel for almost fifteen years. They'd met in college and had liked each other immediately. Even after getting her art degree and applying to the FBI

Academy, they'd kept in touch. Now they lived only five miles apart, but even so, their schedules didn't leave much time for 'girls' day out' as they referred to it. She and Rachel always had fun when they were together. They laughed, talked and reminisced about their college days and the guys they'd dated.

Rachel was happily married and had kids, so only worked part-time at the hospital. Maybe that was the problem, Noreen thought. Rachel had a husband, three great kids *and* a career; her life was full and going somewhere. She had a man to come home to, someone she could talk to about how her day went and someone who loved and desired her. Noreen had the FBI and waiting for her at home, her love bird, Bo. She wasn't getting any warm, fuzzy feelings from Bo; he'd always been a biter.

At the beginning of her career, being a member of the FBI and working for the Department of Justice was thrilling, rewarding and everything she'd hoped it would be. She loved art and art history, though had no artistic talent of her own. She could draw a recognizable stick figure, but that was about it. But that didn't take anything away from her love of beautiful artwork. She appreciated the mastery and talent of the great Renaissance painters and this job allowed her to travel to some of the world's finest galleries and museums. Florence, home of the Uffizi Gallery and Pitti Palace Museum, was one of her favorite places to be sent on assignment. She was going again in two days and now was trying to figure out why that knowledge didn't send her heart racing with excitement as it usually did.

"Maybe I do know," Noreen continued.

"Well tell me, okay? Because you know there are times that I would gladly trade places with you. Not forever; I'd miss Tony and the kids. But there are some days that I dream about driving around Italy on the back of a Ducati driven by some gorgeous Italian guy with no laundry waiting to be folded and no kids screaming at each other!"

Noreen laughed. That was the best thing about Rachel. She was funny, outrageous and passionate about life. Right now, Noreen wanted some of that passion.

"On second thought, don't tell me," Rachel went on. "I think I know why the blue mood. You need a man: a beautiful, tanned, muscled Italian who will wait on you hand-and-foot, who wants nothing more than to kiss you and then when he does, he'll pick you up, carry you into his bedroom and make love to you all night long! Yep! That's what you need! I'm married to an Italian and even though he's only half, he's got to be one of the most passionate guys in the state of Virginia! Imagine a full-blooded Italian!" Rachel fanned her face with her hand as if suddenly overcome with passion's heat.

"Well," Noreen said laughing, "when you're right, you're right!"

"Listen. I've seen it coming on you like a bull charging a matador's cape. It was only a matter of time before you figured out that you need a warm body to cuddle up to at night instead of that pistol the department issued you. You won't get any satisfaction there, girl! I knew you'd figure it out sooner or later and I'm happy it's sooner. Neither of us is getting any younger!" Rachel swallowed the last of her cocoa and then went on.

"How about getting back with that gorgeous agent Alex Channing? If I were you, I'd slap my handcuffs on him and drag him down the aisle of the nearest church before he got away again! You know he's always wanted you. You've had him drooling for a long time now!"

Noreen smiled. "He's gorgeous alright and we've had some great times together, but I heard he got engaged. No prospect there anymore."

Rachel's face fell. "Wow," she said, "that's a bummer. You should have latched on to him while you had the chance." Rachel bit her tongue when she saw the look on Noreen's face. "I'm sorry. I shouldn't have said that."

"It's okay. What's done is done. I'm over him," she said. Sometimes even FBI agents had to lie.

"There are other guys out there," Rachel continued. "Go to Italy and find one! Find an artist! That would be *so* great! I can see you married to a fantastic artist who would have you posing naked for him all day while he sipped Chianti and painted your portrait!"

"Why am I naked if he's painting my portrait?"

"Why not?" Rachel answered and gave Noreen a scowl, then added, "You're worse off than I thought!"

They both laughed for a long time. Just being with Rachel made Noreen feel better. 'Girls' day out' was the best medicine, but it was getting late and she had a few details and some packing to take care of before she left for Italy.

"I've really got to get going," she said. "This has been so much fun and I really feel better about this whole trip. I might just take your advice and look for some hot Michelangelo to flirt with. Who knows, maybe I'll come home with a portrait of myself."

"Skip the portrait and come home with Michelangelo!" Rachel exclaimed and they both laughed as they walked out into the June sunshine.

Chapter 3

THE SIX HUNDRED euro he'd taken from the girl's wallet and the three hundred he'd gotten from selling her credit cards was going to go a long way toward paying off Luca "L'Insegnante" Bocchio. His nickname meant "The Teacher" and he'd come by it honestly. He'd taught secondary school, was fired for some illegal activity on the school grounds and then had gotten into the 'banking business.' He now worked for a local criminal organization and loaned money at ridiculously high interest rates to people who couldn't pass the credit checks required by legitimate banks. If he wasn't paid on time, he would 'teach' you not to be late with your payments in the future.

Bocchio was heavy-set with deceitful, narrow eyes and even in the warm weather, wore his trademark black overcoat. It was a cloak almost, whose extra length accentuated the man's short stature and reminded Travani of the Dracula character in the movies. The association was appropriate: Bocchio's career was sucking the blood out of innocent victims.

Travani had become another victim. He'd been a little short of cash and had gone to Bocchio for the loan of a small sum: one thousand euro. Nine hundred would at least cover some of the fifteen hundred he now owed, which included the inflated interest. Bocchio wasn't going to be happy that it wasn't the full amount, but Travani was fairly certain The Teacher would grant him a reprieve when he was told about the payment for services Travani expected soon. It was a large sum of cash, enough to pay off Bocchio and never need to borrow from him again.

Travani's apartment was off Via del Corso behind the Piazza de' Donati, an area centrally located in the heart of old Florence and on a street so narrow that only scooters could traverse it. He lived up an even narrower staircase in a cramped, one-bedroom place with a monthly rent that kept him living from one petty theft to another, unless he got a commissioned work, drew on the street for tourists or sold one of his paintings. He knew if he put more time into the legal endeavors, he'd be better off financially and his father would be happier, but he enjoyed the thrill of stealing and couldn't imagine giving it up for a full-time job. He didn't dream of being the best pickpocket in Florence…he just liked his freedom.

Lately though, there were times that he wanted a more settled life. He wanted to give up the streets and his apartment and have a small house somewhere away from the crowds and noise…maybe in the country. He wanted more than the occasional liaison with a pretty woman whose name he barely knew. He wanted a good wife like his mother had been, wanted to come home to someone who loved him and lately, he wanted to have children. He was the only male child and if he didn't marry and have a son, his uncles with sons would carry on the family name, but his father's line would end.

And he was starting to get a sinking feeling every time he snatched a purse or wallet. The pretty girl today had photos: there was one of her…with her parents maybe? She looked like them. Her smile and dimples were the same as the older woman's, her hair the color of the man's. And another photo: a handsome, young man and the girl, their arms wrapped around in an affectionate embrace. She loves him very much, too much for the boy to be her brother. He is an American soldier. Did he give her the ruby ring?

He remembered his mother always teaching him about truth and integrity. From the time he was a small child, she'd told him about God and how he should live a good life that honored Him. His father took the family to Mass and kneeling in the massive cathedral, the statues of Christ and his mother Mary larger-than-life, Damiano had listened and obeyed his mother.

But in his teens, he'd started getting into occasional trouble, committing small, petty crimes with friends who didn't know his mother or the values she taught. As time went on and after his mother died quickly from an aggressive cancer, Travani's life continued to spiral downward and the lure of the streets replaced the holiness of Mass. Her death had shaken the very foundations of faith that she had tried to instill into him and he walked away from God, blaming Him for not saving her.

He was thinking about all these things as he held the money and admitted for the first time that his stealing was affecting real people, people with families and friends they loved, people that he'd refused to think of before now. They were people like his mother. He had always been able to justify his stealing if he didn't think about the people he was hurting, but lately it was getting harder to do that.

He heard a knock at the door. "Who is it?" he asked as he stood near the door, his hand ready to disengage the lock. When you lived the life he did, it was never a good idea to open the door without finding out who was on the other side.

"Open the door, Travani," the voice instructed and he knew it was Luca Bocchio.

"I was on my way over to see you," he lied as he opened the door and Bocchio's over-muscled bodyguard stepped forward, peered around the room and then motioned that everything was okay. Bocchio sauntered in, his eyes never leaving Travani.

"You have something for me?" The Teacher smiled, sounding as if he were expecting Travani to hand in some overdue homework. He was wearing the trademark coat and as usual, he was perspiring heavily under the weight of it.

"I have your money right here," he said as he handed over the nine hundred euro and Bocchio immediately went to work counting it.

"You are a little short, are you not?" he asked.

"Yes, but I am expecting a large payment on a special commission I just finished. It has to be approved by my client and as soon as that is done, I will be able to pay you the balance I owe." Travani was getting nervous; Bocchio suddenly looked unhappy.

"You know that is not the way I work." Bocchio frowned as he pocketed the nine hundred. "Who is your client?"

"Giorgio Galiazzi."

"He is dangerous, this man Galiazzi. I told you that," Bocchio warned. "Do not be mistaken by his fine suits and expensive jewelry. If you continue to do business with him, you will end up in prison and consider yourself lucky. If your luck runs out, you will end up dead."

Travani had to chuckle to himself. He could find himself dead by The Teacher's hand too. They were both dangerous, but Galiazzi had connections in the art world and was starting to throw work Travani's way; not often and not legal, but it was good money and he liked copying an original master on canvas more than stealing purses and wallets.

"He said his client is a very wealthy man from Dubai," Travani went on.

The Teacher was interested. He knew that Travani was an exceptional artist. He also knew that if Galiazzi was involved, this 'commission' was illegal and that Travani was keeping that fact to himself.

"He wanted Titan's *Flora*," Travani added.

"Hah! That shows you how stupid these foreigners are!" Bocchio said disdainfully. "That is a small, insignificant painting. He should have asked for the *Mona Lisa*!"

"Well," Travani replied, "I am happy he wants *Flora*. I love to paint her and *Mona Lisa* is a dreary old hag compared to my *Flora!*"

Bocchio chuckled. "I like you Travani, but do not let that go to your head. If you do not get me the rest of my money in ten days, you will see how persuasive I can be. And in ten days, you will owe me the added sum of two hundred euro; interest, you understand." Travani understood and nodded.

Bocchio and the body guard turned to leave and as he walked out the door, The Teacher called over his shoulder, "Ten days!"

Chapter 4

ON THE INTERMINABLY long flight from Dulles International to Paris, Noreen had plenty of time to consider the details of what the FBI knew so far about the theft of the priceless painting. She could never sleep during a flight and it was a good time to go over her notes when all the passengers, especially the small children, were asleep.

Her advancement to lead investigator was deserved as far as she was concerned. She'd worked her heart out on this case because the missing painting was one of her favorites. She knew that the brass higher up were watching her and she knew this assignment could lead to a big promotion. The head of the Art Crime Team was retiring in a few months and she had her sights set on filling that vacancy. Everything depended on the success of finding the painting or at least, finding out how the theft had been accomplished. The notorious workings of the art underworld were not as black and white as what was portrayed in the movies and any knowledge gained would go a long way toward understanding how that underworld operated and toward advancing her career.

She knew from her training that the United States had a very low incidence of art thefts, but that it was the preferred venue to *sell* stolen art. The FBI's Art Crime Team had recovered 2,650 art objects since its inception in 2004, with a combined total value of approximately one hundred, fifty million dollars. She was proud of that fact taking into account that only two to six percent of stolen art objects world-wide were ever recovered and the thieves prosecuted.

The FBI also ran the National Stolen Art File, a database of stolen art and cultural property. Missing objects were submitted for entry by law enforcement agencies in the U.S. and abroad.

Italy topped the list of countries with the most art theft crimes, but also had the world's oldest and largest unit dedicated to the recovery of stolen works. It was known by its acronym, TPC: the *Tutela Patrimonio Culturale* or Division for the Protection of Cultural Heritage. It was founded in 1969 after the theft of Caravaggio's *Nativity* by the Cosa Nostra from a church in Palermo. The TPC was under the jurisdiction of the Carabinieri, the military branch of law enforcement in Italy.

The other major player in trying to stem the rising tide of art crime was Interpol's Stolen Works of Art Department. It acted as an information-gathering point for world art police, keeping track of reported crimes and stolen art in its massive database. Interpol ranked art crime as the fourth highest-grossing criminal business with only drugs, arms and human trafficking ahead of it.

Noreen's love of art, its beauty, history and value served to make her relentless in tracking down the organized crime organizations and wealthy world figures who would steal the very foundation of any country's cultural heritage through acquisition of their art objects.

From Paris to Florence, she'd been able to take a quick power nap and after being awakened by a very vocal and distressed baby, she'd thought about what Rachel had said about needing more than the FBI in her life. She *was* getting older. She felt it more ever day. She felt it especially on the dark, cold nights of winter when she would admit how much she wished she were sleeping next to a warm male body.

That body could have belonged to Alex Channing. He was her age, very smart, athletic, sensitive and very easy to look at. He came from a good, solid family, had had a few serious relationships before her, but had decided that she was the one he wanted permanently in his future.

They had met at the Academy firing range, both getting in some practice time, keeping their skills sharp. He worked in Internal Affairs and she had noticed his good looks even before he introduced himself at the firing range. He carried his well-muscled body with confidence and she had immediately noticed his thick brown hair and blue-green eyes. They had dated, whenever their schedules permitted, keeping their budding romance secret; the FBI didn't approve of agents being romantically involved with each other…not during training anyway.

Noreen knew he was serious about her. The subject of marriage was coming up more often and when he kissed her, she wanted to make *him* permanent in *her* future. But her career took precedence over her private life. Alex knew that and their relationship had ended. She was surprised when she'd found out he'd gotten engaged and convinced herself she was happy for him, but felt the loss of what her life could have been with him.

Her father was sheriff in Cumberland, Virginia, a small town nestled among the forests and farmlands in the central part of the state. He had lived there all his life and had married and raised his family there. He was a man who was admired for his intelligence, honesty and fairness.

Her brother Cody had joined the force after attending the police academy in Richmond and had come back to his hometown to become a deputy, carrying on the tradition of public service of the Issenlowe family. Even her mother was involved in law enforcement in the small town, managing the dual roles of police dispatcher and 911 operator.

Noreen idolized her only brother. He was three years older than she was and was her protector and best friend. He never quit pushing her to get into law enforcement. Cody loved helping people and that's how he saw the job of deputy.

Noreen though, loved art. She'd gotten her master's degree in art history with a minor in criminal justice, planning on a career in the art field until a fateful day in October. Cody, who was only twenty-five at the time, was involved in a high-speed chase with a burglary suspect. It was late on a drenching, windy night when the suspect rammed his four-by-four into Cody's patrol car, causing it to skid off the road and into a tree, killing Cody instantly.

The devastation his death caused her and her parents was indescribable, but it was after the initial shock had worn off, that Noreen knew she wanted to honor her brother. She would use her degree as her ticket into the FBI's Art Crime Team; the perfect blend of her life's love of art with Cody's desire to make a difference in helping people.

Once she'd decided on the FBI Academy, her drive to excel and the demands of being a woman in a mostly male organization, had taught her to put thoughts of love and marriage on a back burner. A family required time and attention and she couldn't have the stressful career she'd chosen and do justice to a husband and children too. She'd always thought that those things would come later. Now she was trying to determine if that time had indeed come, but Alex was no longer available.

As she sat in the back of the taxi on her way to her hotel, she decided that it was time to consider starting a relationship. It was time to start looking for that warm, male body to snuggle up with at night, wherever he might be...maybe even in Italy.

She remembered what Rachel had said about getting married to an artist and suddenly a feeling like a small, electrical charge surged deep within her. Yes, she admitted, the thought of being married to a talented artist excited her. She wanted someone like Michelangelo or Raphael whose talent in rendering the human figure revealed the sensitivity and passion of the artist's soul. She could love a man like that very easily and wanted that kind of passion in her life.

The taxi pulled up in front of her hotel. She paid the driver and finally felt the excitement she always got in coming to Florence. Her attitude had changed, but she knew it had changed for the better. She had let Alex Channing slip through her fingers and she wouldn't make that mistake again with someone else.

ଓ

He was across the street watching from a café when the taxi pulled up in front of the hotel and she got out. The June sun was setting quickly and through the binoculars, he saw the pink glow of the sky over Florence leave her skin radiantly beautiful and the golden highlights of her hair more striking than anything an artist could convey on canvas. He would not give himself away, but would keep his eyes on her wherever she went. He would know everything about every person she came in contact with.

He watched her pay the cab driver, then carry her bag into the hotel. She was beautiful!

Chapter 5

VINCENZO SARTORI WAS the Assistant Head of Acquisitions, a husband and father, dependable and a hard worker and he never gave it a second thought when he was approached by a man named Abdel Kadir about the possibility of 'acquiring' a masterpiece from the Galleria degli Uffizi. Now though, his hands were shaking and he'd been having the distinct feeling that he was being watched. The curator and Sartori's immediate boss, the Head of Acquisitions, wanted to see him in the curator's office.

His background, education, references and work history and were as clean as the shine on a new Ferrari and even though he didn't own one, he planned to in the very near future. He was approaching sixty, still good-looking if you asked Angelina, and was tired of being second dog at the gallery. He should have been promoted when the last head of acquisitions left, but the higher-ups had gone with a younger talent, an Italian who had made himself a solid name and reputation at the Louvre, but who had decided he didn't like life in Paris.

After the announcement of who would be getting the sought-after position, Sartori's loyalty to the gallery's administration had cooled considerably and he had seen the benefits of one or two illicit 'acquisitions.' As long as acquiring them could be executed with minimal risk to himself, replacing a masterpiece with a good forgery would pay off in millions of euro. Those euro would go a long way toward giving him the kind of lifestyle he wanted and would exact revenge on those in power for not giving him the promotion.

Besides, there was Angelina to consider. She had strolled seductively into his life a year ago, statuesque and beautifully alluring just like the model she was. Even though she only worked locally, she was electrifying, twenty years his junior and wanted what he could give her. She wanted him in bed too and that made the risk of the theft worth taking. He was tired of meeting her in secret, tired of the stress of hiding a mistress and tired of his wife. This current plan was perfect and bigger than the last ones he'd orchestrated. It would be a one-time risk and then a trip out of the country with Angelina before the fake was discovered. His life would be good.

The dealings of the art world had, and always would be, secretive and mysterious. Acquiring and selling valuable pieces, whether paintings or precious artifacts, lent itself to illegal opportunities due to the great monetary values involved and the general hush-hush attitude of people in the art world. People who dealt in art theft and forgeries managed and orchestrated them off the radar of law enforcement for the most part and even so, museums and galleries were hesitant to admit to losing any of the works in their keeping and more often than not, didn't even report small losses to law enforcement agencies.

Sartori was a little fish swimming outside the big pond of organized crime syndicates who were the serious players in art theft. He kept his operation small and used local petty criminals who could be trusted to carry out the work of obtaining the forgeries and switching the originals for the fakes.

This new job had a big payoff, one too lucrative to pass up: twenty million euro. He knew that Titan's *Flora* was due to be loaned out to a prestigious museum in the United States and Kadir, the buyer's representative, jumped at the chance to acquire it. Sartori needed a forgery to switch with the original. After he collected the twenty million for the original, he would have time to leave Italy before the fake was detected. The American museum would accept the forgery as the real painting; it would be on display for six weeks and then returned to the Uffizi. By then, he and Angelina would be gone and enjoying their new lives somewhere in the Caribbean. He'd already decided on the color of the Ferrari: he wanted black.

He'd enlisted Giorgio Galiazzi, a legitimate dealer and art collector and a man whom he knew wasn't shy about dealing in the art underworld for the right price. Galiazzi had worked well where the first two thefts were concerned, but expected a generous cut for his services this time. His fee though, would be small compared to the full pay-off. Galiazzi had the important contacts: people who supplied the aged canvases and age-appropriate paints and he had found the right forger, a man he'd used before and whose work was impeccable.

He had blackmailed the head guard for gallery security, Rico Panello, to help with the actual switch. In the recent past, Panello had taken up gambling and hadn't been very lucky at it. His debts mounted, but he'd been able to keep them secret from his employers; that kind of a personal problem always resulting in termination. The integrity of the staff was an important part of maintaining security at the gallery.

Sartori had found out and when the opportunity for the first theft came his way, Sartori had convinced Panello to help, promising to keep Panello's gambling habit hidden and assuring the guard that there would be enough money coming his way to pay off all his debts.

After the second theft, Panello's debts were paid and he'd learned his lesson and had quit gambling. Sartori wouldn't let him leave so easily though and was now blackmailing him. This was to be the last theft, Sartori promising that he was leaving the country afterwards, Panello would make a nice sum of money and his gambling history would never come to light. Panello had agreed to help, looking forward to several thousand euro under the table and to getting Sartori off his back for good. Everything had gone well. As far as Sartori knew, the forged painting was now in the museum in the United States and nobody was the wiser.

The problem was that his contact, Abdel Kadir, had not made it to the appointed rendezvous to receive the real painting and deliver the twenty million euro. Calls to Kadir's cell number had not gone through and Kadir had not contacted Sartori. Only Kadir knew who the buyer was or how to contact him. The exchange was to take place seven days ago and now Sartori feared he was out his twenty million. *Flora* was at Angelina's apartment under her watchful eye. They should be sunning themselves on some Caribbean beach right now and instead, Sartori's ulcer was acting up and Galiazzi was breathing down his neck for his money. Angelina was nagging him to find Kadir, get the money owed them and get rid of the painting and he was trying to convince himself that it was only his nerves playing tricks on him, that he wasn't actually being followed. Sartori was dangerously close to a full-blown panic attack.

As he walked down the hall toward the curator's office, he tried to control the shaking of his hands. Nobody had told him what the meeting was about. Perhaps there was a new painting that had become available and he was needed to handle the details. Perhaps it was another boring budgetary meeting. No matter what he wanted to believe, he knew he might be in big trouble. His ulcer was gnawing away at his insides and by the time he knocked and heard the curator call him in, he was feeling nauseous.

Chapter 6

THE PIAZZA DELLA Signoria was a large open plaza and a welcomed relief from the crowded streets. Since the fourteenth century, it had been an assembly point for the citizens of Florence. Excavations done during the 1980's had uncovered many archeological finds dating back to medieval, Roman and Etruscan times, some even dating to the Bronze Age. Now it was a favorite gathering place of tourists and was surrounded by a plethora of shops and cafés with outdoor seating.

The iconic and familiar cathedral Santa Maria del Fiore, also called the Duomo, dominated the surrounding area and was only a short walk away, as were most of the popular tourist sites including the Galleria degli Uffizi, the Palazzo Pitti, the Ponte Vecchio and Santa Croce. People from all over the world came year-round to visit this historic city and the streets, shops, cafés and museums were always full and busy.

It felt good to be in the open plaza headed to the Uffizi on this mild June day. Noreen had gotten some sleep the night before and was now on her way to meet with the head of security for the Uffizi, Signore Umberto Castagno. She would start at the bottom of the gallery's staff today; her jet lag was still plaguing her and she knew a meeting was scheduled for the next day with the administrative staff.

The Galleria degli Uffizi was a massive, three-story, U-shaped building, the short end of the 'U' facing the Arno River. Noreen had studied its history purely for her own information and because it was one of her favorite galleries.

It was originally commissioned by Cosimo I de' Medici as a central office for the city administration, hence the name *ufficio*, which means 'office'. Giorgio Vasari became the chief architect in 1559 and because of space limitations and its proximity to the river, Vasari had to deal with many problems in its design owing to the poor load-bearing capacity of the soil.

The gallery had been converted and renovated many times, including in the aftermath of a shocking bomb attack in 1993. Much of the gallery was now being redesigned so that the eventual exhibition area would be tripled to 215,000 square feet. Treasures which were previously stored were now being made accessible to the public, much of this taking place since 2004.

After getting some directions, she found Castagno's office tucked away on the first floor, knocked at the door and heard him instruct her to enter. He rose from his rather messy desk, his arm extended to shake her hand. He was short, about fifty and balding, but had a pleasant smile and gentle eyes; not at all what she expected from a man in charge of protecting some of the most valuable treasures of the Western world.

"Signorina Issenlowe, it is my pleasure to meet you at last. I must say, you are not what I expected for an FBI agent."

She smiled. "I'm happy to finally meet you too, Signore, and I too am surprised. You seem much more congenial in person. On the phone, you sounded much more...serious. I hope that doesn't offend you." He motioned her to a chair opposite his desk and then took his seat.

"Not at all. Sometimes it is necessary to be somewhat firm in our business. Is that not so?" He held a pack of cigarettes out to her, but she waved her hand to decline. She had never smoked and wasn't about to take up the habit.

"Do you mind if I smoke?" he asked. She shook her head and he lit up, taking a long drag before the smoke exited his nose and mouth and formed a heavy cloud above his head. Smoking in buildings was now so uncommon in the United States that she was always taken aback when she traveled overseas and saw how prevalent the habit still was in other countries. It was his office and she wasn't about to deny him his vice.

"Now Signorina, if I understand our phone conversation, you believe the original painting was exchanged for the forgery *before* it left Italy. Is that correct?" He took another drag on the cigarette and carefully tapped the ashes into a metal ashtray. Noreen couldn't remember the last time she'd seen an ashtray.

"Yes, I believe it was exchanged after it left the Uffizi, probably at Aeroporto di Firenze or en route before it arrived there."

"And how have you come to this conclusion?"

"When the painting arrived in Denver, its first stop on its way to Seattle, our department had two agents meet the plane and supervise the ground crew who loaded and unloaded passenger baggage. They watched everything that came off that plane and everything that went back in. The crate that contained the painting was never touched, except to be examined by customs agents. Even then, our agents accompanied the crate, which was never opened. They had their eyes on it at all times.

"Two of our agents from the Seattle office met the plane when it landed there. After the passenger baggage was unloaded, the agents supervised the unloading of the crate, its transfer to the armored truck and rode with it to the museum." She took a shallow breath. The cigarette smoke had drifted her way and was stinging her eyes. She continued.

"The curator of the museum and the head of acquisitions both checked the painting over thoroughly shortly after its arrival. Foremost, they wanted to be sure that the painting hadn't been damaged in transit. It was the head of acquisitions who noticed the tiny imperfection in the left hand corner of the painting. It was so miniscule that he had to use a magnifying glass to see it clearly and it was then that he discovered it was a cross."

She blinked hard, her eyes stinging worse now. He must have noticed because he promptly pressed the remaining half of the cigarette into the bottom of the ashtray and put the ashtray behind him on the windowsill.

"Yes, our experts have gone over the painting very carefully. It is an exquisite forgery, that is certain. The canvas, the paint...they are exceptional. But Signorina, does it not seem strange, unheard of even, that a forger would go to so much trouble to create such a perfect copy and then destroy the illusion of authenticity by painting a cross in the corner? Who would do such a thing? Any artist worth his talent would not give the fake away. The worth of a master forger is that his fake is never discovered for what it truly is."

"I have no answer to your question, Signore Castagno. I've never come across anything like this before and I've no idea why a forger would do that, unless that's exactly what he wanted to do."

"But why? That is the question, is it not?"

"Yes, it certainly is," she said. She'd thought about that for quite a while and even with her advanced training in the Behavioral Analysis Unit, she couldn't shed any light on that question. The only reason that made any sense was that the artist was narcissistic and just *had* to leave his mark, as if to say 'Kilroy was here!'

"Have you spoken with anyone at the TPC?" Castagno was starting to look like he needed the other half of that cigarette; he kept glancing at the pack on his desk.

"Yes. The museum in Seattle initially notified your office. Our office was contacted by the TPC. They were advised that the FBI would do everything to determine if the painting was switched after it entered the United States. I was initially assigned to handle the case and after my report, the TPC asked for the FBI's help in recovering the painting."

"Well, Signorina, anything that I can do to aid you in that pursuit, please let me know. Everyone here at the Uffizi is anxious to solve this puzzle and bring our painting back to its home. We are all proud and protective of our collection and we are very happy that you will be helping us."

He glanced at the pack of cigarettes again and she decided it was time to go before his withdrawals got any worse. She could see his hands shaking and then realized that maybe it wasn't the lack of a cigarette that was bothering him; maybe it was nervousness.

She got up and Castagno did likewise. "I'll want to speak with some of your employees, but I'll do that tomorrow. It was a very long flight and I'm afraid I have a very bad case of jet lag. I'm anxious to continue my investigation, but I really need this day to rest and to prepare for the meeting with the administration."

"I know just what you mean. I am the same way. So I will be seeing you tomorrow, yes? We will get started then and see if we can solve the mystery of this master forger and I pray, find the real painting."

He shook her hand again and saw her to the door. On her way out, she thought about just spending an hour or so in the Uffizi, wandering the rooms and enjoying the art. Even the few times she'd been in Florence, she'd never really seen all of it. She'd never been able to see it at a tourist's pace with no work obligations attached. But she *was* jetlagged and after being in Castagno's smoke-filled office, she needed some fresh air.

☙

He waited in the courtyard, well-hidden so that she wouldn't see him and close enough not to need the binoculars. Her meeting with the Head of Security didn't last long and as he waited, he watched the street artists setting up for the day.

After twenty minutes, he saw her emerge from the security office. He didn't wonder about what was said at their meeting; he could find out later. For now, he kept his eyes on her as she strolled the courtyard. She was watching the human statues, in particular, a man posing as Michelangelo.

Chapter 7

THE COURTYARD BETWEEN the long sides of the gallery wings was called the Piazzale degli Uffizi and Noreen strolled there, watching the street artists, their easels set up and their paints and pencils ready for work. For a reasonable fee, you could have your portrait drawn, choosing from a serious likeness or a caricature depending on the artist. There were watercolor artists creating familiar sights of Florence, mostly the Duomo and Ponte Vecchio, and they worked seemingly unaware of the tourists unless it looked like they might be able to make a sale.

She loved watching the street performers who would dress in costumes to make themselves look like human statues. To her way of thinking, they were artists in their own right. The body and hair paint and detailed costumes were remarkable in obtaining the look of hard stone. Sometimes they would be able to hold a pose so perfectly still that when they purposefully moved, it completely startled an unsuspecting tourist who never realized the statue was a living person.

All along the facing wings of the gallery were twenty-eight columns with niches containing stone statues of famous Italians: Dante, Galileo, Donatello, da Vinci and Machiavelli, to name a few. She was now in front of a man who was dressed and posed exactly like the real statue located above him. He was Michelangelo's human twin and she had seen him in this same spot during her last trip to Florence five years before.

Of all the 'human statues' she'd seen on her previous trips to Florence, he was the best in her opinion. No matter how long she watched him, she never saw him move…not even his chest as he breathed. Today though, as she stared at him, his eyes moved and fixed on hers. Even this imperceptible movement from him startled her.

"I have seen you before, Signorina!" he exclaimed, continuing to hold his pose, but smiling now as if she were a close friend that he had missed and was excited to see again. For a moment, she was so taken aback that she didn't know how to respond. She returned his smile.

"Yes, I was here five years ago and I remember you too. You're very good at what you do," she said finally, watching him come down off the box he was perched on. She couldn't believe he was actually moving, let alone coming toward her and giving her the standard European greeting: kissing the air by each of her cheeks. He didn't actually touch her so as not to spoil his makeup.

"I never forget a beautiful face! I am glad you have come back to Florence! Did you come just to see me or are you here for other reasons?" She could tell that under the makeup, he was old enough to be her father.

"I come occasionally for business. My name is Noreen." He didn't need to know what kind of business, even though she knew that people who 'worked' the streets were very astute about what went on around them; they knew all kinds of people and knew what they were up to. Michelangelo here might provide her with some usable clues as to the theft of the painting.

"I am Giulio and I am pleased to meet you." He was smiling at her, a look of expectation on his face and she was getting uncomfortable. When Rachel had told her to come back from Italy with Michelangelo, this isn't what Noreen had pictured! If this man was making a move right now, she was going to excuse herself and escape into the crowds in the Piazza della Signoria.

"You were visiting the Uffizi, no? That means you are a lover of fine works of art!" The expectant look was still in his eyes, mixed with excitement now.

"I love art, especially Italian art," she said. His eyes seemed to light up even more with that comment.

"Your business? It deals with art?"

"Yes. I'm working this trip."

"It is time for my break. Would you have coffee with me?" He pointed and continued, "You see, there? It is a café and we could get some espresso. My feet are...how is it said...killing me? I stand for many hours a day and I would like to talk to you about art while I rest them. I would be honored if you would join me."

She was tired too and could use an espresso. The café was located on the plaza, a public place and safe enough.

She reminded herself that sometimes more information was passed on in idle chat over coffee than through any other means. "I think that would be a wonderful idea," she said.

Giulio tucked his money box under his arm and they walked the short distance toward the café and took a table outside.

He was a pleasant gentleman, one who reminded her of her father in many ways. In the time they'd spent sipping their coffee and chatting, they had talked about different artists who worked the streets in front of the Uffizi. Most of them worked this area regularly as the tourists were always thick here. Giulio seemed to know them all; they were almost like a family according to him. He told her most of them had worked this area for years.

He really seemed more interested in telling her all about his son, who he pointed out quite early in the conversation, was about her age and unmarried. According to Giulio, his son was a good man and a masterful artist.

Noreen had to admit that the minute the word 'artist' had come out of Giulio's mouth, it reminded her again about what Rachel had said about marrying an artist and about how that thought had intrigued her. Giulio was very interested in getting them together and she realized it might be worth her while to meet him for two reasons: Giulio worked the streets and could be a wealth of information that would help her with her investigation and she could tell Rachel that she'd met an Italian artist and therefore, her love life wasn't as desperate as Rachel made it out to be.

They made a date for dinner that evening, eight o'clock at the same café and after touching up his lips with a tube of gray face paint, they said 'good-bye' and Michelangelo walked back toward the Uffizi.

After he'd gone, she realized that he was such a personable man that she hadn't even given a thought to how odd if must have been to onlookers to see a woman having a cup of coffee with a statue and she wished she'd had a photo to show Rachel.

☙

It surprised him to see the street performer talk to her, but shocked him that they'd left together.

He watched them for almost thirty minutes as they sat outside Café Tortino, sipping their coffees and chatting. It seemed a pleasant meeting; she was smiling anyway and didn't look nervous. Did she know this guy?

He took out his notepad and pen and made a note to check into 'Michelangleo's' background. There were ways of getting any information he needed about anybody she came in contact with. He wanted to know why she had obviously agreed to have coffee with him.

He put the notebook back into his pocket and after her back was turned, he took up a position far enough behind to keep hidden, but close enough to see every move she made.

Chapter 8

AFTER THE PREPARED canvas and paints were delivered, Travani was left to his work. He didn't know the man who had made the delivery, but as before, he knew this man would also pick up the copy when it was finished. He also knew that he would not have any contact with Galiazzi until it was time to get paid for his work. Galiazzi always delivered the money himself; nobody could be trusted with that much cash.

It had taken Travani eight weeks of ten-hour days to complete *Flora.* For those eight weeks, he had been her intimate lover as he applied the paint carefully to the canvas and brought her radiance to life. He was familiar with every inch of her exquisite body, having drawn her many times in chalk on the streets of Florence. He knew that she would eventually leave him, a substitute for the real *Flora,* who would probably leave the country and though he pushed that thought out of his mind, he knew someone was going to pay a heavy price for the original. He knew too, that if he was caught, what he was doing could put him in prison for a long time.

The other two forgeries he had done were less important paintings, but beautiful in their own right. Without being told, he knew they were only a test to see how good he was and if he could copy an important work sometime in the future. He also wondered if that test included determining if he could keep his mouth shut about what he was doing. As *Flora* had taken shape before him, he wondered if he'd passed the test.

Though he loved painting her, this time his work had left him with a bad feeling. When he'd finished and had finally turned over the forgery, he was left feeling her loss as though she were real. She was gone now and losing her saddened him in ways he hadn't even expected. It was the same feeling he had about his mother.

Today he would draw her again, his *Flora*, but not on canvas. After he retrieved his chalk and put on his knee pads, he searched his backpack for the photo of her. Bringing it out, he laid it reverently on the street next to his money box and taking a piece of chalk, laid down the first lines of her rebirth, this time on the streets of Florence. He knew that having a photo of the original for comparison would impress upon tourists the extent of his artistic abilities and that in turn, would mean a fuller money box.

The tourists were already starting to gather and watch, but he kept his head down, his eyes intent as he gazed into the beginnings of hers. As he continued, the comments and the sighs of appreciation started as the tourists nudged each other and pointed at the beginnings of her sensuous, heart-shaped lips.

As the beauty of her image emerged from the gray, dreary stones, the inevitable questions started. How long would the drawing last? Was he sad when it rained and his work was washed away? Where did he study art? Did he do canvas paintings too? They were all questions he had heard and answered many times before, but he enjoyed talking about his *Flora*, her history and about the original master who created her in 1515, Tiziano Vecellio, known by only one name: Titan. And so again, he would tell their story.

Titan was one of the most important artists of the sixteenth century and mastered the use of color, making his portraits rise above those of any other artist of the age. He was able to create perfect skin tones and preferred to use simple, plain backgrounds in his portraits in order that the viewer's eyes focused on the model.

Flora was so beautiful that many of that era thought the model must have been a contemporary Venetian courtesan, but the flowers in her right hand pointed to her as the representation of the ancient goddess of flowers and spring. She was sensual, serene, graceful and charming and Travani loved her and loved creating her. When the street sweeper's brushes twirled over her at midnight and erased her beauty, he would come back in the morning and bring her faded image to life once again.

Flora consumed his attention. When he was with her, he could forget the disappointment he'd caused his mother. He could forget that his father thought of him as a street thug; someone with no future. He could forget about the money he owed Bocchio. In the mental solitude it took to draw her, *Flora* was all he knew and was all he wanted to think about.

It was the innocence of her face that he loved. That innocence seemed to imply that as seductive as she was, there was no man worthy to have her and that her beauty was so rare, that no man had ever touched her. Just like spring itself, she was new, unspoiled and virginal. Creating her was the only time he would dream about loving a woman like her.

☙

She watched him fill in the golden highlights on the auburn hair. This man was very talented. The movements of his body as he worked hinted that he seemed to imagine himself alone with *Flora*, just the two of them in an intimate encounter of creation: he was the Master and she was his labor.

As a street artist, he must be used to people staring at him while he worked, but there was something more to the way this man moved, as if it were a dance between the two of them and he wasn't aware that a large crowd was watching. He kept his head bowed to her as if he were telling her secrets as he worked the flesh-colored chalk down her chest, using his fingers to lightly blend the colors between her breasts, gently stroking her like a tender lover. When he picked up a piece of alizarin chalk, she saw his thumb brush across Flora's lips tenderly as he applied it, as if he could feel their smoothness.

Noreen had spotted the crowd as she walked back to her hotel. Now she tried to get a better look at him, but there were so many people gathered around him that she could barely get close enough to see the entire drawing, let alone his face. She watched for a few more minutes, captivated by the intimacy of his work, and then finally left the crowd behind and walked back to her hotel.

She thought about *Flora* and how the chalk artist had 'danced' with her. He loved her. He was having an affair with her. That was what she had seen in his body language. She decided that she would come to the same spot tomorrow and see if he was there again. For now, even the espresso she'd had with Giulio wasn't keeping her awake and she wanted a nap before her dinner date.

Once in her hotel room, she slipped off her shoes, rubbed her feet and wondered how 'Michelangelo' could stand unmoving for hours at a time and if the chalk artist went home to a real woman and loved her the way he loved *Flora.*

ଔ

She was back at her hotel. He would be able to get some lunch at a nearby café and still have his eyes on the hotel entrance; he didn't know how long she would be there.

He'd followed her from the café and saw her approach a crowd of tourists watching a chalk artist. He could see the look on her face and it excited him. She was totally absorbed in the execution as the artist applied the chalk to the street and the form of a woman took shape. That was what was so amazing about her: her love of art and how her emotional response to it took over her entire body until she 'glowed.' That was the only word he could think of to describe her.

He didn't know this artist. He would check this guy out too and made a note of the street address and that the artist was drawing Titan's Flora. It was a painting he was very familiar with.

Chapter 9

"PAPA, I AM a grown man! You cannot raise me any longer!" Travani's voice was loud; he was angry. Giulio was on him again about giving up the life of a petty criminal and settling down. He was an exceptionally talented artist, his father reminded him, and should be using his talent to make beautiful works like the masters instead of scrounging for whatever he could find in some unsuspecting tourist's wallet. Besides, Giulio continued, it wasn't moral. If his Mama was here, she would not approve and what he was doing would only lead to worse things. Damiano had heard it all many times before.

"I know you are right, Papa," he relented, only to get the elder Travani off his back for now. His father didn't need to know that all of his 'commission' work was coming from Galiazzi. His father knew of Galiazzi and knew his reputation. Giulio didn't know about the loan from Bocchio either.

He finished up the pasta on his plate and grabbed another piece of bread. He usually ate lunch at his father's house. There wasn't much of a kitchen to speak of at the apartment and his father was a good cook. Lately though,

Giulio had been more aggressive about Damiano's illegal leanings and he was thinking it might be time to eat lunch at his apartment; he hated seeing the look of disappointment on his father's face.

Giulio lived across the Arno River in a quiet, but crowded, old neighborhood. The buildings in this area continued for blocks, row after row, all joined to each other and for the most part, only fifteen feet across the narrowest of streets from more buildings on the other side. Most of the streets were one-way owing to the fact that only one car at a time could navigate them, along with numerous scooters and bicycles. Florence proper was densely populated and one of the reasons Damiano dreamed of the countryside.

His father lived at Number 22 Via Garibaldi, a two-bedroom place with high ceilings and no yard in front; the entry door opened directly on to the street. Nobody had front yards in this neighborhood.

"Tell me about the piece you just did. How much are you getting paid?" Giulio was hoping his son would get interested in doing more commissioned work. It would be a start in the right direction.

"I will get five thousand euro when the buyer accepts the work. That is a very good sum of money, no?" He wouldn't tell his father that he'd just lied, that he was getting a hundred times that amount. His father would know instantly what his son was involved in and things would explode.

Giulio huffed. "Of course it is! That is exactly what I have been telling you all this time. You could be making so much more money if you would just put your mind to it. But you will not listen to me!" Now it was Giulio who was mad.

"I am telling you now, Damiano," he continued. "I will not pay one more euro to bail you out of jail! You said I cannot raise you any longer. Well, here is where I stop. From this day on, if you go to jail or if you are in other trouble, I will not bail you out! Do you understand?"

Damiano shrugged, his eyes downcast. This same subject was the only one that had caused major arguments between his father and mother. Carlotta would insist that Giulio bail their son out of jail and if he refused, she would do it herself. She told her son and her husband that God would change Damiano sooner or later.

Now mama was gone and after Galiazzi paid him, Damiano would never need Papa's money again. He would be richer than he ever could have imagined. The problem was that he knew his father was right. It was time to give up the street life, the stealing and the unsatisfying one-night affairs with women he didn't know and didn't love. The commissioned pieces from Galiazzi were starting to make him nervous. He respected art and had never intended to misuse his talent to create forgeries. He fell asleep every night wondering if the next day would see him in prison or worse.

He wasn't a boy anymore. He was thirty-six and it was time to find something else to do, something less risky.

Besides, he loved his father and now sitting across the table from him, Damiano could see Giulio's disappointment again. Mama had been gone for ten years and he hadn't been able to show her that he was an honorable man. That knowledge left him feeling dirty and worthless. He still had a chance to make it up to his father.

"I understand, Papa. I will go back to painting for the tourists and I will try to get more private commissions."

"This will be a good thing! You will see!"Giulio said smiling, the anger gone now.

Somewhere inside him, in a place he'd put away long ago, Damiano Travani wanted to live up to the promise he'd just made. He wanted Bocchio and Galiazzi off his back permanently. Life on the streets was becoming dangerous and he was lucky he wasn't in prison right now.

He'd done two pieces in the past and luckily, those thefts had never been solved. It was then that Damiano had backed off doing 'commissions.' But when Galiazzi had approached him about painting a copy of *Flora*, he'd allowed himself to be pulled back in. He loved her and loved creating her and he would have the chance to paint her on aged canvas and with paints just as Titan had used.

But it was the money that had seduced him more than his love for her; more money than he had ever had in his life! It would be his last commission with Galiazzi, he promised himself that. He would buy that house in the country, taking his father with him, away from the streets of Florence.

"Oh, I have news!" Giulio's eyes were fairly dancing now, especially in light of the promise Damiano had made to mend his ways. "A beautiful woman! We are having dinner tonight with a beautiful woman!"

Damiano gave him a suspicious look. "What woman?"

"I met the most beautiful woman outside the Uffizi today! She is the one I saw a few years ago. You remember when I told you about her?"

Damiano did remember. He remembered how excited his father was about her. "You talked to her?" Damiano asked.

"Yes and I told her all about you. We are having dinner tonight at Café Tortino, eight o'clock!"

"Papa, you know I do not like you to arrange dates for me. I am a grown man. I can get my own dates!"

"But this woman is special! She loves art! She will be perfect for you!"

Damiano shook his head. It was hard to be mad at his father. It was love that propelled him to fix his son up with dates and sometimes the women his father chose were very nice and some were very accommodating *after* the date ended. In light of the fight with Giulio and his encounter with Bocchio, Damiano relented. He could use a pleasant past-time tonight.

"No more, Papa. I will meet this woman tonight, but do not arrange any more dates for me. You promise?"

"*Sì*, I promise."

Damiano saw the glint in his father's eyes and knew the promise wouldn't hold for very long.

Chapter 10

BY SIX-THIRTY, NOREEN was ready for dinner. She'd put on a casual royal-blue dress. The color enhanced her brown eyes and brought out the golden highlights in her hair. Her makeup was perfect, her pierced earrings and necklace matching and her watch tattling on her. She wasn't due at the restaurant until eight and it was only a short walk away. Her speed at getting ready told her she was more excited about meeting Giulio's son than she was willing to admit to herself.

Already she could feel the butterflies in her stomach and her heart rate increasing as she tried to calm herself with negative scenarios: he could be as homely as a Neanderthal, he could have off-putting body odor or missing his front teeth, he could smoke, be conceited, be boring or have any number of bad traits that would turn her off immediately. No matter how many reasons she could think up to try to dispel her excitement, she always came back to the knowledge that he was an artist.

She did the math: it was about noon in Falls Church and she knew Rachel had the day off. She would give her a call and see if that helped relieve her anxiety. Besides, she could inform her friend that she wasn't as bad off as Rachel thought: she had a dinner date with an Italian *and* he was an artist. She wouldn't say anything about Giulio making it a threesome.

Rachel picked up on the fourth ring and Noreen could immediately hear two of the kids in the background.

"Noreen, is that you?"

"Who else would be calling you from Florence? How are you?"

"We're great! Tony just got that promotion at the college. He's head of the English department now! Maisy! Quit hitting your brother on the head with your Barbie!"

"Oh, that's wonderful!" she said, laughing. "Tell him 'congrats' from me, okay?" She could hear the two youngest kids squawking in the background and started to rethink the idea of having kids. She loved Rachel's kids, but she was 'Aunt Nordie' and when their boisterous energy got to be too much, 'Aunt Nordie' could go home to her quiet apartment!

"Sorry about the kids. It's raining here and they've been cooped up all day. So tell me, how's the investigation going?"

"Just starting really. I was so jetlagged today that I met with the head of security and then came back to the hotel for a nap. I have a big meeting tomorrow though with the administration and governing board."

"Well, that sounds exciting," Rachel said sarcastically and then immediately followed with, "Justin David, to your room for a time out! Right now! And Maisy, you'll be doing likewise if I have to speak to you again!" She could hear Rachel let out a deep breath. "Sorry. You know how it is. Now what were you saying?"

"Well, it hasn't been such a boring day after all. For your information, I have a dinner date tonight with an Italian artist." There was an audible gasp at the other end of the line and Noreen smiled.

"Tell me all about him! What's his name? What does he look like? How old is he? How did you meet him?"

"Rachel, get a grip, okay? First of all, I didn't get his name and..."

Rachel interrupted her. "You don't know his name? What does he look like?"

Noreen was afraid of that question and wondered how she was going to answer it without giving away that Giulio would be joining them on the date. "Well, I don't know."

"What do you mean you don't know? How'd you meet him if you've never seen him and don't know his name? Is this a blind date?"

"Well, in a way. His father is one of those human statues. Do you remember when I was in Italy five years ago and I told you about the man dressed as Michelangelo? Well, he was outside the Uffizi today and believe it or not, he looked at me and told me he remembered seeing me before and I never even spoke to him the last time I was in Florence."

"You never even had a conversation with the guy, he only saw you once five years ago and he remembers you? You see, things like that *always* happen to beautiful women like you! I see my ob-gyn every year and he can't remember what *I* look like and he's known me almost twelve years! Of course, he's usually not looking at my face!" They both laughed and Noreen realized how much she missed Rachel.

"Girl," she said, "you crack me up! Really though, I told Michelangelo, whose real name is Giulio by the way, that I remembered him too and he asked me to have coffee with him."

She heard Rachel suck in her breath. "And you did? Wow! I never thought you'd do something like that, but then again with your training, he should have been more afraid of you than you were of him!"

"He's just a nice man, Rachel. It was a public place, lots of Carabinieri around. I was safe. Besides, seems he was more interested in telling me about his son the artist than he was in coming on to me."

"Oh, so your date is with his son?"

"Yeah. That's why I don't know what he looks like. But I'll find out in about an hour. I'm meeting him at eight at the same restaurant where Giulio and I had coffee."

"Sounds exciting, unless he turns out to be some avant-garde, purple-haired twig with nose rings. You know, the kind who throws paint on his old underwear, slops it onto a canvas and then convinces a group of pseudo art experts that what he's done is really worth a cool million."

Noreen laughed again. "Yeah, I know the type. But for your information, his father is a nice looking man...well, from what I could see through the heavy face paint, and I'm going with 'like father, like son!' But I want to tell you about the man I saw doing a chalk drawing of *Flora* on the street. He..."

"Isn't that the painting you like so much? The naked woman with the flowers?" Rachel interrupted.

"You're thinking of the *Venus of Urbino.* Same artist, different painting. Flora's not naked; a little exposed, but not naked. Anyway, this guy was an amazing artist considering he was drawing on the street. The tourists were so thick around him that I couldn't see all of what he was doing or even what he looked like, but he drew *Flora* as if she were part of his soul. It was like he was *dancing* with her. The way he moved as he applied the chalk and the way he caressed her as he blended the colors together was like an intimate moment only the two of them shared. It was wonderful and so erotic!"

"*Sounds* wonderful and very sexy! Too bad your date isn't with him!"

"Most of the time, these chalk artists will work on the same drawing day after day. At night the street sweepers erase most of the drawing, but there's usually a faded image that remains and they come back and fill it in all over again; another day's work is another day of coins in their dish. So I'm going back tomorrow and see if he's there again."

"Good idea! He sounds so passionate. That's the guy you need to be having dinner with!"

"For once we agree, but I like Giulio. He's a very nice man and I think he might be able to give me some information about who might be involved or capable of pulling off the theft from the gallery. People who work on the streets every day know a lot more than most people. In that respect, I think he could be a good source of information."

"Well, if his son doesn't look like a zombie or Frankenstein, you might also get a few more dates under your belt before you get back home. That would be a good thing," Rachel responded.

"It's more important to me who he is on the inside. I've waited a very long time for a guy who's right for me and I don't intend on rushing into any relationship just because I'm getting older."

She was adamant about that and Rachel knew it. Noreen wanted a committed relationship, not a one-night stand or a 'roommate with privileges.' It was too easy to walk away from a 'live-in-without-the-benefit-of-marriage' relationship and she wanted no part of that kind of heartache. She and Rachel both knew couples who had gone through it. She wanted someone who truly loved her…a 'forever' someone. Rachel understood this. She and Tony had been high school sweethearts and had a good, solid marriage.

"You're right. It doesn't matter what he looks like as long as he really loves you and is committed to you," Rachel agreed and added, "Well maybe this guy will be that kind of man. He's got one thing going for him already...he's an artist!"

"Well, I'd better be going. Hey, give the kids a hug for me and tell Tony I said 'hi.' Are you off tomorrow too?"

"Yeah, and the next day, so you'd better call and tell me all about your date tonight. Deal?"

"Oh, you can count on it. I'll talk to you soon, okay? Arrivederci!"

Rachel said 'good-bye' and Noreen closed the cover on her cell phone. She looked at her watch. It was time to leave. She checked her purse before she left as she always did: lipstick, tissues, wallet, identification and her gun loaded with the safety on. She added her cell phone and was as ready as she would ever be.

Chapter 11

"I THOUGHT YOU were coming too, Papa." Damiano was putting on his sport coat. It was cool this evening and he might need it. Sometimes his dates left him cold and it wasn't due to the weather. Damiano had come to Giulio's house after finishing the drawing of *Flora*, to show his father the amount he'd collected in his box. The tourists had been generous and he wanted Giulio to know that he meant what he'd said about getting away from petty crime and becoming a legitimate artist. They were supposed to arrive at the cafe together.

"You are always telling me you are a grown man. You do not need me to hold your hand tonight. Hold the beautiful woman's hand," he replied. Giulio brushed a piece of Damiano's black hair off the left shoulder of the coat.

"You did not even tell me what she looks like."

"I told you she was beautiful. What more do you need to know?"

"Beauty is in the eye of the beholder, is that not so? You may think she is beautiful, but I may not." Damiano was tired and wanted to go back to his apartment in case his money for doing the forgery was delivered. "Tell me what she looks like. What color are her eyes, her hair? Is she fat?"

Giulio placed both of his hands on his son's shoulders and looked directly into his eyes. "She looks like *Flora*, Damiano. *Just like Flora*!" There was an unmistakable twinkle in the old man's eyes that made Damiano instantly excited. If there was one thing the elder Travani knew, it was beautiful women and if he had that sparkle in his eyes, this woman must be very beautiful!

"Her hair is the same, the same golden light that shines when the sun strikes it. Her eyes are dark and have the same tenderness and clarity, but much more light. Her face…the same innocence. Her lips...not quite the shape of a heart like *Flora's*, but full and sensuous and she is not as plump as your *Flora*! Her body is perfect and she moves like an angel!"

"You're right, Papa. I won't need you tonight! I'll give the signorina your apologies!"

"Listen to me! You must be on your best behavior. This is not an ordinary woman, the kind you are used to. She is very professional and educated."

"Papa, you're not making her sound very exciting," Damiano replied, his shoulders sagging a bit.

"Believe me! I can tell she is *very* exciting! She excited me!"

"Papa! It is a good thing Mama cannot hear you!"

They were both smiling. The older Travani had dated a few times since his wife's death, but had decided that no one could replace her. He was content now to remain single, but he could still appreciate a beautiful woman.

"All I am saying is do not treat this woman as you do the others. She has quality. There is something warm and inviting about her eyes, something tender in her soul. I do not want you to hurt her."

Damiano recognized the look on Giulio's face and was stunned for a moment. "You love her, Papa," he said, surprised at the veracity of what he saw in his father's eyes.

"Like she was my own daughter! There is something about her heart that shows in her eyes and I *do* not want you to treat her as if she were just a temporary distraction. If you are not attracted to her, then that is all right. But do not pretend to love her, use her and then cast her aside."

Those words stabbed hard at Damiano's conscience. They hurt and the depth of that pain surprised him. Most of his relationships with women were exactly like that, but hearing it come from his father's mouth and knowing it was true, deepened the guilt he felt about them. He wanted to be married and knew that he couldn't continue using women to satisfy his lust. He would never find a good wife that way and he knew it.

"I promise you, Papa. I will not hurt her. And if it is true that she looks like my *Flora,* you may get the daughter-in-law you have always wanted."

Giulio's grin covered his entire face. "Yes, that would be wonderful! You will see! She is beautiful...and smart and cultured and tender and delicate like a flower and..."

"Papa, enough! I understand!" They both laughed as Damiano started to leave.

"Promise me you will *respect* her and you know what I mean...please, Damiano," Giulio begged.

"I will, Papa. I promise." They hugged before Damiano walked out into the street.

.

ന്ദ

As she came into the restaurant, he sucked in his breath, he hands immediately shaking and wet with perspiration. Papa was right: she looked like *Flora*! He would have known her anywhere! Her hair had the same golden highlights that crowned the auburn beneath, her dark brown eyes the same gentle wistfulness and her skin the same warm, flesh tones he'd blended with his fingers earlier that day. The thought of putting his fingers on her chest as he had done with the drawing made his hands shake even more. He stood, unable to speak, and motioned to her. He knew now why Papa's eyes had sparkled when he'd spoken of her. Could *he* speak to her? He wasn't sure.

"I am Damiano. You are Noreen?" She smiled and he could tell she was excited. Even *Flora* didn't have light dancing in her eyes the way this woman did.

"Yes," she said. He offered his hand, suddenly feeling very unworthy as he felt the delicateness of her touch. He didn't want to let go, but after several seconds she pulled away gently and sat down opposite him.

"I thought your father would be joining us. Is he coming later?" she asked. Her relief was profound. For a blind date, this man was very handsome, not a Neanderthal or a Frankenstein. He was as easy to look at as Alex was.

"He sends his regrets and wants me to tell you that he hopes you will come to the gallery every day to see him."

"I'm sure I'll see him often while I'm here."

The light shawl she was wearing slipped off her left shoulder and he could see the perfect skin of her arm. The gold necklace she was wearing caught his gaze and he followed it down her flawless chest to the neckline of her dress. How many times in painting *Flora* had he wished Titan had painted her left hand open, her gown dropping away and exposing what was hiding shyly underneath?

"Your father tells me that you're an artist. What kind of art interests you?" She replaced the shawl over her shoulder; she'd seen his pupils dilate and knew it was much too early in this relationship to let anything entice him. Those kinds of situations usually left her with regrets and the way this guy looked, she didn't want to have *any* regrets!

"The Renaissance masters," he answered. He took a long, imperceptible breath in and let it out carefully. He couldn't even breathe when he was with her! He sipped at the glass of water above his plate.

"They interest me too," she said.

There was something about the perfect symmetry of his face that made her think that his look could have easily been created by one of the old masters. His eyes were intense in their darkness and perfectly shaped with full black lashes and nicely shaped eyebrows. His nose was strong and straight, his lips perfectly formed with just the right amount of fullness and they framed beautiful, white teeth. The faint five o'clock shadow on his face mirrored the dark hair on his head and what she saw at the top of his unbuttoned polo shirt.

She uncovered both shoulders and put the shawl into her lap. She sipped at her water too. All of a sudden, the night air seemed warmer than it had been just a few minutes before.

"Actually, I like them all, especially Bellini, Michelangelo, Titan, Caravaggio. And you? Who are your favorites?" He couldn't take his eyes off her and her beauty wasn't helping calm his rapid heart rate.

"It's very hard to choose, but I'm drawn to Michelangelo for *David* and the *Holy Family*. The Sistine Chapel too, is amazing, Rafael for *The Alba Madonna* and Titan for *Venus of Urbino* and *Flora*."

She had felt so self-assured when she'd arrived, but now after seeing him, she was feeling anxious. The butterflies were flapping crazily in her stomach, the same feeling she always used to get when she was with Alex.

She took another sip of water. She hated first dates and especially blind dates. She hated the tension, good and bad. This was too much of the good and she was afraid he'd notice. If he was as good as he looked and sounded, she wanted to go slow with him, get to know the man behind the perfect face.

"Yes, Michelangelo. He was great and still is!" he replied. She watched him smile broadly, admiring the way the creases at the corners of his eyes enhanced his good looks. She picked up on the insinuation and smiled back at him.

"Your father is a lovely gentleman," she remarked, relaxing a little. "I enjoyed having coffee with him today, though all he talked about was you."

"I will apologize for him. Sometimes he is very... *ansioso*... anxious...for me to settle down and get married. He is a typical father, no?"

Noreen chuckled, thinking about Rachel who was ever more interested in her getting married than her parents were. "Yes, parents can be like that."

A waiter approached the table. They had been so wrapped up in nervous conversation that she hadn't even looked at the menu in front of her. Now she opened it. She had no idea what she should order. Noticing the frown on her face, Damiano offered to order and she nodded. Italian flew between him and the waiter until the waiter thanked him and left.

He took another sip of water. The wine he'd ordered would come soon, but until then he needed something to do with his hands.

"What kind of work do you do?" he asked. She could tell he was nervous, which didn't seem normal for an Italian man. Having been here before, she knew enough about them to know that for the most part, they were self-assured, confident and loved to prove their attractiveness to women.

They were unabashed flirts and aggressive when it came to scoring.

"I'm here investigating the theft of a stolen painting. I think your father could help me."

Damiano immediately felt his blood go cold; she had to be with the police. He knew she was American and if she were investigating art theft, she had to be with the FBI. His mind raced with the inevitable scenarios as he struggled for a response. Any thread of hope he had of getting to know this woman better was coming unraveled fast.

"How could that be? Papa doesn't know about crimes of that nature. He is a very honest man and does not get involved with business such as that."

Noreen heard the indignation in his voice and didn't blame him. Her comment hadn't come out exactly as she had wanted.

"No, no. I didn't mean to insinuate that your father had anything to do with the theft or even knows about it. I'm sorry if that's what you thought. What I meant was that he's outside the gallery every day and must know a lot about what happens in the streets."

"I understand. No apology is necessary and you are correct. My father has been working outside the Uffizi for almost ten years. He knows much of what goes on in Florence."

He was colder now knowing his chances of being able to be with her, this woman who looked like *Flora,* were evaporating. Then he realized that she hadn't mentioned which painting had been stolen and in the back of his mind, he reminded himself that the original *Flora* was almost certainly out of the country by now, the fake taking her place and hanging in a gallery somewhere else.

The coldness was lifting somewhat, but the resignation was leaving him miserable. He couldn't allow himself to see her again; it was too dangerous for him. He had tonight with her and that was all.

She noticed him fingering his water glass, rotating it slowing in a circular motion as his hand trembled slightly. This guy was more nervous than she was. 'First dates,' she thought. 'You either you hit it off or you didn't, but why sweat it?' Either he was going to like her or not, so why *pretend* to be relaxed and casual. She released the butterflies and felt better immediately. Usually it took several glasses of wine to achieve that state of relaxation.

As soon as she had thought, the waiter returned with two glasses and a bottle. He poured a Chianti, filling her glass first and then Damiano's. He left the bottle and walked away.

"I hope you will not think me too forward, but you are beautiful," he said, holding on to the wine glass now, wanting her as he remembered his promise to his father.

This guy must have gotten relaxed all of a sudden too, Noreen thought, because now he was acting like the quintessential Italian male, the compliment rolling off his luscious lips as though he'd had plenty of practice saying it. Good. Now they could get down to the business of knowing each other better and leave the nerves and butterflies behind.

"I don't think you're forward at all. All women like to know that men appreciate them and telling a woman she's beautiful is always good for her self-esteem."

"Then I will toast to your beauty, to your eyes that speak of the kindness in your soul and to your face that makes me think of beautiful *Flora*." He raised his glass, as did she, and they drank simultaneously.

She enjoyed the sweetness of the wine sliding down her throat and warming her even more. His eyes had become more expressive, if that were possible. She'd noticed they'd been pretty expressive since he'd first seen her. Italian men were known to move fast and apparently he was no different.

"It's my favorite painting and I'm flattered that you would compare me to her."

There was something more she saw in his face now. He was looking directly at her, fixing his eyes on hers, and she suddenly felt naked in front of him. A blush was beginning on her cheeks just as the waiter approached with their first course.

As the evening wore on, the food courses coming slowly, she realized how much she enjoyed being with him. Throughout the delicious meal, the conversation had centered on art, a safe topic for them both, and avoided the more intimate details of their personal lives. Damiano seemed evasive when she'd ask about his art, where he sold his paintings and if they were on exhibit. The only information he gave her was that he mostly did commissioned work, painting for the tourists, and so had nothing to show her. He seemed honest, but there was something about him she couldn't quite put her finger on and she asked herself if she could afford to get emotionally involved with a man right now, even someone as handsome and charming as he was. But then again, could she afford *not* to?

By the time they were ready to leave, she'd decided to keep him at arm's length for now, reminding herself that she was in Florence to work.

He offered to walk her to her hotel. It was after eleven-thirty now and every city was dangerous for a woman alone at that time of night, even a woman with self-defense training and a gun in her purse.

The warmth of the day was gone, replaced with a gentle, refreshing breeze coming from the river. The crowds of tourists had all but disappeared into the numerous hotels and the few cafés that were still open were occupied mostly with locals.

Street sweepers were starting their jobs now, the swishing of the brushes on their vehicles disturbing the tranquility of the night. The few cars and trucks here mostly belonged to the police and Carabinieri or were delivery trucks. The city leaders had seen the advantages of reserving the streets in this area for pedestrians; tourism was all-important to Florence and the major traffic flowed around the central hub.

As they stood at the entrance of her hotel, she could tell he wanted to kiss her, but seemed unsure about initiating it. That too was unusual for an Italian. A 'thank you' kiss surely wasn't too much for him to ask of her and since the awkwardness of the moment was increasing every second, she leaned into him and offered her lips, her eyes closing. She felt his hand cupping her chin slowly as the warmth of his thumb purposely brushed slowly across her lips and he whispered "*Buona notte*, Flora" and then kissed her more passionately than she had ever been kissed before.

He withdrew his hand and walked away as she stood for a moment too stunned to move, her eyes still closed as she told herself that 'arm's length' was too far away from him already.

☙

She had come out of the hotel entrance, the blue of her dress and auburn of her hair more dazzling than the stained glass windows of Santa Maria del Fiore. 'Fiore'...it meant 'flower' and that's what he thought of as he watched her cross the Piazza della Signoria and walk toward a cafe. She was hard to resist when she looked like that and he was having a difficult time keeping his mind on what he was doing.

He found a spot where he wouldn't be seen, relieved he had the binoculars, and watched as she approached a table, the man at the table rising to shake her hand. He could see them inside the cafe, especially her. She had fixed her hair and put on make-up, even though she was beautiful enough not to need it. He could see the excitement in their faces and for the first time, he cursed what he was doing.

This might be a long evening and he prayed this man would not follow her up to her hotel room at the end of it. He didn't think he could endure the pain if that happened. The two of them chatted, smiling between bites of food and sips of wine. He could almost taste her lips and feel the softness of her face.

At eleven-thirty, the man took her back to her hotel, kissing her before he left. The kiss was passionate and he saw her expression when the man pulled away. He wanted her and promised himself he would have her and that she would never want to kiss another man but him.

Chapter 12

SHE UNDRESSED THINKING about how Damiano had purposefully brushed his thumb across her lips. She felt the excitement again. Then she thought about his kiss, her heart beating fast, her desire for him increasing until she couldn't watch the fantasies that were playing out in her mind. She had to calm down. She had to remember that she hadn't come to Florence to fall madly in love with an artist; she had a job to do and had to concentrate on that.

Slipping out of her bra, she put on the cotton tank top and soft knit shorts she used as pajamas and sat on the bed, her cell phone in hand. It was about dinnertime in Falls Church and she'd promised to let Rachel know how the date had gone. After three rings, she heard Tony's 'hello' and Rachel in the background, her voice loud as she told the kids to get started on their homework.

"Hi, Tony. It's Noreen. Did I call in the middle of something?"

"Hey, world traveler! No, we finished dinner early and now we're just riding rough shod on the kids. How's Florence? Rachel tells me you have a hot date."

Noreen liked Tony. He was 'salt of the earth', smart, easy-going and everything good about Italian *and* American men, all put together in one great package.

"*Had* a hot date," she replied. "I just got back to my hotel and I know Rachel will kill me if I don't fill her in on all the details right away."

"Well, I'd love to find out about it too, but she's right here now breathing down my neck, so I'll hand the phone to her. Good to talk to you and don't worry…she'll fill me in after you two hang up."

She heard Rachel giggling, her voice hushed, but clear. "Not when I'm on the phone, Tony!"

"Am I interrupting something?" Noreen asked.

"Oh, you know Tony. He's acting like an Italian again!"

"He *is* Italian!" Noreen said chuckling and pretty sure of what was going on at the other end of the line.

"Yeah…it's great and I love it, but don't tell him! One thing he *doesn't* need is encouragement! So tell me all about your date and don't leave *anything* out! Was he a zombie?"

"Rachel," she started, breathlessly, "he's gorgeous! And sensitive and smart and gorgeous and built and…" Her voice trailed off as she remembered his kiss.

"…and…and what?" Rachel pushed. "Tell me everything!"

"And definitely someone I want to get to know better!"

"You want to be his favorite 'painting'…his *Flora*? Am I right? Like the street artist you saw?" Noreen could almost hear the smile in Rachel's voice. "You want to be the one he 'dances' with?"

"Oh, *yes!*"

"Did he kiss you? How far did he go?"

"Yes, he kissed me. Nothing else happened and you should know that I'm not that type and if something did happen, I wouldn't elaborate."

"You know I'm kidding. How was the kiss?"

"The best I've ever had!" Noreen said truthfully.

"Wow! That's saying something considering what you used to tell me about Alex's kisses."

"Well, Damiano definitely isn't Alex, even though Alex was wonderful."

"Damiano? Is that his name? That sounds *so* sexy!"

"Yeah…it *really* fits him!"

"Cool off girl!" her friend pleaded. "Now you're getting *me* all excited!"

Noreen thought about Rachel and Tony, an instant mental image of how they looked at each other, even now after three kids, a mortgage and busy careers. They hadn't seemed to lose the passion of new love even now. She felt the longing for that kind of intimacy even more acutely, felt the regret of having let Alex go and when she spoke again, she felt heavy inside.

"You have Tony, Rachel. Put the kids to bed early tonight and make love to him. Okay?"

"Are you okay?" Rachel asked. When there was no response, she added, "Don't give up yet. If this Damiano is as good as you think, you could have your very own Italian to make love to."

"You're right. I'm sorry I got all melancholic on you," she apologized.

"Melancholic? I hope that means 'sad' otherwise I have to get the dictionary."

Noreen laughed. "Yes, it means 'sad,' but you're right. This thing with Damiano could work out to be something great. And I already like his father and Damiano loves great art..."

Rachel interrupted her. "That's it! Keep that attitude and you'll be fine."

"I will and thanks. You're a good friend and I always feel better after talking to you."

"Same here."

"I'd better go now. It's midnight and I have a meeting tomorrow with the Uffizi administration staff. Remember what I told you about Tony...what to do."

"Oh, I'll remember! Tony's already warming up!" she giggled and Noreen could hear mock heavy breathing in the background.

Chapter 13

THE MEETING WAS scheduled for eight-thirty and included the head and assistant head curators, the head and assistant head of acquisitions, the Head of Security Umberto Castagno, whom she'd already met, the lead investigator for the TPC, several members of the governing board and an unnamed secretary who looked bored for most of the meeting, but dutifully recorded every word.

For any other woman, being the only female in a room filled with powerful men might be intimidating, especially since culturally she knew that most of the men in this room were probably checking her out and that didn't mean her credentials as an agent of the FBI. She could see their eyes fixing on her at different points in the meeting and the distinct feeling she got was that they weren't sizing up her knowledge of art crime. It was the lascivious smiles that gave them away. Sometimes looking the way she did was a burden, especially with regard to her career. A lot of men wouldn't or couldn't take her seriously and she felt like it was happening again with these guys.

But she put that aside and gave what she knew was a professional, thoughtful presentation about the stolen Titan;

how she'd determined that the theft had taken place before it left Italy and how she thought it had been accomplished.

The representative from the TPC, Carlo Rossini, agreed to get her a printout of the TPC's file of known forgers so that she could co-ordinate with everyone involved in working the case.

The Head Curator, Signore Lorenzo D'Angelo, informed the rest of the group that he had met earlier with the heads of acquisitions and that after scrutinizing the forgery, they wondered if the artist could possibly be new and unknown to law enforcement. They predicated that observation on the fact that the artist had left the miniscule cross in the bottom corner of the painting.

On this point, most of those present began a rather heated discussion. Vincenzo Sartori, Assistant Head of Acquisitions, suggested that perhaps the cross was added to throw law enforcement off on purpose and that the best bet for finding the forger was the TPC's list. She got the impression that the administration didn't want to believe that a new artist, and an excellent one at that, was now operating somewhere and putting their collection at risk.

She offered her theory as to how the theft might have taken place: the forgery could have been switched with the original and placed aboard the plane. Had they gotten any clues when they'd questioned the guards, she asked?

That question was met with head shakes all around, Rossini telling her that the van drivers had been questioned and cleared by his office, while Castagno assured her that the guards and driver had been involved in many transfers and their records were spotless. It was here that she cautioned that even spotless records sometimes hid dirty secrets. That remark didn't sit well with any of the museum higher-ups, but she saw Rossini nod.

Sartori spoke up, appearing somewhat indignant, and told her that as Assistant Head of Acquisitions, he always accompanied any painting that was being loaned out. He said he was in the van from the time it left the Uffizi and that he'd supervised the unloading at the airport and remained with the van until it returned to the gallery. Apparently he and Castagno were immediately responsible for the loading of the painting, accompanied by the curator, and it didn't take a detective to see that he took umbrage at her remark.

The meeting dragged on for almost sixty minutes instead of the scheduled thirty, with no overwhelming insight, much bickering on the part of the staff and only agreement that this case was unusual. It finally ended leaving Noreen even more convinced that any good clues would probably come from the people who saw and heard what went on in the streets.

She shook hands all around, noticing that Sartori had seemed distracted during the meeting and still looked offended and like he wanted her to get lost. He had a very sweaty palm when she'd taken it to shake hands and made eye contact with her for only a nanosecond. Coupled with the distraction and sweat, she was convinced that his background bore further investigation.

The Affair with Flora

ɞ

As she walked out of the Uffizi, Noreen noticed Giulio in his usual spot, several tourists snapping photos of him. Some of them left euros in his dish, some didn't. It wasn't very crowded yet, so when he was alone, she approached him.

"*Buon giorno*, Giulio," she said, making sure her accent was as perfect as she could make it. She had never been very good at foreign languages, but her Italian was getting better each time she was lucky enough to come here. This was her third trip.

"Ah, Signorina Issenlowe, *buon giorno! Come stai*?"

"*Bene*, Giulio. *Bene*!" She was surprised that he came down off his box again, but then the courtyard wasn't too crowed at the moment and he probably needed to rest his feet again. It was more probable that he wanted to know how the date had gone and if she was attracted to Damiano.

"You had a good time with my son last night?"

'Bingo!' she thought, but she knew that Italian families were very close; a father would want to know this, especially one with a thirty-something unmarried son.

"I had a very nice time," she offered, not knowing how much she should say. If Giulio was interested in getting his son married off right away, she didn't want to give him any false hope. Besides, she told herself, anything she said about Damiano would probably make it back to him and she didn't want to give *him* any false hope either.

"Did he offer to show you his paintings?" There was a look of expectation in the older man's eyes and Noreen had to chuckle. She didn't believe he knew that it was an old euphemism having to do with getting a woman into a man's residence for the purpose of seducing her, but it struck her as funny considering that Damiano *was* an artist.

"No, he didn't," she replied. "But I'd love to see his work." Giulio didn't need to know what she was thinking about when she'd answered him. He didn't need to know that she was thinking about Damiano's lips and how they'd felt on hers and that she hoped he would kiss her again.

Giulio pointed toward the Piazza della Signoria, telling her that she should turn right at the statue of Gran Duke Cosimo atop his horse and continue down the street that ran between the Uffizi and the Palazzo Vecchio. She would find Damiano working on his art and then added, "Perhaps we can all enjoy the noon meal together."

"I'd like that very much," she said honestly and then told him she was going to look for Damiano. He smiled at her as she left, the expectant look never leaving his face.

As she walked past the statue of the Gran Duke, she remembered that she wanted to see if the chalk artist was back at work bringing *Flora* to life again. She knew he too was somewhere on this street; it was where she had seen him before.

As a large group of tourists ahead of her turned down a side street, she saw the chalk artist ahead, but this time she could see him clearly: it was Damiano! *He* was the one who had danced with *Flora! He* was the one who had blended the chalk so tenderly; had stroked her like he was her lover! The instant she remembered that, the thought of keeping him at arm's length flew out of her head and the beauty of how he loved *Flora* filled her with thoughts she hadn't had about a man since she'd dated Alex.

His attention was totally on recreating her, even though there weren't as many tourists watching him. Standing at his side as he worked, she watched him applying the white of *Flora's* undergarment, creating the folds that draped seductively across her torso…the folds that almost gave away what was underneath her left hand.

"It's easy to see why you love her," Noreen said, almost whispering. It was a holy thing to watch him, how his hands made love to her, and she felt like she was intruding on them. He looked up immediately and she saw a momentary look of shock on his face.

"I'm sorry," she apologized. "I didn't mean to startle you."

Looking at her, an uncertain smile formed on his lips. "An apology is not necessary. I am just surprised to see you." He wiped his hands on his jeans, depositing the white powder of the chalk on his thighs and greeted her with an 'air kiss' to each cheek. "How did you find me?" he asked.

"I had a meeting at the Uffizi and spoke with your father afterward. He was interested in how our date went last night." She saw someone throw a euro into his coin box and went on. "He said something about the three of us having lunch."

"I would like that very much." He glanced at his watch and then at Flora, waiting for him on the street. There were still people looking at her, probably impatient for him to resume his work.

"It is early yet," he went on. "Papa usually takes lunch at noon. I will meet you were he stands."

She could see the same excitement in his expression, the way his face lit up just as it had the night before. She thought about the sensuality of his kiss and reminded herself that she was going to go slow with him.

"Will you stay and watch me work?" he asked.

"No, I'm sorry, I can't. I have a meeting at ten." She noticed that he looked disappointed and something else...nervous? The thought occurred to her that maybe he wasn't married because he was introverted or maybe shy in his own way. Maybe *she* made him nervous. Sometimes guys were like that with her. Her self-confidence was hard for some of them to deal with…well that and the fact that she worked for the FBI. Being with Alex was easy because he understood that and appreciated that about her.

"Then I will see you at noon. I must get back to *Flora.* She is a hard mistress!" he said, his smile tentative.

Noreen smiled back. "Arrivederci, Damiano," she said and he said the same to her, leaning in to kiss each of her cheeks. He went back to his work, kneeling in front of *Flora*, his head down again as he put the finishing touches on her undergarment. As she turned and walked away, she heard the sound of coins clinking together as they dropped into his box.

ଋ

Florence was laid out conveniently for him. There were so many places he could stay unnoticed while he watched her and the ever-present clusters of tourists made his task all the easier.

He saw him, the man she'd had dinner with the night before. Now he knew the man's name was Damiano Travani and he was an artist. He smiled knowing that there was no one he couldn't get information about if he needed to and after seeing her kiss this guy, he wanted all the information he could get. He wondered if she knew that this man who had kissed her in front of her hotel was also a petty thief and a pickpocket.

He trailed behind her as she headed away from the Uffizi.

Chapter 14

CARLO ROSSINI APPEARED to be about fortyish. He was balding slightly for a man his age, but otherwise was nice-looking. He was neatly dressed in a pair of khaki pants, a blue striped shirt, and navy sport coat and sported the ubiquitous bracelets that most Italian men seemed to wear. He wasn't at all what she expected from someone in the Carabinieri, but then this was the TPC and this branch of the Italian military dealt with art crimes.

He was relaxed and casual. Noreen had glanced to see if he was wearing a wedding band; he was. Well, she told herself, she was in Italy and Rachel would interrogate her when she got back to Falls Church. She wanted to be able to tell her friend that she'd checked out every man she'd come in contact with. She crossed Rossini off the 'available' list. Right now her mind was fixed on Damiano anyway.

"Here are the profiles I promised you." He handed her a computer printout several pages thick and bound in a flimsy presentation folder. "As you can see, we keep them current. Some of these people are in prison now. You see there?" He pointed to the profile at the top of the first page and to the word '*incarcerato*.' "That means the forger is currently in prison," he explained. "Next to that is the date he was sent to prison and then next to that is the length of his sentence."

She looked at the accompanying small, black and white mug shot. This man looked like he could be your neighborhood grocer, not an infamous forger. Even though she couldn't read Italian, she could see the list of his criminal arrests was extensive. It was a good thing he was '*incarcerato*.'

"Inspector Rossini, what do you make of the fact that the forgery of *Flora* had the cross in the bottom corner? Have you ever encountered anything like that before?"

"No and I have been doing this job for almost fifteen years. Whoever did that copy is an excellent craftsman. I believe that if it were not for that cross, the painting may never have come to light as a forgery. The work is better than I have ever seen. To be candid with you, Signorina, I do not think the forger of *Flora* is in our database. I think it is someone we have not arrested before…someone new and quite talented. In that respect, I disagree with the gallery administration."

"I agree with you. I've never known a forger to give his work away by deliberately leaving a clue behind. It's almost as if he were challenging us to discover him."

Rossini took a chair at his desk, leaned back and motioned to her. She sat across from him and continued to thumb through the printout, not really expecting anything would jump out at her with red flags waving and saying "This is the perp!"

"Do you have contacts…informers...who work on the streets that provide you with information?" She still believed that the street people were going to be more helpful than any database to lead her to *Flora's* forger.

"Informants? Signorina, you must understand that here in Italy, criminals have a history of keeping their business very well guarded and private. People who talk to the police many times end up dead and the people on the street know this. Sometimes we will get information from someone who feels they would be safer under the protection of the police, but that is not very often and they usually do not live long enough to make it into our custody."

Noreen thought about this, about the Cosa Nostra and how it operated and protected itself and its businesses. Organized crime was not called that because it was operated sloppily. It *was* organized and that included taking care of people who talked to the police. To do so, could and would have painful and even fatal consequences.

"I understand, Inspector. I'd like to see what I can do, if that's agreeable to you." She heard her inner voice adding '...and even if it's not, I'm going to try anyway. I just want your blessing.'

"You are a guest here and the TPC appreciates any help the FBI can give. Your organization has been very accommodating and we would like to return that favor. By all means, if you feel you can get information that will help us, please use whatever means you like. But Signorina, be careful. These streets are very dangerous for people who are looking for information about criminal activities. Please take care."

Noreen got up and he followed her lead. "I'll let you know immediately if I get any new leads," she said as she put out her hand to shake his.

"I would appreciate that very much and as I said, please be careful." He reached inside his jacket and pulled out a business card. "You may contact me at this number. It is my cell phone and I always answer my calls."

She took the card, thanked him and left his office. It was a relief to get his okay about questioning the people who worked on the streets. When dealing with agencies in other countries, she'd learned it was best not to step on toes. The TPC was in charge of this case. She was making the resources of the FBI available to them and it was better in the long run for the TPC to solve the case. It was their show.

Something was pricking at her brain though as she left the meeting, just a feeling she couldn't put her finger on. Rossini had seemed to be holding back with her, like he had much more information or clues that he wasn't telling her about. Well, she reasoned, this case was his baby and maybe he was just being territorial. She was a woman after all and it wouldn't look good if his case was solved by an outside agency and a woman at that.

In the back of her mind though, breaking this case would go a long way toward advancing her career and giving her points toward that promotion, if that's what she wanted. She wasn't so sure now, not after meeting Damiano and not after his kiss.

ଔ

"Who is she?" he asked, as Travani looked up and saw the familiar coat. "She is very pretty. A girlfriend maybe?"

Bocchio was standing over him with Bruno, the ever-silent body guard always one step behind, shadowing his employer. Today he looked moderately constipated; if he was going for a scowl, he hadn't achieved it.

"She is no one. Just a tourist who likes my art, that is all." Travani tried to play innocent and hoped The Teacher would let it go. He stood up, looking at *Flora* as he did so. She was almost finished…finished so that the street sweepers would have something to do at midnight when they would make her disappear again. Then he remembered that she was already gone, the real *Flora,* and that thought gave him a cold feeling in the pit of his stomach.

"She is lovely, that one. She is giving you more than a few coins, I hope! Or are you paying *her?*" Bocchio's smirk and crude insinuation were not sitting well with Travani, not when it was directed at Noreen. He wouldn't say anything to upset Bocchio though or he could get a lesson he wasn't ready for. Bocchio could add more euro to Travani's balance any time he wanted for no other reason than that Travani had insulted him. He let the comment go.

"She is a tourist, that is all," he replied, hoping the subject was closed.

"That is too bad," Bocchio said, wiping his forehead with the back of his hand. "She looks like she knows how to please a man." He removed a handkerchief from his pocket and continued. "I have come to remind you that you have seven more days until your account is due."

"I am aware of that. I have already contacted Galiazzi about my pay for the work I did. He has always paid me on time before and I do not know why he is late this time. We are meeting this afternoon."

"That is between you and that snake. His business is his business and mine is mine. Just make sure you have the entire balance you owe me when it is due."

Bocchio looked down at the street, a sly smile forming on his portly face as he pocketed the handkerchief. "She is pretty. I will admit that, but a real woman is much more satisfying, no?" He grinned as he made a lewd gesture and then walked away, Bruno close on his heels.

Chapter 15

AS SHE WALKED back toward the Uffizi, Noreen thought about the theft. Her theory was that the original *Flora* had been loaded into the transport van and then had been switched with the forgery at some point en route to Aeroporto di Firenze. Savio Battaglia, Head of Acquisitions, Vincenzo Sartori and Umberto Castagno had all supervised the loading, so the switch must have occurred after it was loaded and somehow the drivers *had* to be involved.

She wanted to meet with Umberto Castagno again and his lead security guard, Rico Panello. Panello had accompanied the painting and had arranged for the van and driver. Castagno had already told her that Panello had used the same driver that had always done the transportation of valuable paintings, but she wanted to be able to question them herself. She wanted to see their body language, to gauge for herself if they were telling the truth. She was instinctive about body language and had even been called on to make presentations on the subject at the Academy.

Once she found out who was involved in the switch, it shouldn't be too hard to find out who had orchestrated it in the first place *if* the suspects would talk. From what Rossini had said, that might be the most difficult part of her investigation: getting people to tell what they knew.

She didn't believe that a low-level staff member could have engineered this theft on his own, especially since the forgery was so good. Someone else, someone with better connections in the art world, had to be involved higher up the ladder. She would start at the bottom of that ladder and see how high up she'd have to climb to get to the top. Giulio and Damiano worked on the streets and that's where she believed the first rung of the ladder was located.

There was just something about this entire affair that didn't smack of organized crime. It was too sloppy. The fact that the forger had left his 'mark' on the fake was proof to her that it was a theft outside of any crime syndicate. Those people were too good to let something like that get through their scrutiny. They were more into outright theft too, just like the theft of Caravaggio's *Nativity*. It was local; she knew that.

In the Piazza della Signoria, she stopped in front of the copy of Michelangelo's *David* and looked up at it. He was flanked by Bandinelli's statue of *Heracles and Cacus* on his left and Ammannati's *Neptune Fountain* on his right.

David had significance in Florence's history. She knew that around the year 1500, Italy was comprised of small city-states and that they would not achieve political unification for almost four more centuries. The city of Florence was heavily populated and wealthy, but at the same time, was constantly under the threat of external attack by its rival city-states: the Duchy of Milan, the Republic of Venice, the

Papal States and the Kingdom of Naples. The people of Florence depended on their own strength and ability to defend themselves and had adopted a piety that guaranteed them divine support in their hour of need. The two Old Testament heroes, David and Judith, were thought to embody the virtues of strength and purity as both had saved their people from threat of annihilation by more powerful armies.

After working on *David* for three years, Michelangelo presented it to his patrons in 1504 and it was to be placed inside the cathedral of Santa Maria del Fiore between a pier of buttresses. But due to its enormous size, six-ton weight and the nakedness of the figure, it was deemed not appropriate for the cathedral and a commission of very famous artists, including Botticelli and Leonardo da Vinci, were chosen to decide where it should rest. It was determined to place *David* in the highly symbolic position at the entrance to the Piazza della Signoria, in front of the main door of city hall and the political heart of the city.

Now she was looking at a forgery of sorts, of *David.* She knew the original was now in the Galleria dell' Accademia, having been removed from the piazza in 1873 in order to protect it from damage. She'd seen the real *David* and he was breathtaking in his execution and size. Somehow the copy, though excellent, didn't seem to have the soul of the original. She thought of the fake *Flora.* It *did* have soul, every bit as much as the original, and that's what was eating at her about this case.

Giulio was standing under the statue of Michelangelo when she walked into the Piazzale degli Uffizi and if he hadn't waved to her, she wouldn't have recognized him without his makeup. He was nice looking with makeup, but even better looking without it. It was easy to see where Damiano got his looks.

"I am happy to see you again!" he said cheerfully as he hugged her and planted the usual cheek kisses, this time actually making contact with her face. "Damiano is not here yet, but he should be coming soon."

"I'm so surprised to see you not working. I guess I just expected to be having lunch with the most revered and talented Michelangelo again today!" She was sad that she'd not gotten that photo of her having lunch with the great master.

"For you, lovely Signorina, I have given myself the day off. I hope you are free this afternoon or do you work?"

"The great part about my job is that I can make my own hours, keeping in mind that I *do* have a job to do. But if my lunch extends beyond an hour, it's okay."

She saw Damiano walking toward them. His smile when he saw her left a lot to be desired. He certainly didn't seem to be as overjoyed to see her as his father was. He did embrace her and give her cheek kisses, but it was almost like he had cooled off from their date the night before. Was he angry that she hadn't stayed to watch him with *Flora*? If so, that was pretty immature on his part and this relationship might be doomed already.

"I am sorry to be late," he said and seemed sincere.

"Come," Giulio said. "We go now."

They followed him out of the Piazzale degli Uffizi toward the Arno River and in a few minutes, they were walking across the Ponte Vecchio. The gold of the jewelry in the shops lining the bridge beckoned Noreen and she couldn't help but stop a few times to look into the windows of the shops, Damiano and Giulio perfectly happy to let her browse.

They continued along the main street, turning off after a few blocks and headed into a quiet neighborhood of two and three-story buildings lining a narrow street. If there was a café in this area, it must be a place only the locals used; she didn't see any tourists here.

They came to a door with the number twenty-two painted next to it and Giulio took a key out of his pocket, inserted it into the lock and they went inside.

"*Benvenuti a casa mia*!" Giulio said excitedly. "Welcome to my home! I thought it would be much more pleasant to eat here away from the crowds and noise."

She smiled. Being in their home was a good way to get to know these men; a house said a lot about a person. Glancing around, this one said that it had been a while since a woman had lived in it. It wasn't extremely messy, just lacking feminine touches.

"I think that's a great idea," she said. It would make getting some usable information from them easier for her; less distractions, no waiters to interrupt.

Giulio seemed relieved and led her to the small kitchen. The smell of basil and garlic reached her nose and she was immediately hungry. "Something smells wonderful!" she said and she saw his eyes light up.

"My papa is a very good chef," Damiano said as he motioned her to a chair at the kitchen table. The table was set with a pretty yellow cloth and beautifully painted earthenware plates, definitely womanly touches, and she wondered about Mrs. Travani and if Damiano lived here with Giulio.

"Today I made for you Damiano's favorite antipasto: roasted sweet peppers with anchovies." He set a plate before her on the table and even though she'd never cared for anchovies, this looked delicious. One taste however, told her that nothing in any restaurant or café would be able to compare to real, Italian home-cooking. In that first bite, she became a fan of anchovies!

"This is wonderful!" she said.

Giulio poured them all a glass of red wine and she sipped it, letting the sweetness linger on her tongue before she swallowed.

"I am not so good a cook as my Carlotta was, may God rest her soul. But I try. She passed away ten years ago. Since that time, I am a bachelor, like my son."

"I'm sorry," Noreen said. "I know that losing someone is very hard. I lost my brother several years ago and I still miss him."

Damiano quickly changed the subject. "How is your investigation going?" he asked.

Giulio eyebrows raised in surprise. "Is this what brings you to Florence? What are you investigating?"

She told him then what she did for a living, even that she worked for the FBI. He seemed totally taken aback, but not in a bad way. He seemed more like a proud father; like her father the day she graduated from the Academy. She saw the look on Damiano's face too, when she'd mentioned the FBI. His look said something else…something unsettling.

She told them about the theft at the Uffizi, but purposefully didn't mention which painting had gone missing. The head of acquisitions and the curator had asked her during the meeting to keep that information from leaking to the public and the press.

Giulio seemed impressed with her credentials, while Damiano looked pale. "You are not eating," he stated, looking at his son.

"I am all right, Papa," Damiano responded. "Not enough sleep last night…that is all." He looked at Noreen and asked, "Which painting was stolen?"

"I'm sorry. I can't tell you that. Orders from the gallery," she answered, "but I can tell you it went missing two weeks ago."

Giulio got up and came back to the table with the next course: fresh pasta with pesto and black and green olives. Noreen could smell the garlic and basil. They were a perfect marriage as far as she was concerned and she closed her eyes momentarily when she tasted the first bite.

"The painting was to be loaned to a museum in the United States. My theory is that the painting was stolen before it left Italy," She speared one of the olives and put it in her mouth.

Giulio scratched his head. "The Uffizi has very sophisticated security! I do not see how this would be possible, to take a valuable painting."

"I believe it was switched for a forgery as it was being transported in the van for its flight to the United States."

She saw a thoughtful look on Giulio's face as he scratched his head again. Damiano just looked paler. He was staring at his plate and had become very quiet. Both she and his father noticed.

"Damiano, are you ill?" Giulio touched the back of his hand to his son's forehead, feeling for a fever, but Damiano pushed it away.

"I am fine, Papa. I told you." Noreen heard the hint of exasperation in the son's voice. Something was obviously bothering him. She'd noticed it earlier when she'd seen him drawing *Flora*. Maybe he *hadn't* gotten enough sleep, but maybe he was upset with her for some reason. Whatever it was, she wanted to know. The memory of how his lips felt on hers, watching his passion as he drew *Flora*… it was all still vivid in her memory and she knew she was very interested in him.

"Take Noreen for a walk. Perhaps that will awaken you," Giulio suggested, the smile giving away his ulterior motives: he wanted them to spend time alone together.

"Yes, please, Damiano. Take me for a walk. I'd love to see this part of Florence."

Damiano nodded and got up and held her chair while she joined him. "We will not be too long, Papa," he said flatly, to which Giulio responded that they take all the time they wanted and when they returned, they would all have some espresso and biscotti with some fresh fruit.

☙

He saw the two of them walk out of number twenty-two Via Garibaldi and turn down the street. He made a note of the address and that it was an ordinary building just like all the others in this area. It was harder to remain hidden here, away from the perfect cover of the crowds. Even though it was sunny, there weren't many people out on this street and very little traffic. This neighborhood was cramped, but quiet.

He wanted to believe she was working. She wouldn't be spending so much time with Travani and his father if she weren't. He wanted to believe that, to believe that she wasn't romantically interested in that artist. She was too good for the likes of him; too innocent and trusting.

He put the thought away and reminded himself that he had a job to do and how he felt about her wasn't pertinent. He was to follow her and report her activities to his superiors; that was all. Depending on his report, they would determine what to do with her. If they knew what he knew though, they never would have let him follow her and so he'd kept that little secret to himself. He wanted her and that in itself, was risky for both of them.

Chapter 16

"ARE YOU SURE you were not followed?"

Sartori nodded his head and sat down. He had come to Trattoria Due Colombe, a forgettable, old tavern on the edge of the Arno River and far enough away from central Florence never to have seen a tourist. It was a family-owned place, a place where people kept their mouths shut and a place where Galiazzi conducted business when he needed secrecy. The owner knew and respected Galiazzi and always gave him the little-used dining room in the back. He knew that Galiazzi was a man of importance in the art world and also knew he had connections with the underbelly of society; the people who could help you if you needed something dirty done and could be trusted to keep their mouths shut.

The fact that the important Assistant Head of Acquisitions had come to *him* for this meeting, pleased Galiazzi and he didn't waste any time getting to the point.

"I have expenses and need my money! I have paid some of my people out of my advance, but I still have debts to pay! It is not my problem if the buyer backed out of the deal! I have fulfilled my part of the agreement and now I want the money that was promised!"

Sartori had agreed to pay him two million euro for securing the supplies needed for the forgery and for the forgery itself. The forgery had been delivered to Sartori and it was past time to be paid. Galiazzi didn't work cheap and he didn't tolerate changes in plans. He was to have his money by now and he was furious with Sartori's excuses.

He wiped the perspiration off his face with a monogrammed handkerchief and pushed aside the plate of veal parmigiana he'd ordered. It was too hot in the tavern today.

If Galiazzi wasn't paid soon, Sartori would be in very real danger of getting hurt bad enough to make being dead the better alternative. He knew there were persuasive means by which Galiazzi could convince him he should pay immediately, but Sartori needed to stall. He needed a good lie. He could see the veins in Galiazzi's temples distended and pulsating as his face turned a dusky red. The perspiration was dripping off his cleanly shaven face and onto his Armani suit.

"Calm down, Galiazzi, before you have a stroke! The buyer did not cancel the deal. The money is coming. There was a little mix-up, that is all. He is very wealthy and you know how the wealthy can be. They operate on their own time system, but he will pay. He promises that and I promise that."

"You have already made promises that you are not keeping! I cannot pay my people with promises! They want cash!"

"And you will get your cash! The buyer assures delivery of the money."

"When?"

"It is on its way. The representative for the buyer is due in Florence in six days with the cash. You will have every euro coming to you," Sartori said. Six days was about as long as he figured he could stall Galiazzi. Maybe Kadir would show up in that time. If not, it was enough time to disappear from Italy with Angelina.

Galiazzi knew that there wasn't much he could do if the buyer was late in keeping his end of the bargain. He would wait the six days and spend that time contemplating a suitable punishment for Sartori if payment was delayed past that time.

Galiazzi's main concern was Damiano Travani. He was new to the game of forgery and had yet to prove himself trustworthy. It wasn't absolutely certain what Travani would do if he didn't get the half million euro Galiazzi had promised him. Travani was young, brash and hungry and that made him dangerous. So far, he'd kept his mouth shut about the smaller forgeries he'd done and had said nothing about copying *Flora.* But he was muscular and strong, no match for a man Galiazzi's age who carried an extra fifty pounds on his body. Travani could have a gun or connections to people who did and would 'take care of business' for him. With Galiazzi gone, there would be no finger to point at Travani as the forger of *Flora*, which gave Travani the upper hand for now unless Galiazzi took matters into his own hands first.

"If you are lying, it will not go well for you. This is my promise," Galiazzi said, then waved Sartori away.

Sartori left, looking visibly shaken and Galiazzi went back to the veal. Travani was due soon. Galiazzi ordered another bottle of wine and waited.

ଋ

He wasn't very talkative. As they passed by a neglected park a few blocks from his father's house, she saw a weathered bench under a shade tree and suggested they sit for a while. Having no idea what was bothering him, she was unsure what to make of his change of demeanor. If he was upset with her about something or had some other personal trouble, it was best to find out now and not later. She liked him a lot, but wasn't so attached to him that if he told her to get lost now it would break her heart…not too badly anyway.

"Have I done something to upset you?" she asked.

"No, Noreen, no! You have done nothing! I am very happy to be spending time with you," he protested.

"You seem very distracted."

That coldness at the center of his being had been increasing. The real *Flora* was gone and he had made that possible and now he knew that this woman was in Florence investigating the loss of a painting, this woman whose face reminded him of *Flora* and of what he had done. Even though she had not said what painting had been stolen, he was fairly sure it was the Titan. The date she told Giulio that the painting had been stolen wasn't far from the time he'd turned over the forgery to Galiazzi.

She saw him inhale deeply and then release the breath. Sometimes people did this to force themselves to relax or it could be a sign of resignation, that whatever was bothering them was about to come spilling out. She hoped it was the latter.

"I am sorry," he began. "I know I am not very good company today. You must believe though, that you have done nothing to upset me. In fact, I like you very much."

He was drawn to her more than any woman he'd been with before, but he was keeping a secret that could end any hope of a serious relationship with her. She was special. She loved art, protected it and she loved *Flora.* The thought of her finding out he was a forger was heavy on his mind. She would hate him, turn him in and he would never be with her again. For now, all he wanted was to be with her.

Noreen took his hand in hers, noticing the warmth of his skin and wondering how it was that he had been given such a wonderful gift, one that she had always wanted for herself. How did God decide these things: which gifts to bestow on which people?

As she held his hand, he didn't pull away and that was a good sign. She remembered the day she told Alex that getting involved with him would jeopardize her career and her career was important to her. She remembered the look of devastation in his face, the way he'd turned away from her so that she wouldn't see his eyes getting red. She remembered asking herself how she could do that to him and still wondered if he hated her.

"I care very much about you too," she said as she squeezed his hand. "And I want to know you better." Her voice was almost a whisper as she continued almost to herself. "I want to know this man who dances with *Flora*, who creates her with his hands and then touches her like a lover!"

The passion of her words excited him and he dared to put his arms around her, watching her eyes for permission. He saw her giving it to him, her pupils dilating in anticipation. Cradling her face in his hand, he kissed her, feeling her silken skin with his fingers and tasting the sweetness of her mouth, knowing that these sensations were exactly as he had imagined they would be every time he drew *Flora*.

His beautiful *Flora*! He had 'sold' her in exchange for money! The image of Judas receiving the thirty pieces of silver for betraying Jesus flashed in his head. He felt like Judas and the fact that he was to receive much more than thirty pieces of silver made his crime weigh even heavier on him.

"I am sorry. I should not have done that," he said, pulling away from her, sure she would see the guilt he felt.

"Don't apologize. I liked it," she said. "I know you're troubled about something and I just want to help." She saw him smile.

"Is that how women help men in the United States?"

She blushed at his question. "I don't know you very well, but I like you, Damiano. You're charming and very talented. You have a passion for your art that I have never seen before and it's very exciting. It would be such a tragedy if you lost that passion. I just want you to know that if there's a problem I can help you with, I'll do whatever I can."

He could tell her now and get it over with. He could tell her that he knew about the theft of *Flora,* that he knew the name of the man who'd contacted him to do the forgery. He could tell her that he was Judas and then she would turn him over to the police, he would go to prison this time, and his life would be effectively over. There would be no house in the country, no wife waiting for him and no children. He would be an old man when he was released and worst of all, his father would be disgraced.

But telling her wouldn't bring *Flora* back. She was gone, somewhere in the Middle East, somewhere in a vault or hanging in the palace of a wealthy sheik, somewhere she didn't belong. He could tell this woman who looked like *Flora* everything he knew, but it wouldn't bring the painting back. So what would be the point? Better to keep what he'd done secret. He needed the money Galiazzi owed him. He had to get Bocchio paid off or it wouldn't matter what he'd done to *Flora.* Bocchio would see to it that Travani would never paint again and that's if Travani was lucky. Besides, he thought, for now at least he could be with *his* Flora, could touch her and dream about making love to her.

"That is very kind of you, Noreen, but it not an important matter. I cannot concern you in my affairs. It would not be right." He concentrated on her hand in his, wanting to feel some comfort from her and a connection to her. "It is very nice, being with you. I want to enjoy our time together, not talk of problems."

He seemed to have let pass whatever it was that was bothering him. She saw him take another cleansing breath and he seemed more relaxed. "I did not know you were from the FBI."

She smiled. It was always like this when a man discovered what she did for a living. They were either very appreciative and interested or nervous and intimidated.

"My father was in law enforcement. I come from a small town in Virginia and he was the sheriff for many years. It just seemed natural for me to follow in his footsteps. I've always been interested in law, but I love art too! I have *no* artistic talent, but this job allows me to visit some of the best galleries and museums in the world!"

He couldn't help but smile at the way she got excited about her work. The urge to kiss her again, to hold her and lose himself in her was strong. He could so *easily* lose himself in her, just like he did with the chalk *Flora.* He wanted to drink in the beauty of her face, the soft pink undertones of her skin and the burnt sienna hues of her hair. He hungered for the sensuality of her body pressed to his, of her beauty becoming part of who he was and recreating in him the person he desperately wanted to be.

"Will you have dinner again with me tonight?" he ventured. The thought of being away from her was starting to weigh on him just like the thought of the real Flora in that vault somewhere in the Middle East.

"I'd like that very much."

"Then I will pick you up at your hotel at seven-thirty. Is that good?" He was much more relaxed now and she was relieved. She wanted it gone: the uncomfortable, uptight way she felt being with him and knew he felt too. She told him the name of her hotel.

"I'll see you then," she said. "I'm sorry, I have to go now. I'm working and should get back to the Uffizi. They will be expecting me." She wanted to add 'but I'd much rather spend the rest of the day *and* night with you,' but knew she wouldn't. Sometimes though, looking into his dark eyes, it was hard not to tell him exactly what she was thinking and how much she wanted to know him better!

"Papa will be expecting us for espresso. Can you not stay just a little longer?" His eyes were pleading as his lips broke into a seductive smile. She wanted to talk to the Assistant Head of Acquisitions, Vincenzo Sartori, but seeing the expectation in Damiano's eyes convinced her that Sartori could wait.

"Then we'd better not keep your Papa waiting," she said and they walked slowly back toward number twenty-two, Damiano's hand never leaving hers.

ɷ

The park was small so he had to find a place to watch them that was farther away than he liked, but he had the binoculars and at least they wouldn't see him.

They talked for a while and he wondered what they were saying, all the while cursing the fact that he couldn't get closer. But sometimes, that was just the way this job went.

He saw Travani take her into his arms and kiss her. She liked it, he could tell, and he felt the ache starting and the anger. He never should have agreed to watch her. He knew it would be like this, knew that if she met someone, it would tear up his insides. He always figured that it didn't matter where she went, some guy would always be hitting on her; she was that beautiful!

Now she seemed to be getting way too close to Travani and there was nothing he could do about it. All he could do was to watch her through the binoculars like some impotent peeping Tom; wanting to have her, but unable to.

He promised himself that he would never agree to this kind of assignment again.

Chapter 17

HE FINISHED THE veal parmigiana and sat sipping the expensive red wine he'd ordered, deciding how long he could stall Travani. Down deep, he was scared. There was something not right about this deal, especially the fact that the buyer was late with the money. That had never happened before and Galiazzi was starting to have doubts about Sartori and his 'wealthy buyer' in the Middle East. Something had made him nervous from the beginning of this entire affair. Galiazzi wondered if there was a weak link in the chain and if Sartori was it; he had never had trusted the man.

This job had come to Sartori initially. He was the only person inside the Uffizi who had ever used Galiazzi's services where a forgery was concerned. Being an art dealer, Galiazzi had numerous contacts in the art world and dealt mostly in legitimate matters. He knew of no one else in the museum who had dealings with the illegal side of the art world. For all Galiazzi knew, Sartori was the only 'dirty' one inside the gallery and had a lot to lose if this deal didn't happen.

He took another sip of his wine, the nervousness making his stomach unsettled; hopefully the wine would help. He noticed his palms were sweaty and wiped them on his napkin as Travani walked into the room. He didn't look happy and for the first time in his career, Galiazzi feared for his well-being.

"Sit down, Travani," he said, trying to sound cordial. "Would you like some wine?"

"I am not here on a social visit."

Galiazzi frowned. "There is no need to be ungracious or to refuse my hospitality." His palms were even wetter now and he wiped them again, this time with the napkin on his lap, out of Travani's sight. Travani relented and sat opposite, his hands folded on top of the table.

"You are sure no one followed you? You came in the back door?"

"Yes, I followed all of your instructions. Now where is my money? I have put myself at great risk to do this job for you and I want to be paid. I have debts, people breathing down my neck…dangerous people."

"I understand that. It is the same with me." He sipped his wine, careful to control his shaking hands. "I must be paid also before I can pay you. There has been a delay, that is all. I have been assured by my contact that the money will arrive in six days."

Travani almost choked. Six days! Bocchio expected full payment of the debt in seven! One day was cutting it too close. Bocchio was nothing if not punctual and the minute the full ten days was up, he'd be banging at Travani's door with his bodyguard in tow and Travani would find himself wishing he were out of the country too, just like *Flora.*

"That is not soon enough," Travani pressed. "I need my money now!"

"Listen," Galiazzi replied, hoping to stall. "My hands are tied in this matter. I need my money too, but it will not be here for six days. It is out of my control."

Travani wasn't going to back down. He was clenching his jaw, his eyes narrowing and his hands forming into fists on top of the table, forcing Galiazzi to fortify himself with a generous gulp of wine."

Travani was mad. He'd always known that getting involved in doing forgeries was dangerous and now it looked as though that danger had caught up with him. He knew what men like Galiazzi were like and no matter what, he couldn't show weakness. If you were weak, your chances of surviving dropped to zero.

"Do not think that because I am new to this game you can cheat me, Galiazzi. If I do not have the half-million euro in my hands in exactly six days, you will not need to worry about paying *your* debts!" He slammed his fists down on the table as he rose to leave, accidentally knocking over the chair.

☙

Walking back from Giulio's house, Noreen had time to think about Damiano, about the complications to her career of getting involved with him. Whenever she considered her career, she always came back to her desire to honor Cody, to join him in fighting for "truth, justice and the American way." Cody saw law enforcement as just that: a job for heroes like Superman, his favorite. He saw himself like that and wanted her to join him. After his death, going into police work was the major factor that kept her looking forward and helped lessen her grief. She knew it helped her father too, knowing the Issenlowe name would continue serving and that their family would survive even in the face of such a tragic loss.

There was something special about Cody, and about his faith in God, that Noreen had always admired. Her family attended church together every Sunday when they weren't on duty. They all had a relationship with God and great faith, but Cody had a special gift: he loved people and gravitated to the lost and hurting victims that he came in contact with almost every day. He gave of his time and energy, he gave what money he could for worthy causes and he gave all of himself. His joy, smile, laughter and sense of humor were contagious and many times, had helped in diffusing what could have been dangerous situations as he fulfilled his duties.

Even though her decision to join the FBI was made with some trepidation, her job did infuse her with the sense that she too was making a difference just as Cody had. But somehow, knowing that had not given her the joy that was so evident with Cody. She helped recover valuable works of art and that brought joy to the people who owned them, but lately that didn't seem to be enough. Maybe that's why she hadn't been excited by this case, about being able to be in Florence again.

Now a handsome, passionate artist had come into her life and her desire was being pulled in another direction. If Cody were alive, what would he tell her to do? What would he think? What would God think?

She stood in front of Castagno's office and took a deep breath. For now, she reminded herself that she was an FBI agent and that *Flora* was missing.

As she entered the office, she saw Castagno snub out a cigarette in the metal ashtray as he, Sartori, the lead transfer guard, Rico Panello and van driver Emilio Tavolaro, stood as she entered. After introducing Panello and Tavolaro, they all took seats, Castagno again looking like he needed a cigarette. Sartori didn't look much better. He looked pale and stressed.

"Thank you, gentlemen, for taking time to meet with me," she said. "I just have a few questions and promise not to take too much of your time." They all nodded politely and she turned her attention to Panello.

He had light brown hair, blue-green eyes and needed a haircut. Noreen knew he was thirty-eight, married with three children and had worked for the gallery for ten years. His record was clean: no complaints, problems or disciplinary actions. She had read all of their personnel files before the meeting, even Castagno's.

"I understand, Signore Panello, that you are the head guard?" He nodded as he fingered a cigarette, though he hadn't lit it yet. Castagno must have said something about her not smoking. If he had, she was grateful.

"Can you go over your duties the day the painting was shipped?" She noticed he suddenly looked a little annoyed.

"I have told everything to the TPC and Signore D'Angelo." As he spoke, he kept rolling the cigarette between his right thumb and first two fingers. She noted that he'd only made tentative eye contact with her and that Sartori was trying to look bored…trying hard.

"I understand that, but I would like to hear your version, you understand, so that there are no misinterpretations." She may be female, but she could play hardball just like a man and these guys better figure that out now. "Were you present when the painting was crated?"

"*Sì.* From the time the painting was brought to the preparation room until the time it was loaded on the plane, I was with it."

"It never left your sight? You didn't leave for a moment, maybe to use the restroom or get a cup of coffee?"

"No, Signorina. It never left my sight." He was making better eye contact now, but the cigarette in his hand was paying the price; tiny bits of tobacco were dropping out of both ends and onto his lap; Italians didn't use filtered cigarettes.

Sartori cut in. "From the time *Flora* was taken off the wall, until it was put on the plane, it was *always* accompanied by at least three museum personnel. That is our policy."

Noreen smiled politely, thanked him and went back to Panello. Sartori didn't seem quite as bored now.

"Did you inspect the van before the painting was loaded?"

"Inspect it? For what purpose? It is a van, the same one we use for every transfer. I checked the fuel gauge to make sure we had enough fuel to get to the airport and back. That is all I checked." He brushed the bits of tobacco off his pants.

"Tell me about the inside of the van." Here, Panello gave her an incredulous look.

"There is nothing to tell. It is a van!"

"How many seats does it have? Is the back carpeted or bare? Is there any place where a copy of Flora, crated to look like the real painting, could be hidden away so that nobody knew it was there?"

She saw the immediate recognition in his face; he knew what she was going after. He worked the cigarette even more intently now. Either he was hiding something or he needed a smoke even worse than Castagno.

"Signorina, I appreciate your tenacity in solving this case, but personally, I do not like this line of questioning. Signore Panello and I escorted the painting and your questions seem to suggest that either he or I had something to do with the disappearance." Sartori's disguised boredom was gone now, replaced with indignation. Noreen saw him run his palms across his pant legs. The room was cool; he shouldn't be sweating. That clinched it for her; he'd given himself away. He was lying.

"I didn't mean to suggest that you or Signore Panello had anything to do with the theft and if I offended you, I'm sorry. I'm just trying to get a picture in my mind of exactly what took place that day. You understand I'm sure." She could play hardball, but it wouldn't do to get these guys mad at her; they'd close off completely if she did. She wanted them relaxed and confident. Sartori gave her a look that told her the apology was accepted and she continued, looking at Panello and waiting for his answer.

"It is an unmarked, white delivery van, two seats, passenger and driver with a single seat behind. The floor is carpeted and there is a sectioned built-in container in back where the crates are kept." Panello's cigarette was almost empty of tobacco, all of the bits either on his lap or on the floor. He put it into his shirt pocket and started rubbing his thumb and forefinger together in small circles, his hand resting on his thigh.

"Tell me about the container. Are the paintings stored vertically or horizontally?" Panello looked confused, so she elaborated. "Do the paintings stand up or lie down?"

"Up," he said tersely.

"So they stand up in slots?" He nodded. "How many slots are there? How many paintings could be transported at one time?"

He shrugged his shoulders. "I have never counted them. Maybe six. I can show you the van if you would like."

She ignored his offer; he was being condescending. "Were there any other paintings being transported that evening or just the Titan?"

"The Titan was the only painting." Panello's eyes darted up and to the right. She almost smiled; so much could be given away without one word being spoken because the eyes said more than any other body part…even the mouth!

She had to be careful now about what she asked. She didn't want to scare any of these men and have them turn up out of the country, especially in another country that didn't have extradition agreements.

The driver, Emilio Tavolaro, had been sitting quietly, intent on the conversation. She decided to let Panello calm down for now.

"How many years have you driven for the museum?" she asked. Tavolaro seemed younger than the other men, but relaxed and maybe a little excited.

"Five years, Signorina," he said. He was tall and thin with piercing blue eyes and a ready smile; maybe too ready?

"Are you the only person who drives the van?"

"Yes. If I am sick, then a substitute is found, but I drove *Flora* that night." He smiled and it reminded her of Cody's smile. She smiled back as he added, "I hope you will find her. She is beautiful and she belongs in the Uffizi."

"I'm going to do my best," Noreen assured him. "Did you leave the van at any time?"

"No, Signorina. I was with her all the time. I did not get out until we arrived at the airport." This man too, who she remembered was twenty-four, but looked nineteen, had a clean work history. He was an art student, but from what information she'd gotten, he was no Michelangelo *or* Titan. Apparently, he didn't have much talent.

"Did you get into the van before or after Flora was loaded in the back?"

"After."

"When you got out at the airport, what did you do?"

"I had a smoke! The museum will not let us smoke in the van." He smiled at her and she wondered if there was anyone is Italy that didn't smoke.

"Was the painting still in the van at that time?"

Tavolaro nodded. "The men who load the plane had not arrived."

"Did you ever get into the back of the van? Did you see the painting once it was in the van?"

"No, there is never any reason. I sit in the driver's seat all the time."

She saw Castagno check his watch. Sartori was definitely trying to look bored again and was rolling a pen between two fingers, Panello was brushing a few remaining stray bits of tobacco off his pants and Castagno was eyeing the cigarette butt in his ashtray.

"That's all I need for now. Thank you gentlemen for your cooperation." She stood and they did likewise. Castagno added his thanks and thanked Noreen for her efforts on behalf of the gallery. With that, she shook hands with each man as they filed out of the room, leaving her alone with Castagno.

It seemed odd that he didn't ask her how her investigation was going. For some reason, he didn't broach the subject with her and she wondered why. He was head of security and it seemed to her that he would be under great pressure to get this case solved, that he'd want any help he could get. But he asked nothing and just smiled as she left.

She checked her watch again. It was getting late and she needed to get ready for her dinner date with Damiano.

Chapter 18

AT SEVEN-THIRTY exactly, the phone in her room rang and the desk clerk told her a Signore Travani was waiting in the lobby. She thanked him, grabbed her shawl and took the elevator downstairs.

His face lit up when he saw her and that got her butterflies flapping madly again.

"You are beautiful!" he said. He wasted no time in taking her hand as he kissed her cheeks, pressing his lips firmly this time and then kissing her on the lips. She noticed the warmth of his breath on her skin and the spicy scent of his cologne. Tonight she was hoping they could get past the polite, safe conversations that always marked a new relationship. She wanted to leave the awkwardness of that behind and get to know who he really was. She was very attracted to him and felt the constraints of time pressing on her. She would not be in Italy for many more days and if this relationship was going to get serious, she needed to know that. Her future, and all that entailed, would be affected.

"I have made reservations at a restaurant near here. I hope you do not mind a short walk." She shook her head as he took her hand and they walked out into the evening, the sun low on the horizon and casting everything in its crimson glow.

There was something magical about Florence at sunset and this was the first time she'd noticed it. The air was warm, with just enough humidity to wrap around her like a luxurious towel after a relaxing shower. It caressed her skin and soothed the butterflies until she couldn't feel them as much. The scent of jasmine drifted to her and mixed with his cologne and at that moment, the missing Flora, the FBI and everything else fell away and there was only the night and him, his hand in hers, his touch warming her in all the right places. They said nothing as they walked. It was as though they both wanted only to enjoy being together and the lack of inane conversation served to achieve that.

The streets were still active with tourists; the café's busy and noisy as they passed by. There was music coming from the Piazza della Signoria as they strolled across and headed toward the Uffizi.

The fake *David* stared down at them as they passed by and entered the courtyard. Still silent, they made their way toward the Arno River, the stone statues outside the gallery giving the impression of a double receiving line. She felt as though all the great Italians of the past were watching them as they headed out of the courtyard. They walked past the Ponte Vecchio along the street that ran parallel to the river until they entered the restaurant.

It wasn't as busy here. There was no outside seating and this place didn't seem to be as crowded as the cafés that faced Piazza della Signoria. The maitre d' nodded at Damiano and Noreen could tell they knew each other. She wondered if he'd brought other women to this place, but pushed that thought out of her head. *She* was with him tonight and that was all that mattered.

They were seated at very private corner table, one that Noreen was fairly certain he was accustomed to occupying. She could tell from the look on the face of the maitre d'. Now though, she was trying to convince herself that she wasn't just a one-night stand for him, that he was interested in a serious relationship with her. That's what his eyes were telling her and so that's what she would choose to believe.

"This is a very nice place," she said at last. The silence between them was out of place now, here where the chatter and laughter of other people swirled around them like cream stirred into a cup of coffee.

"I come here often. The food is very good." That was all he said and even though she could see he desired her, he seemed hesitant to keep eye contact with her. He was fingering the base of his empty wine glass. Was he still nervous, she wondered? She knew men thought she was pretty, but she'd never been with a man like this, one who seemed almost speechless in front of her.

As the waiter approached the table, she said, "Then please order something you like and I know I'll like it too." He scanned the menu, giving the order to the waiter, who wrote it down, then left and Damiano went back to quietly fingering the wine glass.

He seemed very distant, as though his mind was somewhere else and she wondered why. Maybe it had something to do with the problem he'd mentioned at the park. Whatever it was, she wanted to enjoy this meal with him. She was determined to pull him back from where ever he'd gone.

"I'm very attracted to you, Damiano, but you seem very uncomfortable being with me. I don't want to make you feel that way."

"You do not make me uncomfortable. Please do not think that and I am sorry if I have made that impression." He'd pushed the wine glass away and was looking at her now.

The waiter brought a bottle of red wine and filled both their glasses. Damiano held his up and said, "To *Flora* and to her beauty that takes men's breath away."

Noreen smiled. Maybe he was just overcome being with her, the fact that he thought she looked like the woman in the painting. She reminded herself how he had 'danced' with *Flora*, had stroked her as he blended the colors between her breasts, how one only had to watch him to know he loved her.

She took a large swallow of the wine; the butterflies were becoming unruly again, so much so they were making her tremble. She realized then that she was very hungry, but not for dinner and that thought required another large gulp of wine. She saw him smile and smiled back, almost laughing.

"You like the wine?" he asked, winking at her.

"Yes," she replied. "It's very good!" The alcohol was warming her cheeks, making her flush.

From then on, the conversation flowed unheeded. They ate, savoring the meal, while they talked about Italian food, their families, art, Florence, their childhoods and more topics than she thought possible in the course of one dinner. The barriers between them came down, whatever problem he had seemed to be put away for now and the butterflies had taken off for parts unknown.

The wine had worked its magic and by the time their dessert plates were cleared, they were holding hands across the table, Damiano's eyes never leaving hers and the desire in them making her heart race again.

As they left the restaurant and went outside into the night, she glanced at her wristwatch. Four hours had passed and yet it seemed as though it had only been a few minutes. He was close to her now, his right arm around her waist as they headed back toward the Uffizi.

The streets weren't as busy now, but the cafés still buzzed with activity and the multitude of lights gave Florence a carnival atmosphere. She could hear music and singing coming from somewhere. They passed the Ponte Vecchio and she felt him pull her closer to his body until they stopped, his eyes locked onto hers. He held her chin and kissed her just as passionately as he had before.

Letting herself soften into him, she released the newness of being with him and wanted only to feel the warmth of his body next to hers and the strength of his arms holding her. She wanted to be his *Flora*, to be recreated by him the way he recreated the painting on the streets, to be loved by him the way he loved her.

At the entrance to her hotel, he kissed her again, his lips exploring hers until her heart was beating wildly in her chest and her body ached to have him. Her passion rose like a fire burning inside, consuming her control until there was nothing left but the hunger to make love to him.

"Come up to my room," she said.

"I cannot," he answered, stepping back, but holding her hands.

How could he make her understand? She was beautiful and good and he was a criminal and dirty. If he touched her, made love to her, he would dirty her too, he would hurt her and he couldn't do that even if he hadn't promised his father. She deserved better, this *Flora.* She was a masterpiece and he would not make love to her and cheapen her, take away her innocence and leave her less than perfect like the forged *Flora*, the one he'd put his mark on.

"I don't understand. Have I done something wrong?"

"I cannot. That is all I can tell you," he answered. He stood looking down at their joined hands for several seconds. After what seemed an eternity, he finally met her gaze and saw that her hunger was still there.

"Are you married? Is there someone else? Tell me. I'll understand."

"I am not married and there is no one else," he said slowly. "Believe me when I tell you that if I make love to you, you will regret it. I cannot come up, Noreen."

The fire was gone now and leaving her feeling empty, only ashes left of the passion within her. She remembered the image of him chalking Flora, the way he loved her, and knew even then she wanted him to love *her* like that. She wanted him then and she knew she would always want him.

"Will I see you again?" she asked.

"I do not think that would be a good idea," he said. "It would only cause more pain."

"I don't understand any of this!" She gripped his hands, but he pulled away from her. "Do you love me?" She heard him let out a long breath as he took her in his arms again and held her closely.

"Yes, I love you more than I have ever loved anyone. But you must let me go. If you stay with me, you will get hurt and I cannot have that. You must understand that I do this *because* I love you."

"I can't let you go, Damiano. I've loved you since the first day I saw you drawing *Flora* on the street. I love your passion and your talent and I want you to love *me* like that. I want to love you like that and have you in my life."

"It cannot be. I am sorry, *mi bella Flora.*" He walked away, never turning back to look at her. She stood unmoving at the hotel entrance, the shock of how this evening had ended making her legs weak and the grief pressing in on her. When she finally turned and went through the door, she heard the same music playing that she'd heard on the way to the restaurant, her heart heavy in her chest and the tears dripping down her cheeks.

Chapter 19

HE'D FOLLOWED THEM *from her hotel to the café, but unfortunately there was no good place to stay hidden. The café fronted a narrow street and beyond that, there was a chest-high brick retaining wall with the river behind it; no shrubs, trees or other spots that would conceal him. So he'd waited in the doorway of a closed shop, waited for almost four hours wondering what they were talking about and cursing under his breath that he couldn't see her.*

She was smart when it came to knowing where to find the information she needed. She almost had a natural intuition about that and he was sure that was why she was hanging around this street scum; a guy who lived by stealing from tourists and probably had never had a real job with real responsibility.

She wasn't the kind to string a man along, to seduce him in order to get the information she needed and then drop him. She was too moral for that. Her integrity was solid and she knew where her priorities were. And she would never jeopardize her career for a low-life like him. She wouldn't jeopardize it for an educated, honest man either. He knew that.

But he'd seen the look in her face when they came out of the restaurant. She wasn't using Travani to get information. She was interested in him and that meant that she didn't know about his criminal record.

He felt it more now, the pain of not having her, of seeing her with Travani and holding his hand. He thought about how good it would feel to be with her, to be the one to hold her and feel her passion burning when he kissed her.

When they'd come out of the restaurant, he had wanted to run up to her and tell her who Travani really was, to warn her that getting involved with him would hurt her, but he had a job to do.

More than once since seeing her with Travani, he'd thought about ways to protect her, to keep her from being hurt, but the best he could do was to watch her. He knew though that there would come a time when he would have to report and the thought of lying to cover up her relationship with Travani had crossed his mind several times. He would do that for her. He would give up his integrity to protect hers. She was worth it.

Then something happened in front of her hotel. He saw them kiss and knew that look of utter submission she had when Travani held her, knew how she was giving all of herself to him. He was scared for her. If she took Travani up to her room, all that she wanted for her life would be thrown away for a one-night stand. He knew that was all it would be for Travani, but it would be devastating for her and he couldn't let that happen.

But after the kiss, he saw Travani pull away. He saw the questioning on her face and then the pain and tears as he kissed her again and then walked away. She stood there for several seconds. The urge to rush up to her, to tell her how much he wanted her and loved her was so strong. It took everything he had to watch through the binoculars, to see her tears and then see her enter the hotel knowing the pain in her heart. He knew that same pain and never wanted that for her, but there was nothing he could do.

He walked back to his hotel thinking about her, about how he wanted to comfort her, to make love to her so that she would never want to think about Travani again. Maybe it was over now and he would have his chance when this was all finished. He smiled at that thought. Yes, he might get another chance with her.

Chapter 20

SHE HELD THE cold washcloth to her face, willing herself not to cry. As it was, she was having a hard time getting the puffiness of her eyelids to subside and crying again wouldn't help. She tried not to think about last night, about wanting Damiano. She wondered how it could have happened so fast. She'd seen him 'dancing' with *Flora* and had fallen instantly in love. Until he'd told her he wouldn't come up to her room, she hadn't even realized she loved him so completely and the fact that she really didn't know him just added to her astonishment. This just wasn't like her. As she applied her makeup, she thought about how it could have happened.

Obviously, Rachel was right. She needed someone more than she was willing to admit and when her friend had mentioned falling in love with an artist, that idea had taken root in her subconscious. For someone who loved art and the beauty of great art as much as she did, it was no wonder she fell in love with Damiano as she watched him with *Flora.* Maybe it wasn't him that she was in love with. Maybe it was the idea of a man loving her the way he loved creating *Flora*, his tenderness as he applied the flesh colors and stroked her skin.

She grabbed her concealing cream and patted some beneath both eyes. The puffiness was still there, but would go away soon. The dark circles from lying awake all night would take much longer and the cream would help.

Was she in love with the idea of being loved by an artist and Damiano just happened to come along? She thought about that while she lightly brushed some eye shadow on her upper lids, deciding that the answer was 'no.' There was something that drew her to *him*, something in his soul that she knew was there, but that he wouldn't or couldn't allow her to see. It felt almost as if he needed her in some way, the way a child needs his mother when he's hurt himself and is crying. That thought made her chuckle and she almost poked her eye as she brushed mascara on her lashes. In no way did she want a man so that she could 'mother' him. But that was the only way she could express to herself the sense he gave her.

As she glided the lipstick across her lips, she remembered his thumb doing the same thing before he'd kissed her the first time. Her eyes filled immediately and she dabbed them with a tissue, inhaling deeply and mentally pushing him out of her mind as she exhaled. It was over and that's where she had to leave it. She had a job to do and it was best if she forget about Damiano. She needed to help get this case wrapped up and then go back to Falls Church as soon as possible. Any delay in returning home was only going to prolong the pain she felt this morning. There was too much here that reminded her of him and even now, she was on her way to the Uffizi to interview Sartori and she knew Giulio would be standing outside, posing for the tourists. Did he know? What would she tell him?

Her eyes were filling again, the pain from her night of sobbing still pressing on her as she inhaled deeply a second time and cautiously wiped them, careful not to smear her mascara.

She was due at the Uffizi. Vincenzo Sartori was waiting, but keeping him on ice for a while was part of her plan. If he was hiding something, she wanted him to have time to sweat about this meeting. She grabbed her purse and headed for the elevator, pushing the memory of Damiano's kiss out of her mind. It was time to go and time to let go.

☙

After the date ended, Damiano hid away in his apartment. He couldn't get the image of her beautiful tear-streaked face out of his head and couldn't chase away the thought of how he'd hurt her, even though he'd hoped a few bottles of wine would help erase his memory. They didn't. They just reminded him of how she'd gulped her wine twice because she wanted him so much, that she'd tried to hide it, but that it showed all over her. He remembered her dark eyes smoldering with desire and her breathing making her chest rise and fall quickly. The pain of not making love to her, to his *Flora*, was still new and so he tried to make his world small, too small for thoughts of her. Just like the wine, that wasn't working either.

He took two aspirin, hoping his headache would let up and was lying on the sofa when there was a knock at the door. He jumped up. Maybe it was the five hundred thousand euro that Galiazzi owed him. In anticipation, he opened the door quickly without a thought of checking who was on the other side.

"Travani, time is running out." It was Bocchio and that was a bad sign. "Do you have my money or will you put me off again?"

"I still have six days."

"I am checking, that is all, and to remind you that I am granting you special leeway in this matter. I do not do that for anyone else." Bocchio's face was redder than usual, but it was warm in the apartment and Bocchio was wearing his trademark cloak, the perspiration dripping off his chin. Travani had never been able to figure out why Bocchio wore that coat in this warm weather, unless it was to make himself appear more sinister. If that was the reason, today it was working.

"I know that and I appreciate that," Travani replied.

Bocchio looked even more like the Dracula character today, if that was possible. His eyes were bloodshot as if he'd just filled himself with another victim and the blood feast was seeping into his eyes. He wiped the perspiration from his face and continued.

"I cannot live on appreciation. I have been more than generous with you because I respect your talent, but respect will not pay my bills." Travani could guess what was coming. "Due to circumstances that I cannot control, I must add another three hundred euro interest to your account. You now owe me eleven hundred and I *will* get the full amount in six days."

Bocchio didn't have to elaborate. Travani could make an educated guess about what would happen if the debt wasn't paid. A coldness passed through him and it was all he could do to keep from shuddering. He couldn't let Bocchio see him scared.

"You will have your money. As I told you, there was a delay, but it is on its way."

"For your sake, Travani, I hope so." With that, The Teacher turned and left and at that moment, Travani noticed that Bocchio's bodyguard had not come with him.

As he locked the door, Travani noticed his hands were shaking. The coldness was still with him as he imagined both his arms broken so badly that he would never be able to unzip his fly and urinate by himself again without help. He knew it was a very real possibility. Bocchio and men like him needed to make examples of what could happen when loans were not repaid. Alone now and with only six days until payment was due, Travani couldn't help the sinking feeling that was starting in the pit of his stomach. He needed a plan.

He went to his easel and picked up the brush. He loaded some titanium white from the palette and applied it to the canvas, refining what he had started earlier. It was coming along nicely, this painting. Painting relaxed him. He would work for several more hours and hope that he wouldn't think about Bocchio and about the money he didn't have to repay the loan. He would concentrate on his work and that would help. But he knew he wouldn't be able to quit thinking about her. He saw her face clearly, the tears he'd caused, the pain in her eyes right before he turned around and walked away.

Cleaning his brush, he picked up a dab of burnt sienna and applied it to the canvas. He loved her and he hated himself for what he'd become. He'd sold his soul for a half-million euro and in the process, Titan's *Flora* was gone and now so was his *Flora*. As he worked the burnt sienna into the canvas, the more he thought about her and the more he felt his eyes stinging.

He cleaned the brush in the turpentine, and then laid it with the others. He couldn't continue today. He couldn't stop thinking about how he'd hurt her and this time, painting wasn't helping him to forget and wasn't helping the ache he had for her.

He couldn't go back to the street to re-do the chalk of *Flora*. She might try to find him and he was afraid that if he saw her again, he would tell her everything just to be able to hold her in his arms and kiss her one last time. But he needed as much money as he could make before his payment with Bocchio was due in full. He'd neither seen nor heard anything about the half-million euro, so it was best to make as much money off the tourists as he could in the time he had left. He needed to get some real cash now, not the euro coins the tourists threw into his bowl.

He left his apartment and wandered away from the Piazza della Signoria. It was too close to the Uffizi and he knew she would be in that area.

He made his way toward the Arno by way of a side street and headed for the Ponte Vecchio. This bridge, which was thought to have been built in ancient Roman times and was at one time a place of butcher shops, was now home to some of the world's most beautiful jewelry. Gold, silver and coral beaconed from the shop windows lining either side of the bridge and this area was always crowded with people. A score here might even be enough to pay off Bocchio in full.

He stood in at the mid-point of the bridge, in front of the statue of Benvenuto Cellini. It was open on both sides here; there were no shops, just views up and down the Arno. He watched and waited, sizing up the unsuspecting people who walked by snapping photos or staring into the shop windows. It didn't take long before he spotted them.

She was short, heavy-set and walked very cautiously as if she had problems with her hips. She looked about seventy-five. He was thin, and was about her age. He thought they might be Americans or maybe Australians, he wasn't sure, but he knew they had money. He was wearing a large-carat diamond man's ring and she had rings on every finger of both hands: diamonds, rubies and sapphires set in gold. She even had a star opal on her left index finger. If they were carrying that much wealth on their hands, he could imagine what they were carrying in their pockets and the large, heavy-looking purse that hung over her right shoulder.

They had stopped directly across from him and were taking a photo of the river. She seemed to be having a problem with her camera and was upset with the man about it. Maybe he was trying to help, but she was having none of it. Maybe he could 'help', Damiano thought, and approached them.

"Do you have trouble with your camera?" he asked.

"Oh, this silly thing won't focus," the woman said. She held it out to him while the skinny man tapped her arm, told her he was going to find a place to sit and walked to the other side, sitting down at the base of the Cellini statue. There was a narrow ledge, about eight inches off the ground and he sat there, his back resting against the wrought iron fence around the statue. Damiano watched the old man sit and wondered if he'd be able to get up again without help.

"Do you know anything about cameras?" she was asking.

"May I look?" Damiano held out his hand and she handed over the camera. Tourists! They were so trusting of strangers, he thought. He could run off with the camera right then and she wouldn't be able to catch him and yet, she'd handed it over without even thinking. It was an expensive camera too, but he needed cash and he needed to get it without being caught. He could run off with the camera, but she would probably scream and he'd have some good-hearted by-stander chasing after him or worse, the police. This too had happened in the past and he'd only escaped jail by dropping what he'd stolen as he was running away. Stealing was the same as any other endevour: you learned from your mistakes.

"I think it will work now," he said. He hadn't done anything to it, but she didn't know that. "You want a photo of the Arno, yes?" She nodded and he continued, "Take the camera, hold it up to your eye." She did as he said as he positioned himself behind her after a quick check of his surroundings. It was crowded here today and that would help him.

He stood directly behind her over-sized purse so that when he reached into it, what he was doing was hidden by his body. He kept talking to her, giving her explicit instructions as to how to aim the camera and then when to shoot the photo; a stalling tactic that worked well in this kind of situation. By the time she'd pressed the shutter button, her wallet was safely tucked into the inside pocket of his jacket and she was admiring the photo in the camera's viewing screen and thanking him for his help.

She hurried over to the old man to show him and Damiano could see that she was trying to help him stand, but not having success with this either. Damiano rushed over and helped the man to his feet as they thanked him profusely. He turned and walked back toward his apartment, the immorality of what he'd just done weighting heavy on him. He tried convincing himself that they could afford the loss, but nothing eased his conscience. Then he realized he'd just gone back on his word to his father.

He was getting scared. He feared he would give up, turn himself in for all his crimes, even the forged *Flora* and spend the rest of his life in prison. He fought not to think about that, but when he did, the memory of Noreen crying came back. If she knew what he'd just done, would she still love him?

He shook his head, took a deep breath and sped up his pace. He needed to get back to his apartment and see how much money was in the wallet. He had to get Bocchio off his back.

Chapter 21

SARTORI'S OFFICE WAS much neater than Castagno's and the Assistant Head of Acquisitions wasn't smoking when she came in and sat opposite him. She was thankful for that. Her eyes were still stinging from having cried all night and she didn't need the irritation of cigarette smoke to add to the dryness and discomfort she already felt.

She wanted to meet with him outside of his office, somewhere that wasn't his 'home ground', somewhere he felt uncomfortable like a police interrogation room, but there was no evidence to take the man into custody and question him like he was a common criminal. After all, he was the Assistant Head of Acquisitions at one of the world's greatest galleries. He would be comfortable here and would be less likely to make a mistake in answering her questions. Well, she decided, she was just going to have to work with what she had.

"Thank you for your time," she began. If she got him comfortable at the beginning, he might get over-confident and let something slip; sometimes interrogation worked both ways.

"We are very anxious to get the Titan returned, Signorina, and will help in any way we can."

He wasn't as nervous this time…that was for sure. She saw him lean back in his chair, his hands folded in his lap, his facial muscles relaxed and a slight smile on his lips. Was he checking her out?

"You told me during our last meeting that you accompanied the painting from the time it was loaded into the van until the van returned to the Uffizi. Do I have that correct?" He nodded and brushed an invisible something off his coat sleeve. Whatever it was, she didn't see it, but made note that he'd done it.

"Yes, Panello sits up front with Tavolaro and I sit in the seat in back with the art."

"Were you the one who handed off the painting to the person who loaded it on the plane?"

"Yes. We have a protocol here, similar to what you police use with your crime evidence. Our protocol demands that each phase of the transfer is done precisely so that there is no break in the chain of events, that one person is never alone with the painting. Does that make sense?"

She nodded her head and asked, "Were all three of you with the van when it was returned to the Uffizi?" That pesky piece of invisible lint seemed to have found its way back to his sleeve because he brushed it away again. It was a good tactic to use if a person wanted time to think and to avoid eye contact with the questioner. Then he straightened his tie. It wasn't out of place and she made another mental note.

"Yes, we were all together. Remember, we were following our protocol." He had a very condescending tone, one that she'd heard the first time she'd questioned him. His eyes glanced up and to the right momentarily; a sign that he was probably lying.

"Signore Tavolaro told me that he'd gotten out of the van to smoke a cigarette. Where exactly was the painting when he was smoking? Had it already been loaded or was it still in the van?"

Sartori's eyes darted to the left this time and his face blanched as if he'd seen a ghost. His reaction was quick, subtle and would have been missed by anyone not trained in interrogation, but she'd seen it. He was getting nervous. She was sure he was trying to remember what Tavolaro had said at the last meeting.

"Signore, where was the painting?" she repeated.

Sartori cleared his throat. "The painting had already been loaded into the plane. Tavolaro had finished his smoke and we all left."

Even being in his own territory had not saved him. Noreen had just caught him in a lie, but now, what was she to do with it? Better to check with Carlo Rossini before confronting Sartori. It was the TPC's investigation and she was only helping.

"Thank you again for your time," she said with enough appreciation in her voice that she saw him relax. She wanted him relaxed until she talked to Rossini. She got up and he followed her to the office door.

"If I can be of any further assistance, please do not hesitate to call on me. This is a very unfortunate matter and we would like to find the Titan. We are grateful that the FBI is helping." He smiled at her. It was a fake smile, but apparently all he could manage at the moment, so she smiled back. Hers was fake too.

She walked down the hall, stopping at Castagno's office. She knocked, heard his 'come in' and entered just as he was putting out a cigarette. The metal ashtray was full of ashes and butts.

"Signorina Issenlowe, how nice to see you again! Please sit down." She took a chair. She liked Castagno. Even though she got the feeling he was hiding information from her, he had a genuinely pleasing, relaxed personality and it lightened her mood.

"I won't take up your time, Signore. I just wondered if I might talk to Emilio Tavolaro again."

"But of course." Here he picked up his phone, dialed an extension, said something in Italian and then hung up. "He will join us shortly. How is your investigation coming?"

She hesitated and that surprised her. She honestly didn't want to tell him anything about catching Sartori in a lie, but she didn't know why she felt like that. He was Head of Security after all and she should be able to be truthful with him. It was that feeling that he was keeping things from her. Better to say nothing for now, she decided.

"As with most cases such as this, investigation is a lengthy process I'm afraid." She smiled and hoped he would be satisfied with her answer.

"May I say again how happy we are for the help we receive and have received in the past, from your agency?" He reached for his pack of cigarettes, but didn't remove one. He put them into his desk drawer instead.

"The FBI Art Crime Team is happy to help. Interagency collaboration is important if we are to stop art forgery and theft."

"I am still puzzled, Signorina, about the cross on the forgery. It is so very unusual; something we have never encountered before. If this case is solved, or should I say "*when* this case is solved," I hope we will know the meaning of the cross and why it was put there."

His hands were folded together on top of his desk and she could see the yellow nicotine stains on his fingers. The compulsion for nicotine was so strong in some people, she thought. Maybe the forger of Flora had an addiction too, one that wouldn't let him copy the original without 'signing' it. It was something to think about.

"I too hope we will know the reason." Before she finished the sentence, there was a knock at the door and Tavolaro came in.

"You wanted to see me, Signore Castagno?" He was still wearing that smile she'd seen during the first interview.

"Actually, I wanted to see you. May I ask you a few more questions?" Noreen asked and he nodded, the smile gone now. "Did you come back to the Uffizi with the van?

"No, Signorina. My shift was over and so I had Rico drop me off at my house. It is on the way to the Uffizi. It was my sister's birthday and I was late for her party."

"Did you tell that to Inspector Rossini?"

"No, Signorina. He did not ask and I did not think it was important."

"At any time did you actually see the painting in the holding container? Did you look at the container at all?"

He shook his head. "No, Signorina. I never do. The others load it and I drive. That is all. But I did see it when it was loaded into the plane."

"Thank you very much. That's all I wanted to know." Sartori had told her in no uncertain terms that all three of the men had ridden back from the airport to the Uffizi. That was lie number two and Tavolaro had never looked at the container. The slots could have been full of crates and he never would have been the wiser. She couldn't wait to talk to Rossini about what she'd learned. Tavolaro nodded at her, then at Castagno as he left the room.

"I won't keep you any longer, Signore Castagno. Thank you again for your patience and help." Castagno stood as she got up and told her good-bye as he saw her to the door.

On her way to TPC headquarters, she thought about Sartori. Obviously he hadn't followed security protocol because at two separate times, he and Panello were alone with the painting. If he hadn't exhibited clear signs of lying, she would have chalked it up to a sloppy work ethic on Sartori's part. But if Panello was with him while Tavolaro was missing from the van twice, it stood to reason that Panello was as much a suspect as Sartori.

She smiled as she walked into TPC headquarters. She just might get that promotion when this investigation was completed.

ೲ

They were smarter than he'd given them credit for…the old man and woman. She had only twenty euro in cash and a VISA card. The card might bring him two hundred euro if he was lucky. They must have been keeping their money hidden in a money belt or maybe it was stashed down her bra. It surely wasn't in her purse. The old woman didn't even have a cell phone, which would have gotten him another forty to fifty euro. Even so, it wouldn't be enough to pay off Bocchio and Damiano was left right about where he'd started unless he could score better next time.

It was the 'next time' that was bothering him. When he'd helped the old man up to his feet, he'd realized how much that man reminded him of his father. This old guy had children and grandchild; he'd seen the photos in the woman's wallet and it just added to his guilt, erasing any thrill he used to get from the danger of picking pockets.

That was what kept him doing it; the danger. But now even that was gone, replaced with shame for what he had become. He knew that if he kept it up, he'd end up in jail again sooner or later.

He had to go back to chalking on the streets and maybe he'd even set up an easel and paint. Surely the tourists would buy an original oil painting. He still had four days until Bocchio would come for his money. Four days might be enough time if he worked hard.

He grabbed his backpack and headed back out to the streets. He would draw for the tourists, but he would have to do it in a place where he wouldn't be likely to see Noreen. It would be too hard to face her, even though he couldn't stop thinking about her.

Heading toward the Galleria dell' Accademia, he reminded himself again that walking out was the best thing he could do for her. He would have to try to forget her now, to get back to his life before she had completely taken his breath away, before she had captured his imagination and had become his *Flora.*

After setting up, he put out his money dish and a picture of Rafael's *La Donna Velata.* The painting's title meant 'the veiled woman.' She was beautiful too, with her large black eyes, rosy cheeks and sumptuous costume. She even reminded him of *Flora*, but *La Donna Velata's* pose was formal, staid and lacking the allure and sensuality of *Flora.* Damiano hoped drawing her would help him forget about the real woman, and about how much he wanted her.

It didn't take long to attract a crowd of onlookers and for the usual questions to start. The coins started too and every clink in his dish was one step closer to paying off Bocchio. He was still holding out hope that Galiazzi would come through with the half million euro, but having a back-up plan was a good idea when dealing with men like Bocchio.

After two hours, he finished *La Donna Velata.* Every time he painted or drew, he thought of Carlotta, thought about how he'd disappointed her. She loved his art, had encouraged his talent and education all of his life. He was six when she'd taken him to the Uffizi for the first time and told him all about the art and artists. It became a tradition: every year on his birthday, she would take him to a gallery and then buy him an Italian soda.

It was his special time with her and now, all he could remember was her face the first time she had to come to the police station to bail him out. He was sixteen. She never talked about what he'd done, never lectured him about his life. She didn't need to; he could see it in her face and he could still see it today.

He packed up his supplies, counted the money in his dish, pocketed the euros and headed toward the Piazza Santa Maria Novella. This plaza was large and the street was perfect for chalking. It was also far enough away from the Uffizi that he wouldn't run into Noreen.

Chapter 22

CARLO ROSSINI WAS out of his office when she arrived, but she was told she could wait there for him, that he wouldn't be long.

She still had the feeling that she wasn't being given all the information that was known about this theft. That bothered her. If the TPC wanted the FBI's help, wouldn't it be wise to share what clues they had? Something didn't feel right about this case, but she chalked it up to male ego. It was the TPC's case and of course, *they* wanted to solve it. It wouldn't do to have some American woman solve it for them. She tried not to think about that. She was here to help and that's all she was required to do. Besides, she was more upset about how things had turned out with Damiano than about male egos.

Something bothered her about him too. He'd said he couldn't love her because he would hurt her. What did he mean by that? Hurt her how? Every time she thought about that evening, she remembered their conversation in the park. Something was bothering him and now she wondered if it had something to do with her being with the FBI, with investigating the theft of *Flora.* Did he know something?

Was he keeping information from her too? She jumped when Rossini entered the room, startled away from her thoughts.

"I received your call. You have new information for us?" He shook her hand and took his seat behind the desk.

"Yes. I interviewed Sartori, alone this time and also interviewed Tavolaro again. When I first met with the gallery staff, Sartori seemed distant and when I shook his hand, his palms were sweaty. He didn't make good eye contact with me and all of that combined, got my attention."

Rossini looked interested. He leaned forward and folded his hands together on top of his desk. "And what did you learn?" he asked. He seemed genuinely excited that she may have stumbled onto something; the intensity of his gaze was unnerving. She was committed now. She had to tell him what she knew and she wondered how he was going to take it. After all, he'd already questioned Sartori and if he hadn't picked up on the lies, why not?

"He lied on two points. He said all three of them…himself, Panello and Tavolaro…were always together while the painting was in their possession. But Tavolaro told me that he'd gotten out of the van to smoke a cigarette and that the painting was still in the van at that time."

She waited, noticing his expression remained the same and then continued. "Sartori also said that all three of them returned to the Uffizi after the painting was loaded at the airport, but Tavolaro told me that Panello dropped him off at a party for his sister *before* they arrived at the gallery."

Rossini leaned back in his chair. He didn't seem to be surprised at what she'd told him, but looked as though he was deep in thought, trying to make a decision; his brow was furrowed and his jaw firmly set. After a few seconds, he sat up in his chair and rested his arms on his desk.

"What you have told me, Signorina, confirms what we have suspected from the beginning." He was looking directly at her, the intensity still there, but his eyes softening as he continued.

"I hope you will forgive me when I tell you that I have not been open with you. There are things that I have not told you about this investigation, but I assure you it was only because the curator of the Uffizi felt it necessary."

So they *were* keeping information from her! She wondered if Rossini was passing the buck by implying that the decision to withhold had come from higher authority. She liked Rossini, liked his professional manner and wanted to believe that he trusted her and wanted the FBI's help. She didn't say anything, but let him continue.

"There have been two lesser-known paintings stolen from the Uffizi in recent months. The gallery board chose to keep the thefts secret, but was convinced that the thefts were accomplished with help from someone inside. Just like with the Titan, both paintings were removed from the gallery for legitimate reasons: to be loaned to other galleries."

He pulled a file out of his desk and handed it to her. Inside were photos of the two paintings, pieces that she was not familiar with. One had turned up missing almost a year ago and the other, nine months ago.

"May I get you some coffee?" he asked. He was pouring a cup for himself from a carafe on a cabinet behind him. She told him 'no, thank you' and he went on.

"The gallery has very good security. There are cameras located in every room and hallway and some that are hidden in other areas, places such as the maintenance areas, employee break rooms and the room where the paintings are repaired and cleaned. As I said, the security is excellent.

"We knew the paintings had been switched when the forgeries were discovered and like the Titan, the forgeries were excellent. They were so good in fact, that the after the theft was discovered, every painting in the gallery that had been cleaned or loaned previously was examined by experts to make sure that no other work had been replaced with a forgery. I was told that that was the first time it was ever necessary to do that. The curator and administrative board are very anxious to find this forger and whoever else may be involved. You understand, I am sure, how important this operation is to the Uffizi."

She nodded. "Yes, I understand. You must be very anxious for the return of *Flora*." Here, Rossini smiled and she was mystified.

"Signorina, I assure you the Titan is safe."

Noreen was shocked. "*Flora* is safe?" she asked.

"Yes. You see, this is what you Americans call a 'sting' operation. Is that the correct word?"

For a moment, she couldn't speak. On one hand, she was so relieved that the painting was safe and on the other hand, shocked to find out the entire investigation was part of a sting and that that information had been kept from the FBI. All of a sudden she felt like a pawn in a rigged chess game: disposable and insignificant.

"You'll forgive me, Inspector. I'm just…I mean, I had no idea this was an undercover operation."

"And I apologize for that, Signorina. But I can see that you are very perceptive in your interrogations and feel that you will be much more help to us if you know exactly what is going on."

Even though she was taken aback and somewhat angry that she'd been kept in the dark, she felt better knowing that Rossini now wanted her input. That was better than thinking it was his male ego that kept her at arm's length, but knowing that did nothing to make her feel like she had contributed anything to solving this case so far.

"I believe Sartori is definitely involved and that Panello is helping him," she offered.

"Yes, we also believe this, although we are not sure if Panello is involved. When your office informed the TPC that the painting was not switched in the United States, we realized that it must have been switched during transport. But it was possible that Panello had no idea that the switch had taken place.

"Sartori is working with others, people who supply the canvas and paint and of course, the forger. We want to know who he contacts on the outside and especially, who is doing the forgeries. We do not believe this theft involves organized crime, but these thefts are managed in much the same way: there are contacts and most of the time, one contact does not know the other. Sartori is using someone on the outside, someone who can acquire the canvas and paints and someone who knows the forger. Those are also the people we want to find."

She nodded her understanding and then asked, "So the real *Flora* never left the museum?"

"No. It was always safe. The museum has legitimate artists that it contracts to do copies of originals. When an original is scheduled to be cleaned or loaned out, a copy is hung in its place so that the walls will not be bare for the public's viewing or in some instances, a copy is sent out on loan if the original is extremely valuable. The gallery borrowing the art is always informed when a copy is being sent."

"Did the Seattle museum know the Flora was a fake?" She already knew about copies being substituted for originals.

"No. It was felt that that information would not be disclosed in order to maintain the illusion of a genuine theft having taken place. You must understand that at that time, we did not know if there were people involved in the United States. We know that in many cases, the art is sold through the United States and so we had to make sure this was not the case in this instance."

"Then if Sartori is the one involved inside the Uffizi, he stole a copy and then switched it for another copy; the forgery with the cross?"

Rossini nodded. "Sartori was contacted about stealing the painting by one of our agents posing as a representative for a Middle Eastern buyer. The real Titan was removed before the date it was to be crated and shipped to the United States. This entire operation depended on Sartori not discovering that the *Flora* that was removed from the gallery and crated was a forgery. We had the help of the curator in that respect, who was able to distract Sartori at certain times to make sure he never got a good look at the painting.

"In order to put pressure on Sartori, our agent did not show up to receive the 'original.' We hoped this would cause Sartori to make contact with the person or persons helping him, but thus far, we have not discovered who that is. We do have agents following him. Whatever information you can obtain from people on the street would be of great help in solving this crime."

She let out her breath. This was a much more complicated operation than she'd first imagined and for the moment at least, she wasn't sure about what part she was to play. "Now that I know this is a sting operation, how can I help you?"

"I believe you were correct when you said that people on the streets would be more apt to speak with you because you are a woman. Perhaps you would be willing to follow up in that respect. Most of the petty criminals who work the streets of Florence know who the police and the Carabinieri are, so perhaps we could use your help best there, if that is acceptable to you."

She rose, effectively ending the meeting. "You have my cell number?" she asked. He nodded. "Then I'll be in touch with you." He shook her hand again and she thanked him as she left his office.

As she walked out of TPC headquarters, she thought about everything Rossini had told her. She wasn't as sure as Rossini was about what further contributions she could make toward solving this case, but she was determined to do all she could. That promotion was still uppermost on her mind, well…maybe right behind Damiano.

Ever since she'd met him, he'd been front and center where her thoughts were concerned. She wanted to talk to Giulio and maybe get some idea why Damiano had walked out on her. She headed back to the Uffizi, now wondering how important that promotion really was to her.

Chapter 23

HE SMILED BROADLY as she approached him. Looking at her watch, she knew he would be ready for his mid-morning break and so she wasn't surprised that he stepped down from his box and greeted her with air kisses to each cheek. His grin was ear-to-ear. She tried to give him a smile in return, but knew she hadn't succeeded. She still hadn't decided what to tell him about the date.

"*Buon giorno*, Noreen!" he said, excitedly. "You have come to have coffee with me, no?"

"Yes, that would be very nice," she replied, thankful that if he had noticed her weak smile, he'd chosen not to say anything. Maybe he already knew what had happened between Damiano and herself.

They walked to Tortino's again and sat outside. She figured that Giulio must take all of his coffee breaks here because the waiter saw him, brought a cup of espresso and then asked her what she would like. He left for another cup and Noreen cleared her throat. It was better to get this over with.

"I wanted to talk to you about Damiano," she began.

It was obvious now that he realized that what she had to say was serious, because he immediately lost his pleasant countenance, his eyebrows knitted together in a look of irritation or worry; she didn't know which.

"Something is wrong? What did he do?" He seemed very agitated. She wanted to put her hand on his, to reassure him, but his skin was covered in gray paint.

She took a deep breath, hoping she wouldn't cry again; she didn't want to upset him. After all, this wasn't his problem. Damiano was a grown man and his father wasn't responsible for his son's actions.

"I want you to know how much I like him and I'm pretty sure he likes me too. But he told me we couldn't see each other." So far, so good. She'd managed to keep her tears in check.

"What did he say?" Giulio seemed to soften, almost like he'd been through this before with Damiano. That didn't bode well.

"He said if we continued to see each other, he'd end up hurting me. I don't understand why he said that."

Giulio hung his head for a moment and stared into his cup of espresso. "You will forgive him, I hope. He has had a difficult time knowing what he wants from life. His mama could always steer him in the right direction, but now I think he is like a ship without a rudder." He sipped the espresso again and continued, knowing he wouldn't say anything about the illegal ways Damiano earned his money. His son would have to confess that himself.

"I think maybe he is afraid he will use you…you know, to satisfy his desires, and then get tired of you. He has been with woman before, but he does not know how to…to connect? You understand? I think he fears that if he loves a woman, she will leave him, so he makes love to them, but will not stay with them. I know Damiano well and after your first date with him, I know he liked you very much…not like other women he has been with. You are special to him. You understand this, yes?"

Yes, she understood. It made perfect sense now why he said he would end up hurting her. How could he date her, love her, and wonder at what point she would leave Italy and be gone from his life…just like his mother was gone?

She was staring into *her* cup of espresso now. "I love him, Giulio," she said. She wanted him to know the truth about how she felt. The relationship with Damiano might be over, but she respected his father and didn't want to cover up how she truly felt. She looked up from her cup and saw a faint smile cross his lips.

"I knew the first time I saw you that you were a special woman. It is in the eyes, no? The soul of a person shines in the eyes; the tenderness, the compassion and the love that God gives them. My Carlotta had eyes like that and I could see you had them too. I see how much you love my son. That too, is in your eyes."

He sat quietly for a long moment, just looking at her until she wished he'd look away. Nobody had ever said that to her before, but in her heart she realized that was how she'd always seen Cody. He had eyes like that and she'd never thought she did too. She didn't think so now and that's why his gaze made her uncomfortable.

He finished his espresso and she was relieved that he'd looked away. "He is very talented," he went on. "He does not need to draw on the streets. Drawing for the tourists is below him. He could be a great master, just like the great Renaissance artists. He could be making much money, but like I told you, he is without a rudder and so he cannot seem to get himself set on working on his art. If his mother were still alive, things would be different."

"Carlotta must have been a wonderful woman."

"Yes, she was. Damiano feels her loss very much." He seemed to brighten a little now. "You said you love him and I know he loves you too. Will you give my son another chance? Will you talk to him?"

Now what was she to say? She'd already decided that she didn't want a man she had to mother and yet Giulio had just told her about how Carlotta was Damiano's rudder; the woman who kept him in-line.

Then the image of him chalking *Flora* flashed in her head and any reservation she had about mothering him was lost in the pure beauty of *his* soul and how that beauty came through his talent. Damiano had something too valuable to lose and the thought of him wasting his life leaving his art on the streets only to be swept away, filled her with an emptiness and sorrow that surprised her.

"I'll talk to him if he'll let me," she replied.

"I will make sure he talks to you. Do not concern yourself about that. Tonight you come to my house at eight o'clock for dinner. I will make sure Damiano is there and you two will talk." The excitement was back in his eyes as he continued.

"I know you love him. It will take a woman who loves him to make him see that he cannot waste his talent. I know you value beautiful art and that you see his talent too. I want him to be the magnificent artist that I know he is, to use the gift God has given him and to bring beauty and joy to people. That is what I want."

"I want that for him too and I'll do everything I can to help him."

A cold feeling overtook her as soon as the words came out of her mouth. She was committed now. She couldn't and wouldn't go back on her word to this man. She thought of Cody and his honor. She wanted to be like her brother; she wanted to help Giulio and Damiano and if that hurt her career, then she would deal with that problem when the time came.

Giulio got up and left money for the coffees. "I must work now, but I will see you tonight?"

"Yes, tonight at eight," she replied. He smiled and walked back across the Piazza della Signoria. As she watched him leave, Noreen noticed her hands were shaking.

❧

She was beautiful today. She could make a sterile business suit look like an expensive designer gown on a fashion model. The sunlight caught the golden highlights of her hair and made it appear as if she had an angel's halo. He loved that about her because she was an angel to him.

She was talking with Giulio Travani again. Now he was worried. This statue guy was the father of Damiano Travani and he was afraid that she was getting too involved with both of them. Was the father in partnership with his son, an accomplice in the business of stealing from tourists? If so, what other, larger crimes might they both be involved with?

There was sadness in her face today. Was she still upset about the way Travani left her after their dinner together? If she was, it meant that she was very attached to him…too attached. Whatever was going on between her and these two men, he forced himself to remember that he had a job to do and that he had to put his personal feelings aside and just do it. 'Yeah,' he thought sarcastically, 'it's just as simple as that.'

Chapter 24

HE POPPED TWO antacids into his mouth and swallowed them without water. The tension was overwhelming now and he couldn't think straight. He knew he had to keep calm, to think things through, but it was all he could do to remember what day it was. How many days were left until the supposed Abdel Kadir was to bring the twenty million euro so that Sartori could pay off Galiazzi? Four more, he reminded himself.

He should have just told Galiazzi the truth: Kadir had vanished and no money was coming. But that would have had dangerous ramifications. He knew that whoever had done the forgery would want his share and that the forger would be putting the pressure on Galiazzi for it. Galiazzi could be a dangerous man when he was pressured.

To make matters worse, he'd had a big fight with Angelina this morning. She was even more nervous than he was. She wanted *Flora* out of her apartment and he was afraid she'd take matters into her own hands and dispose of the painting. Even if she didn't, she'd threatened to leave him, telling him that when they'd started their affair, she hadn't signed on for this kind of trouble. Before he'd had a chance to calm her down, she'd left, slamming the door behind her and he hadn't been able to get hold of her. She wouldn't take his calls and wasn't at her apartment. He knew she was probably staying with a girlfriend, but he didn't know who. He hoped she wasn't staying with some other man.

Now there were only four days left until Galiazzi would be expecting his money and Sartori's ulcer was keeping him in constant pain. He'd considered every alternative, but there was no way for him to come up with the two million euro he'd promised Galiazzi. In his mounting panic, he had even considered stealing a smaller painting and making a quick sale to someone else; he knew of a couple of people who might buy it, but that plan was too dangerous. Time was running short and the possibility of getting caught was assured when plans were made in haste; the security system in the Uffizi was daunting and very effective. That's why the best thefts were done when paintings were cleaned or loaned out and then switched during transportation.

On top of everything, there was the feeling he'd had for a week now that he was being followed, that someone was watching him. He was constantly looking over his shoulder, watching people as he arrived at the Uffizi in the mornings and left in the late afternoon. It would be so easy for someone to dress like a tourist, insinuate themselves into the crowds and Sartori wouldn't be any the wiser. He worried it was someone from the Carabinieri and was scared to death that it might be someone hired by Galiazzi because Galiazzi had become suspicious that there was no payday.

He fingered his new purchase, a nine millimeter Beretta, and then slipped it into the pocket of his suit coat. Maybe he'd come up with a solution to his problem, a solution for getting Galiazzi off his back. The forger would be out his money, but then the forger didn't know Sartori; for the forger, the trail ended with Galiazzi.

His bags were packed. He would try to reach Angelina again on his way home, but if he couldn't locate her and patch things up, he'd purchase his airline ticket and leave the country without her. His freedom was more important than Angelina. He straightened his desk, pushed in his chair and locked the door of his office. Depending on how things went, his days as Assistant Head of Acquisitions at the Uffizi might soon be ending.

☙

"You invited her for supper?" Damiano was furious. He stood up and pounded his fists on the kitchen table while Giulio turned sharply from the marinara sauce he'd been stirring and glared.

"Do not raise your voice to me! I am still your papa and you will respect me!"

Damiano sat back down, his head lowered as his father continued. "You need to talk to her. Her heart is broken and you promised me you would not hurt her."

"What was I supposed to do? If I continued to see her, she would have been even more hurt when she found out who I really am. Is that not so? It was better to send her away now."

Giulio stirred the sauce once more, and then added the spaghetti to the pot of boiling water. "You do not give her any credit for the kind of person she is! You should have been honest with her at the beginning. Then she could make up her own mind about seeing you. She should have made that decision, not you."

Giulio's anger was gone now and he sat down at the table and put his hand on Damiano's shoulder. "She is in love with you. She told me this and I can see it in her eyes. You must let *her* decide if she wants to be with you. You must be honest with her."

Damiano went limp, his sudden outburst leaving him defeated and exhausted. It was hard to want her so much and have to keep who he really was hidden from her. The guilt of pretending to be someone he wasn't and the pain of not being with her was wearing on him. Compounding his stress was knowing that if he didn't get Bocchio paid off soon, The Teacher would keep adding interest to the money already owed until Damiano would never have enough to pay the debt, no matter how big a score he made from the tourists. When all was said and done, he was in a bad place.

Damiano wouldn't look up. He couldn't face Giulio any more than he could face Noreen. "Papa, I have something to tell you," he said, hoping that a confession would relieve the stress that was now making his head ache again. "I borrowed money from Luca Bocchio." He said it simply and waited for his father's anger. It didn't come.

Giulio wanted to blow up, to strike his son across the face for being so foolish, for not using his talent to make money so that he would never have to go to the loan sharks. But that would only put Damiano on the defensive and that hadn't ever worked with him, not even when he was a little boy. Carlotta's way was better: say nothing. Let the boy live with his parents' disappointment and pray that the regret would be too much for him to bear and he would change his ways. Giulio was too old now to fight with his son; too old and too tired. "How much?" he asked in a surprisingly calm voice.

"Originally a thousand euro. Now with interest, I owe eleven hundred." He couldn't tell his father that he'd already given Bocchio nine-hundred, because then he'd have to tell about the pretty, young girl with the map. He saw Giulio shake his head and since his father hadn't gotten angry, Damiano figured he would surely get a lecture. Just like the anger, it never came.

Giulio sighed and then got up to check the spaghetti. Damiano sat in silence, his guilt heavier than ever now. He still hoped that the half million euro was coming and he knew that he didn't have the courage to tell Noreen about his illegal activities. He loved her and couldn't bear the thought of what she would think of him. He'd seen how disappointed his mother was that day she bailed him out of jail. He'd seen the look on her face and couldn't bear seeing that same look on Noreen's face.

Giulio tested the pasta. "It is time to eat," he said quietly as he dished up two plates. He set one down in front of his son and the other at his place. As usual, he bowed his head and gave thanks for the meal, this time adding a request that Carlotta watch over Damiano.

The mention of his mother's name, the vision of her at the jail on his behalf and the thought of what Noreen would think of him was too much for Damiano. He pushed the plate of food away and with his elbows on the table, put his hands up to his face, covering it. Immediately, he felt his father's hand on his shoulder again.

"We will work this out, Damiano. You will see and you will speak with Noreen when she comes for supper tonight. Now eat your spaghetti and we will talk no more of this."

ଋ

As he walked out of the Uffizi, Sartori dialed Angelina's apartment number on his cell phone. He almost choked when he heard her answer. He was certain she wouldn't be there or that if she was, she wouldn't answer when she found out it was him. She was like all beautiful, spoiled models: she used her temper to her advantage.

"Angelina, I need to see you. It is important." She didn't answer right away and he held his breath.

"What more can you say to me than what you have already said?" He heard the irritation in her voice, but he knew how to get around her temper.

"Please my love, let me come over. I need to be with you. Forgive me for what happened and let me see you again." He heard her sigh. She had an insatiable appetite when it came to making love and he had always been willing to satisfy it for her. Sometimes that worked to his advantage, especially where her temper was concerned.

"For a moment only and I expect your apology," she replied and hung up.

Her apartment was located in a high-rent neighborhood of large houses and too many newer apartments shoved too close together. It was a one-bedroom, nicely furnished, though too feminine for his taste, but it was comfortable. When he was over, they didn't spend much time in the living area or kitchen. She nearly always dragged him right into the bedroom, the pink décor so overwhelming that it made him nauseous. The walls were thin and from the beginning of their affair, that had put a damper on their love-making. She tended to appreciate his abilities in bed very vocally and more than once, they'd heard someone pounding on the walls and yelling for them to be quiet. That didn't seem to faze Angelina; it only excited her for more of him.

Only once had he taken her to his place. His wife and children had gone to Milan to visit his mother-in-law for a week and he had taken advantage of the empty house as Angelina's apartment was being repainted. When his wife had come home, she'd immediately smelled Angelina's perfume on the couch and after a hasty but believable lie, he'd decided two things: he would never bring Angelina to his home again and he should never have made love to her on the couch.

She greeted him at the door in a seductive silk robe that barely hung to the middle of her gloriously firm thighs. It was tied around her waist with a loose bow, the edges of the robe barely overlapping, leaving her nakedness underneath generously exposed and his mouth watering to get at her.

After a long appreciative look, he locked eyes with her and untied the bow. He knew that she didn't care about an apology. She wanted him and wanted him right away. Her hand was already loosening the belt on his slacks. He kissed her hard as they made their way into her bedroom and he noticed the crate with *Flora* still leaning against the wall by her bed. He was relieved; he still had *Flora* and he still had Angelina.

Chapter 25

"I DIDN'T REALLY expect to get you. I thought you had to work today." Noreen had dialed Rachel's number. In her anxiety again, she had gotten ready for the dinner at Giulio's early and had thirty minutes to kill. This time, she'd put on a form-fitting red dress. The silky fabric hugged her body the way she hoped Damiano would tonight. It had cap sleeves, a low scooped neckline and was shorter than most of her dresses. She'd finished off the look with red stiletto heels and a gold necklace, matching earrings and a bracelet. She'd added the outfit to her suitcase after her lunch at Angie's with Rachel. Her red dress was the top of the line in her arsenal of dating apparel. If she did meet a handsome artist, she wanted to be ready.

"Well, you know how the hospital is. They scheduled too many of us, so I volunteered to take the day off. How are things in Italy? Or more importantly, how are things going between you and your artist?"

For a second, Noreen regretted calling. It had seemed like a good idea at first because she was unsettled about having dinner with Damiano, but all of a sudden she didn't want to tell Rachel about what had happened. 'Too late now,' she thought.

"Work first, okay?" she answered. "I found out that the missing *Flora* is part of a sting operation." She didn't hear the kids in the background, but then they were still in school. She reminded herself that it was only about one-thirty in the afternoon in Falls Church.

"Really? Didn't the FBI know about it?" Rachel asked.

"No. The head of the TPC here said it was kept secret because the Italians weren't sure that the painting wasn't going to be sold in the U.S. So I was surprised, to say the least."

"Any surprises from your Italian artist? Have you been out on another date yet?"

Noreen checked her wristwatch. Did she have time to explain everything to Rachel or should she opt out for a short answer?

"Yes," she answered. "He took me out to a nice restaurant away from the tourist places. The food was great."

"Yeah, Italian food is great. I get it. Was *he* great? You don't sound too excited."

"He was great too, but when he took me back to the hotel, he told me we couldn't see each other anymore."

"OMG! Is he gay?" Rachel asked. Noreen had to smile. That *would* be her friend's first assumption. Rachel thought all impossibly beautiful men were gay.

"No, he's not...*definitely* not!" she replied, still smiling as she remembered his delicious kiss. Then the sadness overtook her as she remembered him walking away.

"So what happened?"

"I have no idea. He told me he loves me, but that if we saw each other, he'd end up hurting me."

"You don't suppose he's into bondage or some weird stuff like that, do you?"

"Rachel, get real, will you? How do you live with your mind working overtime like that?" Noreen wasn't mad. In fact, she was feeling better just talking to Rachel; her imagination was one of the things she liked about her friend.

"Sorry. I know...I got carried away. So really, why do you think he told you that?"

"Well, I hope to find out tonight. His father invited me over to their house for dinner. He and I talked earlier today and apparently Damiano has had trouble dealing with the death of his mother. Giulio told me that she was Damiano's "rudder," at least, that's the expression he used. All I know is that Damiano has an extraordinary talent and his father is worried about him wasting it. He doesn't want Damiano to end up drawing on the streets for tourists. I'm in perfect agreement with Giulio on that. You'd have to see him chalk *Flora* to really understand what I'm talking about."

"Oh, I understand. Really I do. You know more about art than anyone I know and if you think he's that talented, then he must be amazing." Rachel was quiet for a moment and Noreen was lost in thought. She was remembering being so close to Damiano that she could feel the heat coming from his body.

"So what are you going to do?" Rachel asked at last.

"Well, I'm going to dinner at his house and hopefully he'll tell me why he doesn't want to see me. It might be hard though, talking to him with his father there."

"His dad's going to be there?"

"Don't worry. I know how to get alone with Damiano. I'll just ask him to take me for a walk."

Rachel laughed. "That's why you graduated top in your class at the Academy! You're a consummate planner!"

"Listen, I have to go. It will take me about ten minutes to walk to Giulio's house and I don't want to be late."

"Well, promise to call me again and let me know what you find out. Okay? I have to work the next two days, and then I have another four off."

"Sure. I'll talk to you then." Noreen and Rachel said their good-byes and Noreen turned her phone off and put it into her purse. She checked her makeup, made sure she had her hotel key and gun and left, wondering if she would be crying again after this date.

☙

When she knocked at the door, she hadn't expected it would be Damiano who answered. His smile was cautious, but he gave her kisses to each cheek and asked her to come in.

The first thing she noticed was a delicious smell coming from the kitchen and to break the tension that she felt filling the space between them, she commented. "Did your father cook again tonight?"

Damiano closed the door behind her. "No, he is not here. I am afraid you will have to settle for my cooking." His smile was weak, but at least he was smiling.

She noticed that he looked wonderful this evening, telling herself that if he ever gave up art, he would have no problem getting modeling contracts. He didn't have the pretty-boy, sterile look that so many male models had nowadays. They all seemed to be excessively body-waxed: the arms, legs, chest and even hands, taking away any hint that they were human mammals and not store mannequins. Their bodies were perfectly muscled, which wasn't a bad thing, but they had no blemishes and no calluses to prove they worked those muscles. Their eyebrows were plucked to perfection, but in that perfection, they again reminded her of mannequins: pretty dolls to dress, pose, set on a bed and only look at. Sometimes she doubted any of them even knew how to make love to a real woman; they seemed too in love with themselves.

Damiano exuded rugged masculinity, the kind that men who worked hard for their living possessed, and the kind that showed in the way they moved and by the roughness of their hands. But he also had the grace of an artist and the combination of both of those traits was making it difficult for her to remain calm.

"Did he escape from us again?" she asked.

"No, he did not escape," he responded, the smile gone now. "He wanted us to be alone. Come and sit down. I must watch the sauce or it will burn."

He led her into the kitchen, held a chair for her as she sat and then stepped over to the stove. He busied himself for a few moments, stirring a pot and checking into the oven. If she thought she was nervous, he was even more so. When he tasted the sauce, his hand was shaking. She felt sorry for him. After all, he was the one who called off their relationship and she suspected that she was here tonight only because Giulio had insisted he see her again.

"What are you cooking?" she asked. A little innocent chit chat might help both of them relax.

"Something my mother used to make although I am not as good a cook as she was. It is called *polpettone ripieno.* I think in your country you would call it…meat loaf? It is ground pork and beef that is stuffed with carrots, spinach, prosciutto and cheese. It was my favorite as a boy."

Remembering what Giulio had said about Damiano not taking the death of his mother well, the fact that he was cooking one of her dishes and his favorite no less, made Noreen's heart ache for him, the way hers still ached for Cody. On the other hand, he'd taken extra effort to cook something special for her and that was encouraging.

She got up and stood next to him at the stove. "What's in the pot?"

"Gnocchi in alfredo sauce," he replied. Then he lifted the lid of another pot and she saw fresh green beans.

"It all looks wonderful," she said, realizing how hungry she was. Italians ate dinner late and it was all she could do not to grab a snack earlier. Now she was famished.

"In Italy, the noon meal is our large meal of the day, but I know in your country, the evening meal is the largest." He seemed to be relaxing and for that, she was thankful.

"I'm glad you know that. I'm really hungry!"

He set the spoon down and lowered the heat on the sauce. He turned and looked at her, his dark eyes pinning her in place until she couldn't have moved even if she had wanted to and being this close to him, she didn't want to. She was barely breathing, her heart beating fast.

His voice was almost a whisper. "I am sorry for what I said. I did not want to hurt you or make you cry."

He was no more than a foot away from her and even at that distance, she could feel his body heat. She didn't need his apology or even want it now. She wanted him. She wanted him to hold her and love her the way he loved *Flora*, to feel his hands on her body the way he had blended the chalk on hers. She didn't even want an explanation from him anymore, didn't need to know why he'd turned his back and had walked away from her. She just wanted him; to belong to him and that would be enough.

He stood before her, holding her with his eyes, until he finally turned back to the stove, leaving her lightheaded. She inhaled deeply, tried to slow her heartbeat and wondered what to say to him, finally deciding that maybe silence was better for now.

He pulled the meat loaf out of the oven and then dished up two plates, the aromas making her stomach growl. She hadn't ever considered that Italians ate meat loaf. It had always been one of her favorites too and still was. It was comfort food and tonight she wanted comfort.

They sat and he poured two glasses of red wine. As he held his glass up, he said, "To new beginnings" and she repeated, hoping that this night would be exactly that: a new beginning for them.

☙

His assignment was almost finished. It was never intended that he would stay as long as she did, but only that he would remain long enough to gather sufficient information to give his superiors an accurate report. He would be leaving in two days and the thought of leaving her behind was eating away at his insides.

He knew now that she was definitely involved with Travani. He knew it when he saw her walk out of her hotel wearing the red dress. It was special in more ways than Travani could ever appreciate and now she was inside his house in that dress! He wanted to run up to her and shake her and ask her why the hell she was getting involved with a bum like Travani, but he wouldn't; those urges had to be kept under control. He wouldn't hurt her like that.

As much as that bothered him, he knew he had a bigger problem to deal with: how much to tell his superiors about her involvement with this guy. If he told the truth, she would find out and he'd have absolutely no chance of ever getting her back. If he lied and his bosses found out, they'd both lose everything. Regardless of which choice he made, her career would suffer and he'd be without her. Right now, the way he felt, not having her was not an option. There had to be some way to do his job without compromising his integrity, but keeping his options open as far as she was concerned.

He wanted to leave now. He didn't want to know if she was staying the night. He didn't want to see her walk out of Travani's house in the morning in that dress. If it was going to happen, he knew it would happen while she was wearing that dress. He didn't want to think about them like that, but the picture of them together in bed was already stuck in his brain. He had to stay for as long as it took. He had to find out; his future depended on it.

Chapter 26

AS SHE LAY next to him, satisfied at last, he lit a cigarette and stared at the crate. She was pouting as usual, but what did she expect from him? He wasn't a machine. She'd had him twice and now all he wanted was a smoke and to think about how he was going to take care of Galiazzi. She cuddled closer, content for now.

He wasn't worried about Panello. He would pay him out of his own money; what he owed the guard wasn't much. He could come up with enough cash to pay Galiazzi too, but that would effectively leave him bankrupt and unable to make a new life with Angelina. The only option was to make Galiazzi disappear permanently and he would have to make that happen himself. He didn't need anyone else involved in this fiasco.

Then the only problem left was what to do with the Titan. He looked at the crate again. The thought of how much money was leaning up against the pink floral wallpaper made his mouth water. Angelina stroked his chest as he took another drag on the cigarette.

He loved fine art. It's what drew him to working in first-class museums in the first place. He couldn't bear the thought of destroying *Flora*, a painting from a genius like Tiziano Vecellio. He might be a thief, but he had high standards and Titan's work was exceptional and irreplaceable. Besides, there might still be a way to get some money for it.

He was sure he could eventually find another buyer for it after he arrived in the Caribbean, but it would be nearly impossible to get the painting out of the country. Italian customs agents were anal and thorough about any art that left the country. The paperwork was daunting and he didn't have enough time now to arrange it.

He knew people in other countries, like France, that would be willing to pick it up for the right price. Since the establishment of the European Common Market, the borders between member countries were wide open; no customs stops or vehicle searches. But he would get only a fraction of what the painting was worth. That idea immediately caused his ulcer to gnaw at him more fiercely. The thought of selling a painting worth over twenty million euro for only a few thousand grated on him. Time was gone for that idea to materialize too.

"Vincenzo, you are ignoring me. You know I do not like that. Make love to me again and forget about the painting for now." She was running her fingertips over his chest, her sensuous lips pouting, her perfectly manicured nails shiny with red polish and her naked body practically welded to his side. Everything about her was perfect: the way she could use all of what nature had given her in ways that aroused him until he didn't care about anything but satisfying her.

He snubbed the cigarette in the ashtray on the stand beside the bed. He'd deal with Galiazzi and the painting in due time, but not now; she was waiting for him.

☙

He left the dishes in the sink even though she said she'd help wash them. It didn't take a genius to figure out that she was trying too hard, but it made him feel good. She still wanted him and maybe her eagerness to help with dishes meant that he was forgiven.

The second he'd seen her in the doorway in that scorching red dress, he'd decided that admitting to her that he was a thief and pickpocket would destroy him as much as if he were to set fire to *Flora.* The dress was absolutely spectacular on her and he wouldn't be able to survive seeing the look on her face any more than he could bear seeing the paint on Flora's face blistering and then turning black in a fire. He knew that if either of those things happened, he would fall into a deep depression. So he wouldn't tell her, which created another problem: what would he tell his father?

He knew that Noreen and his father talked to each other outside the Uffizi. Giulio wanted him to be honest with her and if he wasn't, his father might find out. Maybe he should just tell her everything and end all the suspense.

Somehow, he'd find a way to go on without her just as he was trying to go on knowing that the other *Flora* was gone.

"You're very quiet," she commented. She was close to him, seated on the sofa. The smell of her perfume was intoxicating. She looked even more like *Flora* in this light and he was finding himself speechless. He kicked himself for not coming up to her hotel room when she'd asked him. He could have made love to her all night and would have, but his guilt wouldn't let him. And now, all he wanted was her and if he could only have her for tonight, it would be enough.

She was waiting quietly for him, her eyes giving him permission, her lips parted in anticipation and her breathing fast. He reached out to touch her, to feel the silk of the dress against the softness of her body and heard a knock at the door. He cursed to himself. His father had come back too soon; he'd promised to stay out until midnight. Well, at least he'd knocked.

As soon as he opened the door, he felt the blood drain out of his face. Even in the darkness, he knew it was Luca Bocchio; the Dracula coat fluttered in the evening breeze and he could see Bruno close behind. Before he could say anything, the bodyguard pushed passed him, shoved the door open wider and peered inside. "He's with that woman," was all he said and then took up his flanking position behind The Teacher again.

"Have I interrupted something, Travani?" Bocchio said, his tone as salacious as when he'd seen Travani with her on the street.

Travani looked at Noreen quickly, told her he'd only be a minute, and then stepped outside, closing the door behind him.

"What are you doing here? You'll get your money! Until then, leave me alone!" Travani's fists were clenched at his side and if Bocchio had shown up tonight without Bruno, Travani would have put one of his fists squarely between Bocchio' piggish eyes.

"Calm down, Travani," The Teacher said, the bodyguard moving in a little closer. "I have every right to check on my accounts, to make sure everything is being done to pay what is owed me." His eyes narrowed even more and his voice lowered into an inhuman growl. His lips were drawn back in an evil snarl and he looked even more like the Dracula character. "Do not *ever* tell me how to do my business! I will check on you whenever I like!"

Travani made a quick assessment of his position: he couldn't afford to get into Bocchio's face about the intrusion, not now with Noreen waiting on the other side of the door.

"Six hundred more for the way you talked to me," Bocchio said, calm now. "One hundred for each day you have left. You would do well to remember that *you* are the one indebted to *me* and that there are ways of getting what is mine! Now, you had better get back to that pretty woman before I decide that maybe cash is not all I want." With that, Bocchio turned and left, his coat flapping wildly behind him like the wings of a bat.

Travani took a deep breath trying to erase the tension that now had all his muscles ready for a fight and his heart pounding wildly. His mind was fixed on Bocchio's last comment, his threatened insinuation. Bocchio was not above taking anything he wanted and that included Noreen.

When he came back into the house, she immediately stood up and approached him.

"I was worried about you. Are you okay?"

"It was nothing. Just business," he said.

"I heard everything, Damiano. Don't lie to me. You're in some sort of trouble."

He needed her more now than she would ever know. He needed her to help him forget how he'd disappointed his mother and father, how he'd wasted his life with other women who meant nothing to him and how he'd helped *Flora* disappear. He needed her to take the fresh image of Bocchio away from him, to replace it with her beautiful eyes full of desire and excitement, but now, he needed to keep her away. It was getting dangerous for her to be with him.

He wrapped his arms around her, holding her tightly to himself and feeling the comforting softness of her beautiful body; a priceless jewel wrapped in red. He didn't ever want to let her go. He wanted to get so lost in loving her that everything else would disappear and there would be nothing else in his life but their bodies blending together as he made love to her.

"Tell me how I can help you," she said, her lips close to his face and her breath warm and moist on his skin. Her lips searched for his until he felt her so firmly against his body that he could feel her heart pounding against his chest.

Right now! She would let him take her right now! He knew it and wanted to have her more than he'd ever wanted anything before. The intensity of his desire for her was making his head hurt. He felt the zipper of her dress under his hand. He slid it down until it stopped well below her waist, then put his hand on the small of her back. Her skin was as smooth as the silk of her dress.

She was saying nothing now, the heat of her passion setting him on fire until he felt himself burning from the inside out. He would take her; she wanted it and he wanted to give it to her. He would lose himself in the glory of her body, lose himself just like he did whenever he chalked Flora and then…

He exhaled. And then…he would leave her with a regret that would haunt her for the rest of her life and a pain that would brand him for what he truly was: a thief. He would steal her body and then her heart, leaving her with nothing.

He was on a one-way road and he wouldn't take her with him. Eventually the police would discover that he was the one who had forged *Flora* and he'd go to prison and if that never happened, he knew he'd never be able to pay Bocchio and would end up floating face down in the Arno. Either way, there was no future for her with him and he wouldn't take her life away from her for a few moments of ecstasy. He released her and stepped back, the small sleeve of her dress falling off her left shoulder. She *was* his *Flora*, the thought of the flesh under her dress mesmerizing and enticing.

He stared at her for a moment. Her eyes were begging him as he watched the fullness of her chest rise and fall with every breath she took. She was breathing hard, still waiting for it…still waiting for him.

"You cannot help me, Noreen," he said at last. Her reaction was immediate.

"Don't say that! I *can* help you. If you need money, I can give you whatever you need." She stepped toward him, the other sleeve of the dress falling down. If she moved again, he knew the dress would fall to the floor and he would be unable to stop himself. He would take her, use her, and then make her go away just as he'd made *Flora* go away.

He looked directly into her eyes as he pulled the sleeves back up over her shoulders. Taking her in his arms again, he gave her a last kiss as he pulled up the zipper.

He released her and saw the questioning in her eyes.

"Someday you will understand why," he said softly.

Chapter 27

THE RELIEF HE *felt when he saw her leave the house was immediately replaced with fury. Travani had done something to hurt her again. When they came outside, he heard her tell Travani that she would walk back by herself, that she didn't want him to come with her.*

The street in front of the house was empty and she wasn't even trying to hide her crying. He heard her sobs and saw her wipe her eyes with a tissue. The need to run to her and comfort her was overwhelming. As she passed under a street light, he could see that her hair wasn't mussed and she didn't look disheveled. If she had, he would have gone back to the house, stormed the door and put a gun directly into that bastard's face, demanding to know what had happened and that scum had better hope that he hadn't put a hand on her or the older Travani would be planning a funeral after he returned home.

He followed at a safe distance as she crossed the Ponte Vecchio and got an even better look at her. This bridge was well-lit at night, probably because of the expensive jewelry stores that lined each side. She turned right after she was off the bridge and headed down the street toward the Piazzale degli Uffizi. It was very dark here and the tourists were gone. He could tell she wasn't paying attention to her surroundings. Her shoulders were slumped, her head down. She didn't seem at all aware that she was a beautiful woman, alone at night and vulnerable as hell. He almost tripped. His shoelace had come untied and he bent over and hurriedly retied it. When he looked up again, she was nowhere in sight. He would catch up to her in the Piazza della Signorina for sure, but when he rushed into the large square, he didn't see her there either. He knew she couldn't have made it back to her hotel yet. She was gone and he had no idea where she was!

☙

She felt two powerful arms grab her from behind and thought Damiano had come after her; that he'd decided he would explain himself to her after all. But that thought vanished as soon as the tape was put over her mouth and the realization of what was happening was clear. Now she could feel the pressure of powerful fingers as they dug into her upper arms, forcing her to drop her purse. The power almost lifted her feet off the ground as she thought about her gun. She knew she couldn't get at it now. With her arms held in the vice-like grip, she was dragged down the street between the Uffizi and the Palazzo Vecchio. The plaza was empty now; it was late. This street was deserted too. No one had noticed her abduction; it had happened in just a few short seconds.

She was forced into a deep door way behind the Uffizi, the powerful man holding her from behind. She couldn't turn around to see who it was, but she did see someone else approaching. He was short, heavy-set and was wearing a long, dark coat. As he came closer, she could see his face: narrow, squinty eyes…too dark to see what color…and a sickening grin. He was sweating.

He crammed himself into the small space, the girth of his abdomen almost pressing against hers. Reaching out his hand, he cupped her chin. She tried to turn away, knowing that this might be her worst nightmare: he was going to rape her and maybe the guy who was holding her would have his turn with her too. Nothing in all her academy self-defense classes could have prepared her for the sheer terror that gripped her now. She realized she only had one shoe on as she tried to steel her mind for what she knew was coming.

"You are very beautiful Signorina, but not very smart," the fleshy man said. His voice was low, his face close to hers and she could smell wine on his breath. She recognized his voice as the one she'd heard outside Giulio's house.

He took his hand away and looked at her for a long moment. He was smiling at her, enjoying his control over her. Was he deciding how best to violate her?

She tried to calm herself. She knew she couldn't overpower these two men, especially the one holding her from behind. He still had his fingers dug into her arms and for the first time, she noticed the pain. He could easily restrain her while the other guy raped her. She couldn't try a kick to the fat guy's crotch either, not with this guy holding her. He was too strong and she had no doubt that he could apply enough pressure to break both of her arms if he'd wanted to.

"Do you know why you are not so smart?" the fat man asked. "I will tell you."

There was a seductiveness in his voice that made her nauseated and she wondered if her dinner would stay down. If she vomited with her mouth taped shut, would she inhale her vomit into her lungs and die that way? Would she choke to death?

His hands were on her shoulders, his fingers feeling the fabric of her dress. He was feeling her up now, his hands sliding over her chest, hesitating as he pressed them against her breasts. Her throat was so dry she couldn't have screamed even if she'd had the opportunity. She felt like she was suffocating. Her breathing was too fast and she couldn't get enough air.

"It is a mistake for you to be involved with Travani." He paused, his hands still on her. "He has… obligations; business that demands his full attention. He does not have time to seduce a woman, even one as pretty as you. You are just a distraction to him, someone he will use and then throw away just as he has always done."

His fingers were feeling the fabric again, his eyes following the path of his hands as he worked down her body until he reached the hem of the dress and began rubbing the fabric between his thumb and index finger. He looked up and smiled at her, his eyes locked on hers.

"I could satisfy you if you would like, but you must leave Travani alone so that he can concentrate on his business. It would not be good for him or you if his attention should stray and I can see that with a woman like you, a man could stray very easily."

His right hand was under her dress, between her legs now. He was stroking her thigh and she could tell he was excited. She just wanted him to get it over with. If she could come out of this with her life, then she could deal with being raped. She was strong mentally and physically. She could handle it; *would* handle it somehow.

The guy behind her released just enough pressure on her arms to slide his hands down to her wrists, pulling her arms back and holding them behind her. The fat guy pulled a roll of tape out of his overcoat pocket and bound her hands, the tape so tight it cut painfully into her wrists and caused her fingers to tingle. At least now his hands were off her.

"Now it is time for you to be smart," he warned, his voice cold now. "Leave Travani alone. I have been a gentleman with you tonight, have I not? I have not hurt you or even mussed your beautiful hair. But if I hear that you are keeping Travani from his business again, I will not be so kind to you next time."

He smoothed the fabric of her dress as if he were doing her a favor; making everything neat so that she looked her best. Saying nothing more, he nodded at the guy behind her, who released her arms.

"*Buona notte, Signorina*," the fat man said as they left her bound and standing in the doorway. They disappeared into the street and she sank to the ground, tears rolling off her face and dripping down the front of her dress.

ଓ

His eye caught site of something at the edge of the square, on a street leading away from the Uffizi. It looked like a purse and as he walked over to it, his throat closed up so tight, he had to suck in a lungful of air. It was her purse! A few feet away, he found her red shoe. He picked them both up. She had to be somewhere near.

"Noreen!" he called and heard a muffled sound coming from somewhere in the dark. It echoed between the walls of the Uffizi and the Palazzo Vecchio, bouncing through the cool air until he couldn't get a bearing on its source. He called several more times and then waited, listening intently until he heard the sound again and thought it was coming from behind the Uffizi. He ran to the spot and saw the red of her dress, the color dim in the darkness of the alley. She was sitting on the ground in a door way. He saw her move and relief flooded through him. She was alive!

As he approached her, she looked at him, disbelief in her eyes. He saw the tears too and the thought that someone had hurt her made his stomach clench.

"Are you alright?" He pulled the tape off her mouth. "Are you hurt?" Her eyes were glassy with tears and a questioning look covered her face.

"Alex?" He tore at the tape on her hands and helped her up. She wrapped her arms around him, her body shivering and her tears coming so hard now that she was sobbing uncontrollably. He held her closer, trying to stop the tremors coursing through her body.

"I have you now, Baby. You're safe. Let me look at you," he insisted. He brushed the hair out of her face. Her mascara was smeared in long black streaks down her cheeks, but he didn't see any injuries; no cuts or bruises. She was still beautiful, even now.

He figured she'd been raped, although he didn't see her panties anywhere; she must still have them on. He would need to get her to a hospital so that she could be examined and a vaginal sample taken for DNA analysis of the semen.

"What happened, Baby? Were you raped?" He asked as gently as he could and was relieved when she told him 'no.' With all she'd been through, he couldn't bear the thought of putting her through that kind of examination, even if it was proper procedure in cases of rape.

"What are you doing here?" she asked. He wiped the tears from her cheeks with his hand, then pulled a handkerchief out of his pocket and gave it to her. "How did you get here, Alex? I don't understand."

"Later, okay? I just want to make sure you're not hurt. Did you get a look at who did this?" She nodded and started to cry again. He put his arms around her, promising himself that whoever had assaulted her, would pay dearly; he'd see to it. "We need to go to the police."

She shoved him away. "No, Alex. I'm okay. I'm just shaken up a little, that's all." She'd seen him drop her purse and shoe. She retrieved the shoe, removed her other one and then picked up her purse. She was shaking so badly, she knew she wouldn't be able to walk in those stiletto heels.

Trying to avoid his questions, she begged him to take

her back to her hotel. She knew who the fat man was. She couldn't tell Alex because all of this had something to do with Damiano.

"Okay, I'll take you back," he agreed and put his arm around her shoulder as they walked back across the Piazza della Signoria. He wanted her to report the assault to the police, but he wasn't about to argue with her or force her to do that. She'd already had enough trauma and didn't seem to have any physical injuries. He would try to convince her tomorrow after she'd had a chance to calm down and get some sleep.

"What are you doing here?" she asked again. Her tears had stopped now and she wasn't shivering as much. He was holding her as close as he could hoping his body would help warm her; he knew she was in shock.

"I was sent here by Internal Affairs to watch how you handle this case."

"Why? Have I done something wrong?" He thought she might be crying again; he heard her sniff and saw her wipe her eyes with her hand.

"No, Baby, no! It's not like that," he said. "The higher-ups are seriously considering you for the job as head of the Art Crimes Team. It's protocol. This is the last requirement before they appoint you head of the department. Anybody in line for that kind of promotion gets the same scrutiny, that's all. You're not in trouble." He heard her sniff again.

As they arrived at the front of her hotel, she stopped and hugged him. "I'm so glad you're here," she said. "Will you come by tomorrow?"

"No, I won't, because I'm not leaving you alone tonight. I'm staying and don't bother arguing with me. You know that never works."

He knew how capable she was, how self-assured and confident. But he also knew her well enough to know her soft spots, to know how far he could push her to get his own way. She would be scared and awake all night if he left her alone. She was a capable and strong agent, but she was a woman and he knew that an assault like this would take its toll on her. She would need the security and comfort of his presence, even if she would never admit it.

"What if your fiancée finds out that you spent the night with your ex-girlfriend?"

He hesitated before he answered. "I'm not engaged anymore" was all he said, but the look of pain in his face was obvious. "Look, we can talk about all of that later. Right now, you need to clean up and then get some sleep."

She nodded in agreement. Her body was beginning to ache. She needed a bath to wash the dirty feeling she had off her body and she needed rest, though she didn't think she'd be able to sleep.

"You're right," she said and reached for the door, but he opened it for her and then followed her up to her room.

Chapter 28

SHE CAME OUT of the bathroom with her hair wrapped in a towel, wearing a knit tank top and shorts. She had the best set of legs he'd ever seen and loved to see her in shorts. She was towel-drying her hair and he was in heaven just sitting in a chair, watching her and happy to be face-to-face with her at last. To watch her with binoculars and to know the thoughts he was having about her had made him feel like a pervert.

Her face was clean now; no mascara streaks and no makeup, but then she was so beautiful she never needed makeup. He always wondered why she even bothered to wear it and she always told him it was 'a girl thing.' She was definitely all girl and being with her now was making it hard for him to keep his hands to himself. It would be so easy to get physical with her, to touch her in all the spots he knew would excite her, but he wouldn't do it. She would need time to heal from this trauma and he knew that.

"I'm okay now…really. You don't have to stay with me. Where will you sleep?"

"Let me take care of that. I'll be fine."

She put the towel over the back of a chair and looked at him looking at her, a very familiar smile on his face. She knew that smile, knew it intimately. He wanted her. She could read it all over his face and after what happened to her tonight, she was thankful to be with him.

Alex was a man through and through. He was passionate about life, about his job, about taking care of the people he loved and most of all, passionate about her. He was honest, strong, kind and smart and their relationship had been one of the happiest times of her life. But things were different now…or were they?

She walked over to the bed and sat down. Her hot shower had helped with the achiness. She thought about the fat man's narrow eyes scanning her body as he put his hand between her legs and the memory made her shiver. All of a sudden, she was extremely tired. A single tear rolled down her cheek and dripped off her face. Alex approached and sat down beside her.

"I'm here. I won't let anything happen to you." His arm was around her waist and he kissed the side of her head, relishing the feel of her clean hair on his face. "Lie down and get some sleep."

She did as he said and he pulled the sheet over her. For a moment, he sat on the bed and just stared at her. She had no idea how beautiful she was or what a great person she was; how full of love and life. He'd wanted her from the second he'd seen her on the firing range at the Academy.

He ran the back of his hand down the side of her face, then bent down and kissed her gently on the lips. "Sweet dreams, Baby," he said and turned off the lamp next to the bed.

Quietly, he removed his jacket and shirt and then his shoes and sox. The room was warm, which was a good thing because he didn't see any extra blankets. He made himself as comfortable as possible by shoving two upholstered chairs together, front-to-front. He was tall and he knew he wouldn't sleep much; he'd be in an almost sitting position, but that didn't matter. What mattered was that he would be with her. He could protect her, but even more than that, just to be in her presence made him happy. He was stupid to even have thought that any other woman could mean to him what she did.

He tried to relax and thought about the day she had told him that she couldn't see him anymore. The pain he felt when that had happened was as sharp now as it had been then. But even so, even knowing she'd chosen her career over him had left some part of him proud of her. Pain or no pain, she'd had the courage to make that decision and he respected her for that.

Maybe somewhere in the back of his mind, he believed she would come around some day, that she would want him in her life and what he could give her that her career never could. He believed that it was the uniqueness of total, committed love for another person that fulfilled the most basic desire of every human being. Humans longed for that perfect love, that perfect relationship. It was what made people turn to God, but it was also what made men and women turn to each other. Some day, she would need that kind of love and he wanted to be there when she came looking for it.

Only a dim light from the street outside filtered through the curtains. He heard her breathing. It was deep and regular. He knew she was asleep and so he closed his eyes and imagined what he always imagined at night in bed: what it would be like to be sleeping next to her, to spend his life loving her.

☙

He heard something, but couldn't tell if he was dreaming or not, so he made himself listen again. She was crying. The clock next to her bed read two-forty. She'd only been asleep a couple of hours.

She was lying on her side with her back to him, her legs curled up tightly against her body in fetal position and she was sobbing quietly. Sitting down on the edge of the bed, he touched her arm. She made a muffled whimper like a wounded animal. "It's okay, Baby. I'm right here," he whispered, gently turning her until she was lying on her back. "Bad dreams?"

She didn't say anything and didn't try to hide her tears from him. "Move over," he told her and after she'd made space, he lay down next to her. "I won't leave you. You're safe."

She turned on her side toward him and nestled against his chest. The sobbing had stopped and as he cradled her in his arms, he felt her body relax. She was so warm and being next to her made him want her more than he ever had before. He wanted to protect her, to spend the rest of his life loving her and being loved by her. Even after they had split up, he'd counted himself lucky that he was able to see her at work. It wasn't much, but it was enough for him. And now, she was in bed lying next to him; something he had dreamed about so many times.

"What happened between you and Claire?" she asked.

"We can talk about that tomorrow," he whispered.

"I can't sleep, Alex. When I close my eyes, I see it all over again. Just talk to me for a while, okay?"

He kissed her forehead, the smell of her shampoo bringing back the good memories of their time together. It was times like now, when she wasn't Agent Issenlowe, but just a woman, that made him want to hold her and never let her go. He loved her strong personality and abilities, but it was the fragility and tenderness of her emotions that made him want to protect her.

"Okay, I'll tell you. About two weeks ago, Claire and I got into an argument over some silly wedding thing. She was really into planning a huge wedding, you know? I mean, she was inviting over two hundred people. I never wanted a wedding that big, but hey, it was her special day so I went along with it."

Her was head resting on his arm. He was running his fingers through her hair; something he knew had always relaxed her and hoped it still did.

"I don't think I *know* two hundred people," she said.

"Neither do I. I don't even remember what the fight was about, but up until then, it was the biggest one we'd had. I was late for work, so I told her we'd talk about it after I got back and that just made her madder. She said if we were going to be married, *I* needed to get my priorities straight.

"I had to go. I knew I was going to be buried in paperwork all day and that we had a departmental meeting. It was going to be a real heavy day, you know? And to top it off, I had a hell of a headache. So I took off and didn't even kiss her good-bye. She was so mad she probably would have slapped me anyway.

"By the time I got to work, my head was pounding. It felt like it was going to explode. Well, Jack came by my desk, took one look at me and told me to go home, that I looked wiped out. I still had about six hours left on my shift, but my headache was worse so I wasn't about to argue with him."

She heard him inhale deeply and then let the air out slowly. He was quiet for a long moment, obviously deep in thought. She pressed closer to him as he began again, his voice much quieter.

"Claire didn't hear me come in when I got back to my apartment. To tell you the truth, I really didn't expect to find her there. All I wanted to do was get some damn aspirin for my headache. On my way to the bathroom, I passed the bedroom and saw her in my bed with some creep. I don't even know who he was, but they were going at it like rabbits. It was all I could do not to punch that bastard's lights out, but he wasn't *forcing* her…know what I mean? I think she knew I was there because I heard her lie to him and tell him he did her better than I did. That *really* got my blood boiling. I swear I thought *real* hard about going for my gun. I don't know why I didn't because right then, I sure as hell wanted to waste them both. You should have seen the look on his face when he finally saw me. I told them both to get out and I told her the engagement was off."

"I'm so sorry, Alex. I didn't know."

"You want to hear the funny part? Before she slammed the door on me, she told me she was keeping the engagement ring, that I owed it to her for and I quote, 'services not rendered.' She was mad at me because I wouldn't make love to her before we were married and tried to blame the whole thing on me. Guess she had other guys who would give her what she wanted…anytime and anywhere, including in her fiancé's bed."

She didn't know what to say to him. Alex would have been crushed by finding Claire in bed with someone else and in *his* bed at that. He might be one of the toughest agents she knew, but he had a tender heart and believed strongly in integrity. He was totally committed when he put his mind to it and something like this would have been devastating for him.

She'd never met Claire and didn't know much about her. The only thing she was sure of now was that Claire had let a great guy slip through her fingers and that she definitely didn't deserve someone as wonderful as Alex.

"Tell me about Travani," he said.

For a moment, she was stunned, but then reminded herself that if Alex was sent to watch her, he would be thorough about getting information on everyone she came in contact with. The FBI was anal about the integrity of its agents. She understood why: agents dealt with all kinds of crimes and all kinds of high security information. A top secret security clearance was mandatory and the FBI was more aggressive about clean backgrounds in their employees than any other branch of the criminal justice system. Only the CIA had more stringent checks.

"What do you want to know?"

"Do you love him?" That was just like Alex: get right to the point.

"That's a complicated question. I don't know how to answer it."

"A simple 'yes' or 'no.' How complicated can that be?"

"Then yes, I think I do."

"You *think*…so you're not sure?"

"I told you, it's complicated. I know I could love him very easily. His passion for art and his talent are very exciting."

"Does he excite you as much as I used to?"

"That isn't fair, Alex. I'm trying to be honest with you. We've always been honest with each other. You told me about Claire and I'm trying to tell you about Damiano. Don't make it harder for me, okay?"

"I'm sorry, Baby. It still hurts…you know? We had such a good thing going back then and it's just hard. I don't want to see you get hurt, that's all. Has he told you he loves you?"

She thought about how to answer. Yes he had, but she didn't want to hurt Alex by telling him. Besides, she was confused and wanted time to sort out how she felt.

"I know he thinks I look like Titan's *Flora* and that he loves *her*. I know he's interested in me." Alex knew how much she loved that painting. He was quiet for a moment, his face close to hers as she lay against his chest.

"Has he made love to you?"

She rolled onto her back, away from him. "You have no right to ask that, Alex! You know the answer anyway, so why did you ask? Have *you* made love to me?"

"You're right. I'm really sorry. I do know the answer. I guess I'm just jealous of him. I've always loved you, Baby. You know that and I still love you, but I don't want you to think that I'm saying that because of him or because of calling it off with Claire. I've thought a lot about why I fell in love with her and I realize that it was always you I wanted. But you didn't want me and I had to get on with my life. Claire came along and I grabbed at the chance to move ahead. I made a mistake. The rest is history."

"What am I supposed to say to that, Alex?"

"You don't have to say anything. You don't have to tell me you love me or that you'll give me another chance. I just want you to know it will always be you."

"I haven't stopped loving you either. I don't think I ever will."

"Then where does that leave us, huh Baby? What am I supposed to do with that? Are you taking me back? Are you over Travani now? Tell me, okay, because being this close to you and not having you is tearing me up and I can't stand that kind of pain anymore."

"I don't know what to say to you because I don't know what I want. I'm sorry, Alex. I am. I just need more time."

He sighed, got up and stood next to the bed. "Do you think you can get back to sleep now?"

She nodded and he covered her up and kissed her forehead. "When you decide what you want, let me know. I'll be waiting. I'll wait as long as it takes," he said. In the darkness of the room, he couldn't see the tears in her eyes.

Chapter 29

TWO DAYS AFTER the fact, Rossini was still mad. Nino Lanzetti stood in front of him, his eyes downcast. His only job was to tail Vincenzo Sartori, to keep him in sight every minute and yet two days ago, he'd let Sartori slip away for over an hour, finally picking him up again as he returned to his mistress's apartment. Rossini was livid thinking that it may have been during that hour that Sartori contacted the outsider who had helped him steal the Titan. There was nothing he could do about it now though, and he'd taken his frustration out on Lanzetti afterward until the kid almost cried. Lanzetti was new to the TPC, low on the ladder and given only the dirty jobs the higher-ups didn't want. Tailing a suspect was one of those jobs and Lanzetti was eager to prove himself, but he'd failed. His future with the TPC didn't look promising and he knew it.

"Go ahead," Rossini started.

"He left the Uffizi at two twenty-two and went straight to the mistress's apartment." Lanzetti was reading from his notes. "She was there with him. I saw her pull the drapes closed in her bedroom. Sartori exited the building exactly three hours later, necktie in his right breast pocket, shirt collar unbuttoned. He got into his car, drove directly to a produce stand three blocks from his house, bought four tomatoes and then went home, arriving at five forty-six."

Lanzetti was still shaking from the dressing down Rossini had given him the two days before. He'd followed Sartori yesterday, but somebody else was tailing Sartori today and all Lanzetti wanted was another chance, even though he knew he probably wouldn't get it.

"Good. Did you get any more information about Angelina Negretti?"

"Yes, sir. I talked to one of her model friends, a guy who calls himself Adamo. He did not want to give me a last name. Said he only used one name, that it is his professional name. I found out from the owner of the agency that his full name is Alfonso Fenucci. It seems he had a brief affair with Angelina over a year ago and was not happy about the split, so he was more than willing to talk to me. He said she was telling people that she was not going to be modeling much longer, that she had other plans and they included living on a tropical island."

"Did she happen to mention when that would happen or what island?"

"She told Fenucci that her lover was an important person who was coming into a lot of money, leaving his job and taking her out of the country for good, but did not say when or where."

Rossini perked up. He knew that Sartori would probably have plans to leave the country after he'd gotten paid for the painting, but apparently he was still planning on leaving even though he must assume by now that the money wasn't ever coming. If Sartori left now, the TPC would never know who he was working with and more importantly, who the forger of *Flora* was.

"Anything else?"

"No, that is all." Lanzetti pocketed his notepad.

"You can go," was all Rossini said and Lanzetti left without looking back.

Rossini got on the phone. He would check back with the reservation desk at the airport and find out if Sartori had made any attempt to purchase tickets. The TPC already had given his name and photo, along with Angelina's, to the airlines. Airport security was to report immediately if either of them called, electronically reserved or came to the airport for tickets. Rossini wanted to bring him in for questioning, but that would have to wait until he had information on everyone who had helped with the theft.

ɷ

Sartori left home earlier than usual, lying to his wife about having a special meeting with the head curator before the museum opened. As he drove off, he called Angelina. It was early, about seven-thirty, and models slept late; that's what she'd always told him anyway. She didn't sound happy when she answered the phone.

"What do you want? I was asleep," she said, yawning.

"I want you to be ready to leave tonight. Pack your things." Sartori stopped at a traffic signal and fingered the gun in his pocket. He'd bought a silencer for it and now he was ready to end this nightmare once and for all.

"Why so soon? The agency just got me a contract with Cristoforo Designs for this year's new line of lingerie. This could be a big opportunity for me. Did you get the money?" She was whining as usual. He hadn't told her that the money he was supposed to receive for the painting wasn't coming.

"Angelina, do you want to be with me or not? If you do, be ready to leave." He heard her sigh, but he wasn't about to answer her question.

"Will you stop by on your way to work?" she asked. He knew what she wanted. It was the same thing she always wanted. That's why he stayed with her. The pouting and temper tantrums drove him crazy, but making love to her drove him crazy too, in much more satisfying ways.

"I will be there in five minutes," he answered and then pressed the 'end call' button. He dialed again and heard the 'hello.'

"I will make delivery of your package tonight, eleven o'clock, outside your meeting place, in the back. Be on time."

He heard Galiazzi gasp. "It has come?"

"Yes. Come alone and if you are late, you will not see me or the package again."

"Eleven, in back of Due Colombe. I will be there."

"You idiot! I told you not to mention names!" Sartori was furious. He worried that he was being followed and wasn't sure if his calls were being monitored too. "Be there!" he growled and hung up.

He would carry out his delivery exactly as he had planned, only he wouldn't be bringing Galiazzi a package of money. He'd be delivering a bullet directly to the idiot's head and then he'd dispose of the body, drive to Angelina's place, make love to her all night and leave with her early the next morning to start their life away from everything he'd ever known.

He'd already withdrawn some of his savings, leaving most for his wife and kids. The bulk of his money was in off-shore accounts on the Caribbean island he planned to make his new home. It wasn't twenty million euro, but what there was, was invested well and enough to make Angelina happy and give him a safe and comfortable life.

He knocked at her apartment door and she greeted him wearing one of *last* year's Cristoforo designs: a black lace, ruffled something that showed most of what she owned and had him salivating to see the parts it didn't show.

"I have fifteen minutes. That is all," he told her and he saw her pout as she put her arms around his neck and pulled him forcibly into the apartment.

Chapter 30

WHEN SHE FINALLY managed to keep her eyes open, she checked the alarm next to the bed. It was nine! She *never* slept that late, but she decided that after the night she'd had, she deserved the extra rest.

She stretched and noticed blue bruises in the shape of finger tips on her upper arms and as she rubbed them, she felt the pain and horror of what had happened all over again. She wanted Alex with her, but didn't see him in the room and that worried her. Had he gone to report the assault? Was he coming back or had he left for good without telling her 'good-bye?' She knew their middle-of-the-night conversation had left him upset.

She dragged herself out of bed and into the bathroom. She urinated, flushed and then realized that her body still ached. Removing her pajamas, she got into the shower and ran the water fairly hot, letting it run over her skin as she tried to relax her muscles.

Why did he leave? Was he upset about what she'd said about wanting to love Damiano? Was he mad because she hadn't offered to give him another chance? She turned the water temperature up and stood under the flow until all she knew, all she could think about was the burning on her skin.

As she began drying off, she heard a knock at the door and for a second, her heart pounded as it flashed through her mind that the fat man might have followed her to the hotel last night, might have wanted to know where she was staying so that he could assault her again if he saw her with Damiano. She wrapped up in the towel and ran to the door to make sure Alex hadn't left it unlocked.

"Noreen, it's me," she heard him say and she quickly opened the door. She tried not to let him know how scared she was.

"I wondered where you'd gone," she said, trying to calm down. He walked past her and laid a tray on the small table near the window. There were two chairs and he sat down on one.

"Thought you might like some breakfast," he explained. His eyes were fixed on her as she stood before him, her hair wet and dripping, her hands holding the towel together above her breasts. He reminded himself that he'd never seen her naked. He turned away, trying to calm the appetite he felt for her, and poured two coffees from a carafe. "Get dressed and we'll eat," he said.

When she came back out of the bathroom, he was sipping his coffee. There were two croissants on a plate. They both worked on the coffee and were silent for a long moment.

"What will you report to IA?" She hesitated to ask him and didn't really expect that he would answer her; that information would be considered confidential, especially where she was concerned.

"I don't know," he said haltingly. "I'm trying to decide if I should lie." He was staring into his cup now and wouldn't make eye contact with her.

She was shocked. Alex *never* lied, especially not where it concerned his job and Internal Affairs. "You mean you won't tell them you broke cover and talked to me."

"No. I mean I'm trying to decide if I should tell them about you and Travani." He still wouldn't look at her and there was an edge to his voice that bothered her.

"What about him? What does the FBI care if I have dinner with him or even love him? I'm not shirking my job and I won't let them have control over my private life! Besides, I think he and his father can help me with the investigation. They both work on the streets and might have seen or heard something."

She was angry now, not at Alex, but with the idea of how much control the FBI thought they could have over her private life. She was still angry every time she remembered hiding her relationship with Alex. They always had to be careful about how they acted around each other at work, always had to be conscious of how much time they spent together. Even in their off-time, they had to worry about running into someone from the Agency and what gossip might get back to their bosses.

He finally looked at her and what she saw in his eyes frightened her.

"There's something you need to know about Travani. He has a criminal record." He said it simply, giving the information to her as gently as he could. He didn't want to hurt her, but saw it in her face anyway.

"You're just saying that because you want me to give him up! Admit it, Alex! You're mad at me for turning you down! You can't stand the fact that I could love someone else! You *are* jealous!" She wanted to believe what she'd just said, but somewhere inside, she knew Alex was telling the truth.

She'd suspected it all along. Maybe the signs had always been there and she was so enamored of his talent that she didn't want to recognize them. She knew Damiano had money problems and knew he was connected to the fat man in some illegal, dangerous way. He was evasive about his art work and Giulio seemed worried about the course his son's life was taking, comparing him to a ship without a rudder. She could tell from his body language that he was hiding himself from her, that part of who he really was, was closed off to her. And now it made sense why he'd told her that it wouldn't be a good idea if they continued their relationship, even though she knew how much he wanted her. She was crying now as he pulled her up and wrapped her in his arms.

"I'm sorry, Baby. I didn't want to tell you. Please believe that."

"Tell me what you know…all of it!" she demanded as she wiped her tears away.

He let out a long sigh before he began.

"He's been arrested several times for stealing, mostly picking pockets. He was arrested the first time when he was sixteen, and…" His voice trailed off.

"And what? Tell me, Alex!"

"And he's been arrested for sexual assault."

He tried to hold her closer, but she pushed herself away from him and sat down again. He stood behind her chair and put his hands on her shoulders.

"I'm so sorry, Baby, but I just want to protect you. I know how much this promotion means to you and I don't want anything to jeopardize your chances of getting it. I won't say anything about him in my report. I promise. I'll do that for you, but I want you to know about him so that you can protect yourself, that's all. I don't want you to get hurt." He sat back down next to her.

All she could think about was the way Damiano 'danced' with *Flora*, how he loved her with such passion and intensity and how *she* wanted to be loved like that by him. But now, there was so much at stake. If found out, she might be able to talk her way out of being in the relationship with him; tell her superiors that she didn't know about his criminal record, which she didn't. But now that had changed and any contact she had with him from now on would be with the knowledge of his past record. She would lose everything she'd worked for, everything she'd done to honor Cody and her family.

And sexual assault? Had she *ever* been safe with him? She thought about how she'd asked him to come up to her room after their date, not even thinking about how dangerous that could have been for her and about how easily she had given up everything she'd been taught at the Academy about protecting herself.

But then she remembered that he wouldn't come up and that he'd said he couldn't because it would hurt her. Was that what he was talking about? If he were into assaulting women, would he have denied himself and refused her offer? There were too many questions begging for answers and she had none to give herself.

"Tell me what the report said about the assault," she demanded. "Tell me, Alex! I know you read it."

"It was just a simple assault, Baby. That's all."

"I want to know. Tell me!"

"He picked up some woman, a tourist I think. She wanted him or so he told the detectives. The woman admitted only that she'd let him seduce her, but then said she had second thoughts before they started to get it on. Her husband came in, she was in bed with Travani and all hell broke loose. The husband pulled a gun on Travani and she called the police."

Noreen was shocked. Damiano had given her no clues at all that he would ever have forced her to do anything against her will. He'd always been polite and gentle with her. Now she had doubts about him and that hurt as much as when he told her they shouldn't see each other.

"Tell me about last night," he said, changing the subject. She'd had enough trauma in the past twelve hours, but he needed to know. "Do you know who assaulted you and why? Did it have something to do with him?"

"I had dinner with Damiano and that same man came to his house. I recognized his voice. They went outside and talked. Before they did, some gorilla checked the house, saw that I was there and then told the other guy. I'm pretty sure he was the other guy's bodyguard. I could hear some of what they were saying outside. Damiano owes the guy some money."

"Sounds like a loan shark," Alex said and she nodded her head in agreement. "Loan sharks aren't independent; they work for someone else. This guy could be part of organized crime."

"I know it was the same pig who assaulted me and I'm pretty sure the bodyguard was the one who held me."

"What did the guy say to you?"

"He told me to leave Damiano alone, that he had business obligations and that he couldn't be distracted by me."

"What else? Tell me, okay? Did he put his hands on you?"

She hung her head. She wanted to forget about what happened, forget about how scared she was and about how she should have been able to defend herself, but couldn't. She was wondering now if she was fit to be an agent at all. She was afraid too…afraid that Alex would try to get revenge and end up destroying *his* career.

"I told you. He didn't rape me. He just felt me up, that's all."

"You did the right thing by telling me. You need to stay away from Travani. Work the investigation and stay clear of him. I won't say anything in my report. If you stop seeing him now, you're okay as far as IA is concerned. You had no way of knowing that this guy was a creep and…"

She interrupted him. "He's not a creep, Alex! You don't know him, so don't pass judgment! You were watching me after he brought me back to the hotel, right?"

He nodded. "I knew he hurt you. I saw you crying and I wanted to deck him."

"I was crying because I asked him to come up to my room and he wouldn't. I wanted him to make love to me and he turned me down. That's the kind of "creep" he is! He told me if I continued to see him, he'd end up hurting me. And last night…I wanted him then too and he wouldn't do it. He told me someday I would understand."

Alex's shoulders slumped. "I'm sorry, Baby. I only knew that he'd hurt you somehow and it made me mad."

"Yeah, he hurt me. I propositioned him…did everything but get naked in front of him and he wouldn't make love to me. I don't believe that sexual assault thing. He wouldn't do that."

She wiped the remaining tears from her face and realized something more clearly than she ever had before. "I do love him, Alex. He may be a thief, but that's not important to me compared to what's in his soul. There's so much beauty there and I want to share it with him."

"Yeah, I get that impression." His tone was harsh as he continued. "You never offered to make love to me, so I guess that proves that you want him more than you want me."

She started crying again, her face in her hands, but he couldn't hug her now. He'd heard the conviction in her voice and knew it was over between them…over for good this time. She'd made her choice.

"I have to go," he said flatly.

"No, Alex! Please don't leave like this!" she begged.

"You can't have it both ways, Noreen. You want him? Then go to him, but don't say I didn't warn you. Don't come running to me later when you find out he isn't who you think he is. But you want me? Then tell me now and you'll have my love for the rest of your life. I won't say anything in my report about him, but I'll do that only as a favor to you. Just remember one thing: I've loved you for a long time and I'll *never* stop loving you."

"Alex, please…," she pleaded, but he turned and walked out the door, leaving her sobbing again.

☙

Everything else faded into the background when he painted. His concentration was so intense that he could forget about Bocchio, about not getting the half million euro Galiazzi owed him and about how empty his life was.

Everything faded, except the thoughts of her. Her beauty was permanently etched into his memory and the heartache of not having her was like a knife twisting in his chest. And so he painted; lost in the smell of linseed oil and the vision talking place on the canvas as it flowed from his memory to his hand.

The doorknob rattled as the door swung open. In his depression over giving up Noreen, he'd forgotten to lock it and now Bocchio and his bodyguard were coming in and there was nothing he could do about it.

"Very nice, Travani. A good likeness," The Teacher said, looking at the canvas. "Do you not think it is a good likeness, Bruno?"

The bodyguard shrugged his shoulders. "Bruno is not much of an art critic, but he has other important qualities," Bocchio said.

After the addition of that last sum of interest, Travani wasn't going to push his luck with some smart come-back and end up owing even more. He imagined Bocchio flying away like the blood-sucking bat he was; leaving forever.

"I had a very lovely time last night," Bocchio went on. "I had a date with a beautiful woman!" The lewd tone of his voice made Travani nervous. "She had on the most beautiful red dress, soft as silk, just like the skin of her thigh!"

Travani clenched his fists, the heat of his hatred building until the only thing that stopped him from turning Bocchio into a piece of raw meat was the look on the face of the bodyguard. Bruno could take him out with one hand tied behind his back. Travani had too much to lose. He took a deep breath and waited.

"She was very beautiful *and* accommodating," Bocchio continued. "We had a lovely talk. She regrets that she is unable to see you any longer."

He was dabbing his forehead with a handkerchief, the smell of his perspiration adding to the stench of the kind of man Travani knew he was until Travani thought he'd vomit from the disgust he felt right then. But he said nothing. He would go to Noreen, make sure she was okay and then figure out a plan to take care of Bocchio once and for all.

"You are very quiet, Travani. Does it not please you that I had such a lovely evening or are you jealous?"

Travani glared at Bocchio, his fists so tight his fingernails were gouging the palms of his hands, but he remained silent, his rage numbing the pain.

"Well then, if you have nothing to say, I will remind you that you now have five days until your debt is to be paid in full." He turned and looked at the canvas on the easel again. "Very nice. I have always said that you are very talented. You have captured the essence of her and she is much more beautiful than the *Mona Lisa!*"

Bocchio nodded to Bruno, turned and left, leaving the door open behind him and Travani as cold as a week-old dead body…a body he intended on seeing belonged to Bocchio.

Chapter 31

HE KNOCKED CAUTIOUSLY. He'd gotten her room number from the front desk, was told she hadn't left for the day and then had asked them not to disturb her by calling up first. He wasn't sure she'd even see him again and hoped he would have a better chance this way.

As she opened the door, he heard her say "Alex, I'm glad…" and then she stopped as soon as she saw him.

"What are you doing here, Damiano?" She looked surprised to see him. He knew she'd been crying; her eyes were red and puffy.

"I was worried about you. Are you all right?"

She didn't answer immediately and he was afraid she would shut the door and he would never have another chance with her. But just to see her one more time was enough.

"Come in," she said and he followed her into the room and watched her as she sat down at a table. There were two coffee cups and he wondered who Alex was.

"What do you want?" she asked, telling herself that he still excited her, but that she wouldn't let her guard down…not yet. He'd excited her before only to push her away and leave her miserable and she wasn't about to let him do it again. Yes, she loved him and wanted him, but he had a nasty habit of leaving her depressed and she hadn't made up her mind yet about being with him…and about the assault.

"I wanted to explain about last night," he started. "That man who interrupted us? I owe him money. He wants to be repaid and I will not lie to you…he is dangerous."

He watched her face and saw the color drain out. He wanted only to hold her, to tell her how sorry he was that he'd gotten her involved in his affairs, to love her and not let anyone hurt her. He had to know what had happened between her and Bocchio. His dealings with The Teacher would depend on what she told him.

"I know he saw you last night," he continued, her face paler now. "He came to my apartment and told me. Did he hurt you?" He was terrified of her answer, but he had to know.

"What happened was not your fault. You warned me about being with you and I should have listened the first time we had dinner together."

"What did he do, Noreen? Tell me and I will make it right for you."

"How will you make it right? What's done is done and I don't want to think about it anymore."

"Please tell me! Do not leave me wondering. I know all of this is my fault and I want to make it right."

She had been running her fingers on the napkin at her plate. She could smell the freshness of the croissants and remembered that Alex was gone for good this time.

Damiano put his hand on hers and held it, waiting for her, loving her now with no reservations. He would give up everything for her…even his freedom.

"He wanted to scare me so that I would leave you alone. His bodyguard held me and the other man ran his hands over me, but nothing else." She couldn't look at him, but concentrated on the napkin under her hand, the warmth of his hand on hers comforting until he pulled it away.

"I have not been honest with you about myself. There is something I must tell you. After I tell you, I want you to decide if you will still love me." He had a slight smile and she noticed. "Papa told me that *you* must decide. I am trying to be a good son and listen to my Papa.

"I have been in trouble with the police; not just once, but several times." He expected her to ask, but she sat quietly and waited for him. "I am a thief. I steal from the tourists; you know…I take their wallets when they are not aware. That is how I make my living, that and drawing on the streets."

He looked away, not wanting to see the rejection he knew was on her beautiful face. But he knew he had to go on. The truth about himself was the only thing standing between them and keeping them apart.

"There is something else. One time, I took a woman's wallet and she discovered what I was doing. I was going to run away, but she grabbed my hand and told me not to go. I could not believe she was not angry with me and did not call the police.

"She said we could have a good time together and that she was lonely. She told me that I was handsome and that she would like to know me."

Noreen watched his expression. If he were lying right now, she'd know it and he definitely wasn't; his hands were shaking, but his eyes were riveted on hers as he spoke.

"She wanted to go back to her hotel and told me her husband was gone and would not be back until late. She was very pretty and I knew she wanted to make love, so I went with her." He took a deep breath as if telling her would relieve his guilt and cleanse him of his sin.

"Her husband came in the room when we were in bed together and I thought he was going to kill me. He had a gun and pointed it at me. She told him that I had forced her to make love, but I did not force her. She lied. I tried to tell him, but he would not listen to what I said. He held the gun on me and she called the police. They arrested me and I went to jail."

Now it was out in the open; everything that is, except how he'd made it possible for *Flora* to go away. Now he waited to find out if his real *Flora* would leave him too.

"I love you and only want to take care of you," he said simply. "I am sorry that I have made you cry, but when you told me that you were from the FBI, I knew I could not keep seeing you. I did not want you to get in trouble and I thought you would hate me."

She knew that she now had a big decision to make. If she continued to see him, to have an intimate relationship with him, her chances for the promotion would be gone and it was unlikely that she would ever be considered for one again in the future. Could she live with that? Could she live knowing that she'd failed to honor the memory of her brother? Her parents would understand, but would that be enough to ease her guilt?

On the other hand, there was something about Damiano that captured her, imprisoned her until she could no more walk away from him than she could stop being a woman. His passion when he drew caught her up in the excitement of the creation until all she wanted was to be created anew by him; to experience the same ecstasy he did when he drew *Flora*. She wanted to share that with him until she was so full of him that nothing else mattered. If her career, the FBI and the Art Crime Team disappeared, she would be fully satisfied in him.

"I need to be alone," she said at last. "I need to think about all of this. Do you understand?" she asked.

"Yes, I understand. Take your time. I will wait for your decision." He sounded very dejected and looked even more so. He got up to leave, saying nothing as he headed for the door.

"Damiano, wait," she said and walked over to him and wrapped her arms around him.

He made no reply, but pulled her securely to himself, breathing in the smell of her and wanting the embrace to last forever. She had already decided: her life would be different now because he would be part of it.

"I'll be leaving in a few days. Can I come to your place?"she asked.

"Tell me when and I will pick you up."

"Tonight. Can we have dinner?"

He smiled, his pupils large with anticipation. "It is better that I take you to a café than cook at my apartment! The kitchen is too small. We will have dinner at Tortino's, yes? And after, we will go to my apartment. I will pick you up at eight."

She smiled and nodded, the butterflies having returned at the thought of being alone with him again. She knew it would happen this time: she would offer herself and he would accept. He kissed her lightly, turned and left the room.

Chapter 32

GIULIO STEPPED DOWN immediately when he saw her approach. He gave her air kisses, but not much of a smile and that worried her. The Uffizi courtyard was crowded today and it looked as though he had quite a bit of money in his box.

"You have come at a good time. I will take my break now. You will get some espresso with me?" he asked.

"Yes, of course. Tortino's again?"

He nodded, grabbed his money box and they walked to the café with no words spoken between them. After the waiter brought the order, Giulio sat sipping the hot liquid and she got the impression that he wasn't going to start a conversation. She had no idea what Damiano might have told him about their dinner, but she couldn't stand the suspense, so she began.

"Damiano came to see me this morning at my hotel." Giulio perked up. "He said that you told him that I should be the one who decides if I want to be with him. He said he was trying to be a good son." She waited a moment and saw him smile.

"The dinner…it went well then?" he asked. Apparently he hadn't spoken to Damiano yet about what had happened. Maybe that was a good thing. She wanted Giulio to like her and she wanted to trust that whatever happened between herself and Damiano when they were together would be private, especially what would happen this evening.

"Yes and no. He told me after dinner that I would get hurt if I was with him and I didn't understand. But when he came to my hotel, he explained about his police record."

Giulio sighed. "He is trying to be better, Noreen. I know this," he stressed. "He loves you and for you, he will change. I knew this would be true when I first talked to you."

"Well, I don't know how much of an influence I have on him, but I do love him and I want to be with him; to get to know him better."

"This is good! You will see! As I said, he is a good man. He just needs a good woman to shape the edges…you know…like Michelangelo when he carved the marble. Damiano has rough edges and a wonderful woman like you can shape him to be as beautiful as *David*."

Noreen chuckled. "Well, I'm no artist and I certainly haven't ever carved marble, but I'll see what I can do!"

"I will pray every night for you, just as I pray for my son. You will see. It will all turn out just as Carlotta said it would. God will change Damiano because you will be helping Him!"

She smiled. She was happy to be alone with him for a few minutes so she could ask him some questions. "Since you are outside the gallery every day, do you know any of the staff who work there?"

"*Sì*, I know some of them."

"Do you know Rico Panello?"

"Sì. He is the head of the guards. I see him often. Why do you ask? Is he part of your investigation?"

"In a way, yes. When a crime is committed, everyone is questioned, even those people who are least likely to be a suspect. It's just part of solving the case. Do you understand?"

She didn't want Giulio to feel uncomfortable about talking about other people. He'd already told her that some street people were dangerous and even though Panello didn't work on the streets, she was hoping Giulio might have heard something that would be of use to her. The TPC already suspected him and Sartori, but she wanted to know for certain if it was Panello.

"I understand. I know Rico. He has a nice wife. I see her with him sometimes and she brings the children for lunch on the days there is no school. They all eat together."

"He sounds like a good husband and father and I know his work history with the gallery is very good," she coached.

"I like Rico. On my birthday, he puts five euro into my box! He is a good man, but I was worried for him one time."

Now she was getting somewhere! "Why were you worried?"

"There was talk that he was gambling. I heard that his wife was going to leave him if he did not quit."

"Did he quit?" she asked.

"Yes. He owed a large sum of money, but he paid off his debt and I do not think he has gambled again."

"Good for him," she encouraged and then asked, "It was a good thing he could come up with so much money to pay his debt."

"That was a worry also. My friend Arturo, he is the one who does the watercolor paintings under the statue of Leonardo da Vinci, told me that Rico was involved in something illegal and that is how he made the money to pay his debts. Arturo knows Rico much better than I."

"Did Arturo say what Rico was involved in?"

Giulio shook his head. "He did not tell me, but you could ask him. Come. I will introduce you." With that, he motioned to the waiter, paid for the coffees and they both walked back to the Uffizi.

Arturo was about eighty years old, maybe older, with wild grey hair and a three-day stubble of beard growing on his weathered skin. His hands were thin and stained with years of his work, but his eyes sparkled when he saw them approach.

He was sitting on a folding chair, his paint box open and balancing precariously on a tiny folding stand. On his lap was a wooden board with watercolor paper taped to it and the beginnings of what looked like a painting of Santa Maria del Fiore and the surrounding buildings. He rinsed his brush in a jar of water next to his chair and got up carefully.

Giulio spoke to him in Italian for a moment and then said, "This is my new friend Signorina Issenlowe." Arturo wiped his hand on his paint smock; a very well-worn large shirt that could easily have been expensively framed and hung in any gallery as an abstract piece of art. The collection and pattern of the different colors on it was dizzying and every bit as interesting as some abstract art she had seen.

"I'm very happy to meet you," she said, taking his hand. He kissed the back of hers and smiled. She noticed the sandwich board next to his chair. Samples of his work were pinned to the board for viewing and for sale. "You're very talented," she said looking at them and he thanked her.

"The signorina is an investigator!" Giulio said. "She is helping the police to find a stolen painting."

"Ah, the Titan!" Arturo exclaimed. "I just heard this morning that *Flora* was missing!"

"Not our *Flora!*" Giulio exclaimed. "Damiano will be so upset! She is his favorite!"

Noreen was shocked. The administration was trying to keep secret which painting had been stolen, but apparently that information had leaked out. She wondered how the gallery administration was going to take the news. Well, she had always believed that the underground communication system was better than most people knew and now she was certain.

"Yes, it was *Flora* that was stolen," she admitted and looked at Arturo. "Giulio said that you might be able to help me. We were talking about your friend Rico Panello. Giulio told me that Rico had had some gambling trouble, but had paid his debts. Do you know where he got the money to do that?"

Arturo's face seized in shock. "You do not think that Rico had anything to do with stealing *Flora*, do you? He is a good man; a family man with children!"

"No, I don't think that," she lied. "But the job of any investigator is to investigate and so I am asking lots of questions about everybody."

"Do you investigate me also?" Arturo asked, looking a bit puzzled, but not nervous or worried as far as she could tell.

"No, of course not. But Rico is an employee of the gallery and it's my job to find out as much as I can about everyone who works there."

Arturo rubbed his chin as if in deep thought, maybe trying to decide if he should tell what he knew. After a few tense moments for Noreen, he finally spoke.

"Rico told me that he had done an extra job for someone at the gallery."

"What kind of job?" she asked.

"He did not say, but he told me that if the gallery found out, he could lose his position. I knew by the way he was talking, that whatever he did was against the law. He said he did it only because his wife was going to leave him."

"Did he say who he did the job for?"

"No, he did not, but he did say it was an important person."

Noreen thanked him and explained again that asking questions was her job and that he shouldn't worry about getting Panello into any trouble. She turned to the sandwich board again, a small watercolor of the Ponte Vecchio and Arno River catching her eye. "How much for this one?" she asked, pointing to it.

"For Giulio's beautiful new friend, it is a gift!"

"Please," she insisted, "I want to pay you for it."

Arturo was shaking his head. "No, Signorina. It is a gift." She thanked him as he removed it from the sandwich board and handed it to her.

"You're very kind and I'll remember you every time I look at this," she said.

"That is the beauty of art, is it not? That in its beauty, it gives to us pleasant memories? I hope you will find *Flora*."

"I hope so too," she said and they left Arturo as a tourist approached and asked the cost of one of the paintings on the sandwich board.

Chapter 33

RICO PANELLO STOOD in front of Sartori's desk. He didn't want to sit. He wanted what was owed him. Sartori had promised the guard he'd have his money by now and Panello was mad. More than the money though, he wanted Sartori out of the country as he'd promised. Panello had agreed to do one more switch only because Sartori would be gone and unlikely to blackmail him any longer.

"Sit down, Panello. There is no reason to be upset."

"You do not have such a tight grip on me as you think you do," he replied, still standing. Sartori understood the innuendo: Panello could turn him over to the police as the perpetrator of the theft of *Flora*.

"I hardly think you would get off free and clear if you went to the police. You would most surely do some time in prison and then how would your wife and children manage without your income? Sit down. I have some good news."

Panello took a chair, not convinced that there was any good news to come out of this meeting. Sartori had been putting off paying him using the excuse that the representative was delayed, but Panello wasn't buying that any more.

"This is what I will do for you," Sartori began. "Since Kadir has been delayed, I will pay you the ten thousand euro out of my own money tomorrow."

Panello frowned. Sartori was stalling again and he knew it. The idea came to him that he could notify the police, tell them about Sartori and still hang on to his job. He'd be out the ten thousand, but he could fake a good enough story as to how he never realized what was happening. Tavolaro wasn't involved at all; he didn't know that the original had been switched with a forgery that was loaded into the van before the original was. Panello could claim likewise and Sartori would be off his back for good. If that story didn't take, he'd lie and tell the police that Sartori threatened to kill him if he didn't help.

"I want my money today…now!"

"Rico, you must understand that I do not have that amount of cash lying around my house! If I did, my wife would spend it all!" Sartori laughed, trying to lighten the mood, but Panello still looked like he'd gladly shove a knife into him and twist it until the Uffizi was short one Assistant Head of Acquisitions.

"I have investments and it will take a short time to draw the cash from them," he continued. "I will stop at the bank and withdraw the money for you. It will be too dangerous for us to meet here, so you come to the back entrance at…" Here he looked at his watch and then went on. "…at eleven-thirty tonight."

"Why so late? My wife will wonder where I am going. This is not a very smart plan." Panello was getting agitated.

His nerves were shot and he wanted the entire affair over with and Sartori gone for good.

"Tell your wife that you have to accompany a painting that is being loaned out tomorrow and the flight leaves very early. Tell her it was necessary to clean the painting first, let it dry and that it still needs to be crated for the flight. We must be very cautious about this. Neither of us wants any suspicions aroused. "

Panello thought about that for a moment. The explanation to his wife was plausible and it would be safer to get his money at night. "And you will have the entire amount: ten thousand euro, just as you promised?"

"*Sì*, just as I promised."

Panello got up. When all was said and done, his only option was to go along with Sartori, whether he liked it or not. Underneath it all, he knew he'd never go to the police. It was too dangerous for him and he had to think about his wife and kids.

"I will be here at eleven-thirty tonight. Make sure you are too or it will not go well for you." Panello turned and walked out the door, giving it a slight slam just for emphasis. He would have slammed it harder, but that would have attracted attention.

His ulcer had him in constant, gripping pain now. Sartori popped two narcotic tablets into his mouth knowing that even the taking the entire bottle wouldn't help. His hands were shaking as he realized that he'd just committed himself to another murder. It was the principle of the thing: he wasn't about to be pushed around by an underling like

Panello and he was worried that the guard just might make good on his implied threat to go to the police. If Panello gave himself up and told everything he knew, he might get off with a very reduced sentence. Sartori couldn't risk it; Panello was going to join Galiazzi in the cemetery. It was the only viable option to insure that Sartori would be safe and living a free life with Angelina in the Caribbean.

He picked up his cell phone and dialed. They wouldn't stay at her apartment after he'd finished with Galiazzi and Panello like he had first planned. He would get a hotel room near the airport under a false name. Their flight left early and he didn't want to take any chances that the police would come knocking at Angelina's door in the middle of the night.

He'd already called and told his wife he was flying to France after work to buy a Rembrandt from a private collector and wouldn't be home for three days. She'd complained about the short notice, but he'd been able to tell a good lie: the seller was hesitant, unsure and might change his mind at any minute. There was someone from the Louvre also interested in acquiring the painting and Sartori was needed to help convince the owner that the Uffizi was where the Rembrandt belonged.

Everything was all taken care of, but knowing that didn't make his ulcer any happier. He still had to get rid of Galiazzi and Panello and that thought was now making his hands shake.

When the desk clerk answered, he made the reservation, telling her he would arrive late with his new wife. She congratulated him after he explained that they were getting married and would require the honeymoon suite. It was a lie, but Angelina would be happy about the room.

He hung up the phone and thought about her, the bottle of champagne that he'd ordered for the room and how excited she'd be when he told her that he was finally going to divorce his wife; something she'd nagged him about since the first time he'd made love to her. He knew how appreciative she'd be, especially after two or three glasses of champagne, and the fantasies playing out in his head were almost enough to make him forget what he was planning before meeting up with her.

ᏈᏋ

The bowl of salad sat in the middle of the kitchen table next to the plate of meat ravioli in marinara. Giulio watched Damiano intently as his son sipped the Chianti and ignored the pasta. He noticed the imperceptible shaking of Damiano's hand and the staring into space. This conversation was going nowhere so far, but Giulio intended on getting some answers.

"Tell me, Damiano, and do not lie to me," he commanded. "Your Mama will turn over in her grave if you lie."

Giulio had used that untruth many times as his son grew up. As a small child, Damiano had believed it. Even though she wasn't dead, he would picture her as she sat up in her coffin, her boney finger pointing directly at him and the look of displeasure on what was left of her rotting face. Then, it scared him, but not now. It did make it harder for him to lie to his father, but he couldn't answer Giulio's question truthfully.

"You are good enough to do it. It is your favorite; the one you draw on the streets ever day. She told us *Flora* was the painting that was stolen, that it was switched with a forgery. Did you make the copy? Did you have anything to do with this?" Giulio waited for the answer.

"No, Papa. I did nothing." He said it coldly as if he were disconnected from everything going on around him and without looking at his father.

"I see your hand shaking. Tell me why it does that if you are telling me the truth."

"Because I am nervous." He took another sip of wine. "She told me she needed time to think about if she wants to be with me. I love her, Papa and I am afraid she does not want me. That is why my hand is shaking." He looked at Giulio when he said this; this part was true.

Giulio wasn't convinced, especially since he knew Damiano's criminal leanings and the extent of his talent. As far as Giulio was concerned, Damiano would have no trouble painting an exact duplicate of *Flora*, one good enough to fool even the people at the gallery.

Giulio sighed. "I do not believe you," he said, his words heavy with disappointment. He knew Damiano was hiding the truth, but wanted to believe otherwise. It *was* possible, he told himself, that someone else had done the forgery. So far, Damiano's criminal record involved petty theft and to undertake forging a painting as valuable as *Flora*, would be too bold a step for his son. That's what he wanted to believe.

"Tell me about the five thousand euro you are getting for the commissioned work. Who is it for? What did you paint? Where is the money? Tell me these things and I will believe you are telling me the truth!"

Damiano looked at him. He felt as bad seeing his father now as he did when he'd seen the hurt in Noreen's face. His life seemed to be defined by the people he loved and ended up hurting. He didn't think he had the strength to go on, especially not if she walked out of his life because she'd found out he had forged her favorite painting.

"Papa, if I copied Flora, I would demand much more than five thousand euro to take such a big chance as that," he lied.

His voice was flat and unemotional. He had no energy left; the lying was leaving him too depressed. "I painted a portrait of a family, a wealthy tourist from Belgium who was here on business with his wife and two children. That is all. He paid me two days ago, but most of that money went to pay my bills. My rent was due. All my bills were due."

"Did you pay off that shark Bocchio?"

"Yes, Papa. I paid Bocchio."

Giulio huffed and started dishing up. He said nothing more. Everything Damiano had said was reasonable and until he had the truth, he would believe his son. That didn't lessen his disappointment though. "Eat your ravioli before they get cold," he said.

Chapter 34

THE ROOM WAS clean, the bed made and the tray gone from the table. She threw her purse on the bed, kicked off her shoes, propped a pillow against the headboard and dropped down, her body still aching. She felt bad physically and emotionally. She thought about Alex and what he'd told her about Claire. She was stuck by how hard it must be for him to have been rejected by two women…two women who supposedly loved and wanted him.

Alex had everything going for him: looks, intelligence, a good job and more strength mixed with compassion than any other man she'd ever met. She knew he'd had lots of women throwing themselves at him, but he'd always been very selective about who he dated and very considerate when he'd break off the relationship. Like her, he wanted someone who was committed to him…committed for life.

His father had walked out on his mother, himself and his two younger sisters when Alex was ten. Within three years, his mother had remarried and the second marriage was very solid and loving. Alex had gained a brother and another sister and to hear him talk, his life from then on was happy and loving. His stepfather was his idol; an ex-

Marine officer who worked at Quantico as an instructor in the JTTF: the Joint Terrorism Task Force. It was from him that Alex learned about discipline, integrity, loyalty, commitment and service. Alex had never given a second thought about any career other than the FBI and that was due to the respect and love he had toward his step-father; Alex wanted to be just like him. His step-father was a deeply religious man too and passed on his values and morals to all of his children, including his new step-children.

Remembering how she had chosen her career over him added to her guilt even more when she realized that it must have brought up all the bad feelings about his biological father leaving him. Alex was strong in every way there was to have strength, but the abandonment by his father was buried deep within him even though he would never admit it. She knew that and she knew she'd walked out on him too, just like his father had. Alex was strong, but rejection was hard for him.

And now, she had in effect rejected him again by throwing it in his face about wanting to make love to Damiano. She didn't even know what had driven her to say anything like that to him.

She sunk further down into the pillow, almost totally reclined on the bed now, and checked her watch. It was seven in the morning in Falls Church. The sadness was becoming all consuming and she needed to talk to Rachel. She needed to laugh. Grabbing her cell phone out of her purse, she dialed the number and after three rings, she heard the small voice.

"Aunt Nordie!" It was Maisy, the seven-year-old.

"Hi, Bug! How are you?"

"I'm not Ladybug. Remember?"

She was right. Noreen had always called Maisy her little Ladybug, but had been informed at the girl's last birthday party that she was too old now for that name.

"I'm sorry. Forgive me, Your Highness. My apologies." Maisy now wanted to be called 'Princess. "Is the Royal Mother about the palace today?"

"Yes, she's right here, but don't talk too long. I'm expecting the Prince to call!" Maisy giggled and Aunt Nordie joined her. It felt good to be connected to this child and to her friend.

"Royal Servant is more like it!" Rachel said sarcastically as she got on the line. "All I do is pick up after Tony and the kids. But enough about me. How are *you*? How's it going with your artist? Has he fallen completely in love with you and become *your* Prince Charming yet?"

"It's complicated," was all she could say.

"Uh oh. Tell me what happened," Rachel replied, the humor quickly gone out of her voice.

"There's so much, I don't know where to begin." That was the truth and for a second, she almost told Rachel she had to go, realizing that it had been a bad idea to call her in the first place; her tears were too close to the surface.

"Listen Sweetie, you know you always feel better when you get stuff like this off your chest. And you know you can tell me anything and I'll keep it to myself."

Noreen did know that. Besides her humor, it was what drew her to Rachel in the first place and kept them friends. They understood each other, but respected their differences; thrived on them, in fact.

"I'll start with the good, okay?" She took a deep breath and began the complicated tale of a budding love now drooping like a bridal bouquet two days after the wedding. "He loves me and I love him."

"And this is bad how? Is he married?"

"No, he's still not married; I told you that before. The problem is that he has a criminal record and that isn't going to help me get that big departmental promotion."

"Oh, Noreen, I'm sorry! That's just too cruel! So what are you going to do?"

"For the first time in my life, I don't know. I mean, I know I'm going to have to decide if I want to stay with him and give up that promotion or give *him* up and stay with the FBI. But there's more."

"Go ahead," Rachel said slowly.

"I spent last night with Alex."

"Alex Channing? That Alex? I'm totally lost now! How did that happen and what do you mean by 'spent the night?'

"Alex was sent by Internal Affairs to watch how I handle this case for the Uffizi. He said it was because I was a shoe-in for the promotion and that it was a security check that all agents go through beforehand. He saw me with

Damiano at dinner; he was tailing me all over Florence so that he could report back to IA."

"So…you knew he was watching you?"

"No, I only found out after I got assaulted."

She heard Rachel let out a loud gasp. "Assaulted? Are you kidding? Are you alright? It wasn't Alex, was it?"

"No, Rachel, it wasn't Alex and yes, I'm okay. It was someone that Damiano owes money to…like a loan shark, if that's what they call those guys over here. Alex was following me, but then must have lost me. It was late and I was walking back from having dinner with Damiano at his dad's house."

"What happened?"

"Some big guy grabbed me and a fat guy told me to stay away from Damiano, that he didn't need to be distracted by me. The fat guy put tape over my mouth and taped my wrists together. I was so scared."

"Oh, Noreen, I'm so sorry. Are you *sure* you're okay?"

"Yeah, thanks to Alex. After the two guys left, Alex found me and took me back to my hotel. I couldn't believe it was him! He stayed the night in my room; he knew I'd be too upset to be by myself. He told me that he'd been watching me and why. He still loves me, Rachel. I know he does."

"So…what about his fiancée?"

"That's the other part of the problem. He isn't engaged anymore." She heard Rachel gasp again. "When I couldn't sleep, we talked for a while and he told me that two weeks ago he called it off with Claire. Let's just say he had proof she'd been unfaithful."

Rachel let out a long breath. "Oh, no…poor Alex!"

"He told me that he's always loved me and that he'd only been interested in Claire because he had to move on with his life after I rejected him."

"Yeah, that does complicate things, doesn't it?"

"No, what complicates things is that I still love Alex, but I love Damiano too."

"Well, for once in my life, I don't know what to say and I don't have any advice," Rachel stated. "Unfortunately, this is one of those decisions in life that a person can only make for themselves and I know how hard that is. I've had patients with terminal cancer have to make the decision if chemotherapy should be continued or stopped and invariably, it's something only the patient can decide. I'm sure deciding between two men that you love is just as hard. I'm so sorry, honey! I wish I could help you."

"Just letting me unload is a lot of help. I don't think you realize that."

"Well, that's what we Royal Servants are for, isn't it? To serve those we love?"

"Yeah, I guess so," she said, smiling at last. "Thanks, Rachel. I'll let you know how things go."

"You'd better! Don't leave me here worrying about you, okay? Hey, I've got to get going or I'll be late for work. Take care, huh? And don't worry. You're smart. You'll make the right decision…I know you will."

She told Rachel 'good-bye,' closed her cell phone and slumped down into the softness of the bed until her eyes closed automatically and she felt herself relax.

When she was almost asleep, she felt the phone vibrate in her hand and checked the caller ID: it was Alex.

ஐ

As he looked around, he realized that his apartment hadn't looked this good since he'd moved in, but then he'd never made a date to bring a woman over before. Not that it was dirty, just always messy. He did all of his painting here and it was more convenient to leave his canvases, easels and paints out. After he'd straightened up, he'd gone back to his current painting and was working on it again. He needed to concentrate on it so that he wouldn't think too hard.

He had to be careful with the titanium white. It had to be applied so that it appeared to the eye that the garment was thin, almost like gauze. He never worked in one area of the painting at a time until it was finished. He moved around, working here for a while, then there. It all depended on his mood.

Today he was excited as he painted, even though he didn't want to admit that to himself. If he did, he'd also have to admit that he was scared of what her decision would be. He also didn't want to think about what would happen if she found out who had forged *Flora.*

He picked up more titanium white and applied it to the canvas, working it into the painting with the same love he always had and for the sheer enjoyment of getting lost in his art. Painting healed him. It took him somewhere else, to a place where he could believe that miracles happened. Wasn't it a miracle to take a blank, white piece of stretched fabric and turn it into something beautiful and something of great value, something as breathtaking as *Flora* or Botticelli's *The Birth of Venus* or as incredibly powerful as Caravaggio's *The Sacrifice of Isaac*?

He cleaned his brush. He had no more time to think about miracles; he needed to get some money. Bocchio would be back. He took the canvas down from the easel, turned it so that the back faced outward and leaned it carefully against the wall in the bedroom closet. Then he covered it with a cloth. He couldn't take the chance she would see what he had done.

He grabbed his backpack and headed out the door. Today was an important day. Today he would know if she would be part of his future and he would find out if his *Flora* loved him as much as he loved her.

Chapter 35

"MY FLIGHT LEAVES at seven tomorrow," he said. "Can we get together for some coffee or something? How about dinner?"

"Why are you calling, Alex? *You* walked out on *me* this morning. Remember?" Part of her was happy that he'd called, but the other part of her…the part that had believed he was gone for good…was confused.

"I know, Baby. I'm sorry about that. I was mad. I admit it, but I wasn't mad at you. I was mad at myself for putting you in that position. I should never have insinuated that you needed to choose between Travani and me. That was just wrong of me and I just want to say 'I'm sorry.'

Alex and his damned, wonderful integrity! Why didn't he just let her think he was gone for good? No, he had to call and get her all soft inside, the kind of soft that made her want to kiss his perfect lips and stare forever into his blue eyes. It was the kind of soft that made her want his body next to hers. She felt like that now as she decided what to say to him.

"I knew you weren't mad at me. I knew you were hurt," she admitted.

"So I'm forgiven?"

"You know you are."

"Dinner then? Seven?"

Now she would hurt him again. "I can't, Alex." The line was dead silent for about ten seconds until he finally spoke. His tone was as dreary as a pauper's funeral on a rainy day.

"Okay," he sighed. "I understand. So I guess this is good-bye then. I'll probably see you sometime later…maybe at work."

"I'm at the hotel. Can you come by now and tell me in person?" She almost choked when she heard the words tumble out of her mouth like she had no control over her tongue. Why had she said that? Why couldn't she just tell him 'good-bye' and let it go? Because she felt guilty; that was the answer and she knew it. She felt guilty about wanting Damiano to make love to her, but even more guilty about telling Alex about it. Maybe she wanted to hurt him for the 'creep' remark.

"I'll be there in ten minutes," was all he said and she heard the phone go dead. She checked her watch: it was two forty-five. She had plenty of time before she had to get ready for dinner.

☙

He was having a hard time staying awake. The narcotic pain medication always made him sleepy. The two he'd taken at noon were working just as they should; his ulcer was quiet, but he couldn't keep his eyes open. Today he was taking a long lunch hour. He'd already gotten permission with the curator, telling him that he wasn't feeling well. Besides, there wasn't much work on his desk right now.

He closed his eyes; he couldn't look at the pink wallpaper any longer. Before he had a chance to drop off to sleep, he heard her come in, drop her keys on the kitchen counter and now she was walking into the bedroom.

"What are you doing here?" she asked, not at all upset with him. He *was* lying in her bed and that excited her even though he was still wearing his suit.

"Taking a long lunch. Are you finished for the day?"

She nodded. "I am finished with the job. I quit this morning. I came home to pack, just as you told me. You did not tell me you were coming over."

She was sitting next to him now, the smell of her expensive perfume hanging over him and taking his mind off the fact that he was doped up on narcotics. He was suddenly in a much happier place; even the wallpaper wasn't bothering him now.

"Angelina, do you want to talk or do you want to enjoy the lunch hour with me?"

She loosened his tie. "Lunch," she said, smiling, and then asked, "Do you really have an hour?"

ଔ

He sat at the table across from her, his hands folded in front of him. As soon as he'd stepped through her door, he could see it in her eyes, but now, he stared at his hands and didn't want her to see it in his. If she had changed her mind, he wanted to be sure it was what she wanted.

"I didn't want you to leave like that…mad at me," she started.

"I told you, I wasn't mad at you." He couldn't keep from looking at her; she was too beautiful. To hell with trying to hide the fact that he wanted her more than he ever had before. If that was because he knew that Travani had her attention, then so be it. He could hold his own against any guy who was making a play for her.

"This isn't easy for me, Alex. It isn't easy because I was so focused on my career and being the best agent I could be, that I hadn't had time to consider my life outside of work."

"So…are you considering it now? Is that why you asked me to come back? Because if you want me, I'm all yours." He couldn't hide what he was giving away in his eyes, but he didn't care anymore. He wanted her. It was that simple and he knew she knew it.

"I was miserable before I left home. I wasn't excited about coming to Florence, about being at the Uffizi *or* about solving this case. And I didn't know why I felt like I did."

"Do you know now?" He was pinning her down with his gaze and doing it on purpose.

"I talked to Rachel before I came…" He interrupted her.

"Advice from the happily married?" he asked, smiling a bit now. Alex liked Rachel and he and Tony got along well together considering that as couples, the four of them hadn't spent much time together; a barbecue now and then, a holiday or Noreen's birthday.

"Yeah, you know Rachel!" She was smiling now too. That was a good sign and he was more optimistic.

"So…what advice did she give you?"

"Actually, she told me to come home with Michelangelo. In reality though, she made me realize that I'm not getting any younger and that what I want at this point in my life is to be married. I want what Rachel has…"

"An Italian, right?"

"That isn't fair, Alex. I'm trying to tell you that I still love you. Do you know how hard it was for me to have to choose between you or my career? I didn't want you out of my life, but I had to decide and just because I chose my career, doesn't mean that I don't regret that choice every day. I know how badly I hurt you and I live with that regret every minute." She was frustrated, her eyes getting moist, but she refused to cry. "Now I don't know what I want."

He reached out his hand to touch hers. "Why does love have to hurt like this?" he asked and saw her shoulders slump and her head drop. "I'm sorry, Baby. I never meant for it to be like this for us, but I guess that's just the way life is. Sometimes it's easy and sometimes it's hard and I know what you're going through now is hard. I can't help you decide what you want though. Only you can do that. But I want you to know that I will always be here for you…even as a friend, if that's what you decide I should be. If you decide you want Travani in your life, then go to him. I only want you to be happy and if that means that I have to give you up, then that's the way it will be. Whatever you decide, don't you worry 'bout me. Do what makes *you* happy."

He stood up to leave, waiting for her. When she got on her feet, he took her in his arms and held her for a moment and then kissed her. Melting into her, he felt her passion cover him like a warm blanket. He could easily take her now and she would have no second thoughts about it. He knew that. He could feel it in her embrace and could taste it as her mouth explored his. But he wouldn't do it.

"You can always call me if you need me. Okay?" he said as he let her go. "Just remember: I'll always love you."

There was nothing she could say even if she had wanted to. She was too overcome with desire for him and thoughts of Damiano as he chalked *Flora*. They were scattered, confusing thoughts that crowded her brain and left her feeling as though a crushing weight had been placed on her chest, the pain of the weight leaving her unable to breathe. She was letting him go and she wondered if she'd just made the biggest mistake of her life. She watched him walk away, the tears coming.

She forced herself to focus. She'd come to Florence as a representative of the FBI, to aid in discovering who was involved in stealing a priceless painting and she'd better get back on the job. She'd never intended on getting sidetracked with an Italian artist or with an ex-boyfriend.

Besides, staying focused on her job was the only way to keep from crying her heart out.

She retrieved her phone from the bedside stand and then searched her purse for the business card. When she found it, she dialed the number and heard him answer.

"Inspector Rossini?" He answered in the affirmative. "I have some information that might help you."

"From your street sources?" he asked and she couldn't be sure, but he sounded like he was being patronizing.

"Yes, as a matter of fact. There is a watercolor artist who works outside the Uffizi and knows some of the staff. A very old man named…"

"Arturo? I know this man."

"Yes, Arturo. Did you question him?" If he was being patronizing with her, she was going to rub a little sand in his eyes as retribution. She was upset and knew it had nothing to do with Rossini. She was mad at herself for letting Alex walk out again.

"No, we did not," Rossini replied, sounding a bit chastised.

"I believe you're on the right track with Rico Panello. He may have been involved in your two previous thefts. Apparently, he had a gambling problem and his wife threatened to leave if he didn't quit. He got some money…quickly and very possibly by illegal means. He told Arturo that he'd done an extra job for someone at the gallery and that if the gallery found out, Panello would be fired. When I read his employee file, I saw no mention of his being reprimanded for anything or that the gallery was aware of his gambling problem, but that doesn't surprise me." She let Rossini digest the information for a few minutes.

"When I interviewed Emilio Tavolaro, I was fairly certain that he had nothing to do with switching the paintings. His body language indicated that he was relaxed and wasn't hiding anything. It's definitely Panello just as you suspected." She felt bad about her tone with him, so threw him that last compliment by way of an apology.

"Apparently, Signorina, our agency needs to listen more to the people on the streets," Rossini was contrite. Was that *his* apology for being condescending before she wondered?

Rossini continued. "I would like nothing better than to bring Panello in for questioning again, but I cannot do that at this time. We know that Sartori is involved; he is the top person. And now we are fairly certain that Panello helped him. But we need to know the intermediary; the person who hired the forger.

"Right now, we have continuous surveillance on Sartori and have been able to listen to calls on his cell phone. He is meeting late tonight with someone. We do not know who, but believe this may be the person who is the go-between. He told his wife that he is leaving for France in the morning for three days and told his mistress to pack her bags and be ready to leave tomorrow. As we have suspected, he is going to leave Italy, but we hope he is contacting the accomplice tonight. If we can get *that* man, we think we may be able to get him to reveal the identity of the forger. Of course, Sartori will be taken into custody tonight."

Noreen was excited. This investigation might be ending sooner than she expected and then she would have time to think about her private life. Ever since the assault by the fat man, she'd lost a lot of her enthusiasm for being a federal agent and noticed it even before that: specifically during the time she'd spent having dinner with Damiano at his father's house.

Damiano had been charming, very desirable and much too tempting for her, but had controlled his desires much better than she had. He'd shown great restraint and instead of being disappointed, she'd felt better about him and his intentions. Even though he'd pushed her away again, she realized that he had every bit as much integrity as Alex had. 'Well,' she thought, 'excluding his criminal record.' Now that she knew why he'd pulled away and knew about his criminal record, she was hopeful that tonight would indeed be that new beginning he'd spoken of.

"Thank you, Signorina, for the information," Rossini concluded. She was pulled back from her reverie. If Rossini said something just before his 'thank you,' she hadn't heard it. She'd been too wrapped up in thinking about Damiano and about being with him at his apartment.

"And you will keep me informed about Sartori's meeting this evening?" she asked.

"Sì. I will call you tomorrow, if that is all right with you," he replied. She told him 'yes' and then 'good-bye,' her thoughts back to Damiano.

Chapter 36

HER DRESS WAS white with a floral print that looked like a watercolor painting. The neckline was low enough to remind him of *Flora's*, and the length of the dress was short, ending about four inches above her knee. It had tiny sleeves that barely hugged her shoulders. The design was casual, but on her it was something so elegant it took his breath away.

They were sitting at a table outside of Tortino's. The sun had just gone down leaving a pink sky that bathed her in a delicate radiance that no artist, not even he, could have painted. 'Only God could create such beauty' he thought as he looked at her.

There was no breeze tonight, but the scent of her perfume drifted his way and it was all he could do to keep his desire under control. He took another sip of his wine, trying to steady his hand. He was afraid to say anything to her. She'd hadn't said anything about whether she would continue to see him.

"Your father was a big help to me today," she said at last, her middle finger tracing the lip of her wine glass.

"Yes? How is that?"

"He introduced me to Arturo. Do you know him?"

"Sì, I know him. He is a very nice man and a fine artist." He was having trouble looking at her; she was too beautiful tonight and he felt unworthy even be sharing a glass of wine with her.

"Yes, he is. He was able to tell me about a man who works in the gallery and that information helped with my investigation."

He took hold of the hand that was tracing the wine glass. "It is a beautiful night," he said softly. "We should not spoil it with talk of work."

She nodded, suddenly embarrassed. The butterflies were making it impossible to get a coherent sentence out of her mouth and her work was about the only topic that she felt comfortable with right now.

He looked every bit as good as the first time they'd had dinner here. The flicker from the candle on the table was reflected in his dark eyes and made them seem to dance and the white, perfect teeth showed every time he smiled. His smile was heavenly and his voice soft and low as if he were telling her secrets that only she was worthy of knowing.

"I am happy to be spending this time with you," he continued. "That is what I want to talk about. I want to know about the things that make you smile and about the things you dream of. I want to know what makes you excited."

"You want to know about us…about our future together." If she were going to enjoy this evening with him, she needed to get that subject out of the way right now before the butterflies got any more unmanageable. He didn't need to say anything or nod. She knew he wanted the answer; it showed on his face, mixed with the desire and hunger for her. She took a few minutes to compose her answer, but he got right to the point.

"There is another man." he said and she was immediately surprised; it had come out so casually. "When I came to your room today…" he continued, but she interrupted him.

"I thought you were Alex and you want to know who he is." Damiano nodded. His dark eyes were pinning her down again; there was no escape from them tonight.

"Do you love him?" His stare wouldn't allow her to move or look away and for a moment, she flashed back to the strong man and how she couldn't get away from him either. She took a sip of wine, hoping it would calm her.

"Yes, I love him. We used to be together, but that's over now."

"But you still love him?"

"Yes." She wasn't about to start a new relationship with ghosts in the closet. "I want to be with *you*, Damiano. Alex is gone and that relationship has ended."

He smiled and took her hand again, his eyes releasing her. "Is it not true that if you are with me, you will have trouble with your job?"

"I worked very hard to have this job. I had good reasons for wanting it. But things are different now."

"Did I make them different for you?"

"Yes and no. I think I wanted something different even before I came to Florence."

"And what do you want now?" He was holding her hand a little more firmly, hoping to hear that what she wanted was him.

The waiter came with their order. He set two salads down and then two plates of pasta with a simple meat sauce and a smaller plate of sautéed squash blossoms and zucchini that they would share.

She let the answer to his question go for now, hoping he wouldn't push her; she still wasn't sure she had one.

He raised his glass to her. "To knowing what we want," he said as they touched glasses, his eyes never leaving hers.

ଓ

When he got home after work, Bianca wasn't happy, but then she never was. She was sulking about the trip to France and how he'd promised her that he would take her the next time he was sent there. It was too late now, she scolded, to find someone to watch the children and she was sure that he had planned it that way.

Sartori shut her voice out of his head and thought about the honeymoon suite he'd reserved for Angelina. It would do no good to try to reason with his wife; it had never worked and wouldn't work now. At least she wasn't screaming at him; she'd stopped doing that a few years ago.

He knew that Bianca's unhappiness with him was deserved. Over the years, he'd grown tired of her, but it wasn't her fault. He'd grown tired of everything and wanted something new and exciting to energize him. That's when Angelina had come into his life.

He'd met her at a party at the gallery given by a group of private donors. The hosts had seen to it that there was a bevy of luscious models to add to the gaiety of the evening, their beauty in direct competition with the display of old masters that adorned the private reception room. Every two years, the donors would put on an invitations-only gala to celebrate the gallery's new acquisitions. The steep cost of attending helped defray the purchase of the new paintings, but even so, there were almost always over three hundred people who attended.

He and Angelina struck it off right away and he knew immediately that she would be his next acquisition. She wanted him; it was as plain as the red color on her full, moist lips. It took her no time to suggest that he show her around, specifically somewhere private like his office, and so they had escaped the festivities and with no encouragement on his part, she had 'posed' nude on his desk. Wouldn't she make a good artist's model, she'd asked him and then suggested that he 'instruct' her how he would 'handle' a new work of art. She was as beautiful as any painting hanging in the gallery and so he had obliged her and she'd been with him ever since.

Bianca wasn't going to be any happier with what he said next, but his mind was on Angelina now.

"My flight leaves very early. I am staying in a hotel near the airport tonight. I will call you when I arrive in France."

Bianca was curiously calm. Perhaps she'd resigned herself to his leaving without her again, but it didn't matter and he didn't care.

"Do not bother coming home, Vincenzo. I know about your mistress and I am finished," she said. It was so unexpected, her voice so calm, that he almost choked and for a minute, couldn't even talk. When he finally recovered, he said nothing. He could tell from her tone that she had thought this through, probably for quite a while. He didn't care enough to try to change her mind.

He went into their bedroom, packed his largest suitcase, took the small photos of the four children that were sitting on his dresser and walked to the front door.

"I will have my lawyer draw up the papers. You will have enough money to take care of the children." He paused as he stared at the resolution in her face. "I am sorry, Bianca. It is not your fault." With that, he left.

ଓ

There was barely enough room for the two of them to climb the staircase side-by-side, but being that close to him excited her. When they came to his door, he unlocked it and let her go inside first.

His apartment wasn't anything like what she had expected, even though she wasn't quite sure what she expected. It was small, but well designed and comfortable and he seemed excited to show her around.

The living area was small, but large enough for a sofa and an accent table, with a small desk and chair in one corner. A doorway led to only the bedroom, with a doorway into the bathroom. He showed her the kitchen and she could see why he'd suggested they have dinner at Tortino's. It was only large enough for a small table and two chairs. Along one wall was a countertop with a sink at one end and a four-burner gas stove at the other. In between, there was a built-in washing machine below the counter and wall-to-wall cabinets above. It was a very small space.

The walls were clean and painted in muted colors. On the wall across from the sofa, she saw an easel and a table with artist's supplies: linseed oil, brush cleaner, tubes of paints with canvases stacked underneath.

He motioned her to sit on the sofa and then asked if she'd like a glass of wine. She told him yes and he went into the kitchen to get it.

"Do you have any paintings you can show me?" she asked, not even having to raise her voice so that he could hear her; the apartment wasn't large enough to have to do that.

"Yes. If you would like, I can show them to you." He brought out two glasses of red wine and handed one to her. Sitting next to her on the sofa, he raised his glass. "You still have not answered my question," he said.

"What question is that?"

"What do you want?" He was waiting, his glass raised.

"I want you," she said. She expected to see him smile, but he didn't. His eyes had her pinned down again. It was the desire she saw in them that wouldn't allow her to move this time and she realized that she was scared, but not in the way she was scared when the fat man was touching her. She was afraid of the feelings inside her, feelings that were building to a crescendo and that she couldn't stop even if she wanted to. She didn't want to and that's what scared her.

"Then we will drink to that, to knowing what we want and thanking God that he has given it to us."

He drank from his glass, his eyes off her now as she sipped her wine too. Her throat was dry, her butterflies active again. She knew he could tell because he immediately relaxed, set his glass down on the table next to the sofa and got up.

"I do not have many paintings here now. I have sold most of them, but I do have some that I can show you." He went into the bedroom and came back with three canvases, all unframed, and stood them up on the floor against the side table.

"This is my favorite." He held up a painting about eleven by fourteen inches. It was a portrait of a woman…a very beautiful woman. Her half-smile reminded Noreen of the *Mona Lisa*, except this woman was much prettier. She had thick, luxurious dark brown hair, beautifully shaped black eyes with long lashes and perfectly formed lips.

"She's so beautiful!" Noreen exclaimed. "Her eyes are so lovely and so intense! There's so much life in her face!"

"I am happy you like it. It is a portrait of my mother."

He said it simply, a smile crossing his face. She looked at him and now saw the resemblance: Damiano had her eyes and gentle smile.

"She was very beautiful," she said again and added, "Your talent is amazing. The technique of how you blended the colors of her skin is wonderful."

She thought about Titan, about how he also excelled at achieving perfect flesh tones in his portraits. In his day, the paints were crudely made and not as technically sophisticated as the oil paints that artists used today. But even with that advantage, she could see the talent it took to blend the flesh tones.

"It is a very special painting to me," he said, his voice almost a whisper. "I disappointed her. My mama talked to God every day. I know she asked Him to make me a better person. I was never able to be that person; the son she wanted me to be. I was trying, but she died before I could show her and then it did not matter to me anymore."

"I'm sorry you didn't get that chance. Sometimes it's hard to live up to other's expectations of us. Sometimes we disappoint them." She was thinking about Cody and about giving up the FBI for Damiano.

Thankfully, he changed the subject. "This one is not my best," he continued as he showed her another canvas. It was smaller. "I am better with portraits than with the scenery," he admitted.

"This is very nice," she said. "I love the play of the shadows cast by the trees." It was a pastoral scene of a countryside in spring, the late afternoon sun casting purple shadows and making her want to go there, to that place he'd created on the canvas. She wanted to be there with him, letting the setting sun cast their shadows in purple.

"Do you like this one?" he asked as he showed her the last canvas. She knew this painting. It was Titan's *Venus of Urbino,* a sensuous and erotic nude posed reclining on white linens, her left hand resting below her abdomen and covering her womanhood, her right arm elevated on a pillow and a bouquet of red flowers in her hand. A puppy is curled up asleep at her feet. There are two servants, one in red, in the background. It was painted about 1538 and was an important example of Titan's mastery as a colorist. Noreen had to admit Damiano's attempt was an excellent copy; the flesh tones every bit as gorgeous as the original.

"It's excellent!" she said at last, overcome by its beauty. She pinned *him* now with *her* eyes. "Why do you steal if you could be using this amazing talent that God has given you?" She looked at *Venus* again, staring at her beauty. "I've always wanted to have talent like this," she said, almost to herself.

He couldn't answer that question for her. He had no answer in light of the fact that he *knew* he had been given a special gift and was wasting it.

"Noreen," he asked, "Will you allow me to do a painting of you? You are so lovely tonight and it would make me very happy."

"Tonight?" she repeated. She checked her watch. It was ten-thirty. She'd never expected to have her portrait done, but then she remembered what Rachel had said about some Italian artist painting her and sipping Chianti. Well, Damiano was an excellent artist and they *were* sipping Chianti. Rachel had joked about it being done in the nude and right now, seeing the anticipation in his gorgeous face, she would gladly pose for him…even nude!

"It will take time to complete of course, but I could start tonight if you will allow me." He stared so intently into her eyes now that she felt like he was invading her soul and that he knew exactly how much she was drawn to him. All she could do was nod her head.

Chapter 37

IT WAS TEN forty-five. He wanted to be in position behind Trattoria Due Colombe before Galiazzi arrived.

"I have to go…some gallery business that I must take care of before we leave tomorrow," he told her as he sat on the side of the bed. She'd had champagne twice and him once and she wanted seconds of him. She was pouting and giving him a come-on look at the same time.

"The night is still young. Do not leave me yet. Come here," she demanded, patting the mattress beside her.

"I told you, Angelina, I have business. I will not be long and when I get back…" He didn't have to say anything more. He dressed and poured her another glass of champagne. "When I get back, we will try out that fancy tub. Be ready." He winked at her, grabbed his suit coat and closed the door gently behind him.

ଓ

"He is leaving the hotel now," he said into his cell phone. Mario De Falco hated surveillance, especially since he had seven years with the TPC and felt that surveillance was below him now. These boring jobs were usually given to the new guys, but Rossini had asked for him personally and that was the only reason he'd agreed to follow Vincenzo Sartori. Well, that and because Sartori had a voluptuous mistress that was very nice to look at. Sartori met her frequently at different locations and De Falco liked looking at her. In that respect, he didn't much mind doing such a low-level job this time.

Rossini had instructed De Falco to keep tight watch and inform him of every move Sartori made and that Rossini would be waiting behind Due Colombe. If they were lucky, he said, they would be making arrests and moving this investigation forward rapidly.

De Falco followed Sartori's car as he drove away from the mistress's apartment. As he kept his eyes on the car ahead, he imagined having a woman like Angelina Negretti.

☙

She came out of his bedroom hesitantly, the sheet wrapped snuggly around her body. The butterflies, which had hitherto remained in her stomach, were now flapping wildly throughout her body. Her hands and feet were tingling, her heart was racing like a thoroughbred at the end of the Kentucky Derby and her legs felt like jelly. She knew it was just nerves. She tried to slow her breathing, knowing she was close to hyperventilating and that it was causing the tingling in her hands and feet. It was no use. Under that sheet, she was naked and Damiano was looking at her, an appreciative smile on his lips.

"Noreen," he said. "Relax. I am just going to paint your picture." His smile broadened. "I promise."

She tried to relax; it wasn't working. He'd placed some pillows on the couch, along with a sheet that he had draped similarly to the one under the *Venus of Urbino.* Right now, she wished she was as cool and relaxed as Titan's model looked in the painting; she knew she was blushing.

He took her elbow as she clutched the sheets tighter to her and led her to the couch. "You do not have to uncover any more than you wish. Perhaps just a leg. You have very beautiful legs!" Alex told her that all the time and she thought about him for a second.

"This is what I will do. I will turn my back. You may pose any way you want. If you do not want to uncover, then do not. If you do, then uncover however you wish. This is your painting and I want to create it to your liking. Is this agreeable to you?"

She hadn't noticed it because of the butterflies and their mad dancing, but he was in 'artist mode.' It was in his eyes: there was excitement, but not the kind she'd seen before, the kind that told her how much he wanted to make love to her. The butterflies were calming down a little.

"Thank you," she said and he turned his back to her, went to the table of supplies and rummaged underneath, searching through the blank canvases.

When she told him she was ready, he turned around and seeing her, dropped the canvas he'd chosen. It hit the bare floor with a muffled thud, and then fell against his shoe. He had never seen anything so beautiful! She was *Flora,* her auburn hair flowing over her bare shoulders, the light from the lamp on the table casting golden highlights in it. Her face was flawless with just a hint of the pink from her embarrassment. Her right arm was at her side, propped with a pillow; the left gently holding the folds of the sheet at her hip; her perfect skin exposed completely down to her lower abdomen. For the first time he could see what had always been hidden in the original painting: what was under the left hand!

She had the same innocence that drew him to Titan's painting, the same look on her face that told him that no man was worthy to touch her or steal that innocence from her.

He couldn't breathe. He couldn't move. *Flora* lay before him waiting…*his Flora*!

ও

"Any sign of him so far?" Rossini whispered.

De Falco shook his head. They were about twenty feet away from the back entrance of the cafe, well hidden behind a large metal garbage container. This alley was very narrow, only about five feet wide, and anyone driving to this location would have to walk from the street to gain access to the back entrance of the building. The street was only fifteen feet away. They were hidden at the far end where the alley abruptly ended against another building.

An outside security light came on and an older man, probably the owner, exited the back door of Due Colombe, turned, locked the door and walked away from them back toward the street. From out of the dark, Rossini saw Sartori walking toward the back entrance. It was obvious he was nervous: he scanned the area continually as he paced back and forth, waiting for his contact. Rossini and De Falco waited along with him.

☙

"First I make a sketch," he explained, "the preliminary drawing to compose the painting." His hand shook badly as he pressed the pencil to the canvas and started the beginnings of her. His heart was beating fast, too fast, and it added to the instability of his hand. This was the under-drawing though, and if it was not perfect, the oils would cover it. He hoped that by then, he wouldn't be shaking as badly.

He sketched her, always breathless when he'd look up from the canvas to look at her. Her body was perfect, even more so than *Venus of Urbino*, and all he wanted was to touch her to make sure she was real. He wanted to feel the silken texture of her auburn hair as it rested on her shoulders, to feel the warmth radiating from her breasts as he sketched their roundness, to touch the smooth skin of her heavenly stomach. He wanted to run his fingers along her silken leg, to trace it up to where it ended under the sheet.

When he looked up again, she was smiling at him. "I think you're more nervous than I am, Damiano," she remarked and he smiled in return at the acknowledgement. She had seen the 'artist mode' suddenly switch off, replaced with even more desire than she'd ever seen on him before. It fed her excitement until the butterflies overtook her again and she shivered at their fluttering.

"In art school, we had models who would pose for us, but they were not as beautiful as you," he said.

He saw her glow, just as she had when the setting sun had tinted her skin rose pink. He put the pencil down and walked to the couch, sitting on the edge and facing her. He said nothing, the silence between them full of desire and knowing.

Taking her right hand in his left, he felt the skin of her forearm, lost in the sensation of its softness and warmth. His hand continue up her arm as he pictured the anatomy charts he'd studied in his art classes, knowing the names of all the muscles and tendons as his fingers glided over them, but realizing that no artist could create the beauty he was touching now…not even Titan. As his hand continued over her shoulder and down her chest, she shuddered and goose bumps appeared on her skin.

There were still no words between them. They didn't need words. Every longing for intimacy that had never been satisfied was pulling them together, until he pressed himself against her and kissed her until he knew the fire of their love would consume them both if he denied her.

Sartori had arrived only five minutes before the man he was waiting for. The two were talking quietly now, but the sound of their voices was magnified enough by the surrounding walls that Rossini and De Falco could hear most of what was said. They didn't recognize the man. He was overweight and short, and appeared to be well-dressed. Rossini was thankful that the owner had turned on the security light over the back entrance door.

"You have my money?" The unidentified man seemed impatient and agitated. Sartori was wearing a business suit, but no necktie, and patted his left breast pocket.

"I have it right here, Galiazzi. I told you I would give it to you." Rossini could see Sartori smile.

"Good. My people have been after me for their money. The forger too. He is young and new to this game and that makes him dangerous."

"You worry too much. I told you the money for *Flora* would come just as I promised."

The TPC agents saw Galiazzi look around the area, apparently making sure no one was watching. As he glanced down the alley toward the street, Sartori pulled something out of the hip pocket of his suit coat. As soon as Galiazzi turned back, a look of complete terror flashed on his face and a distinct 'click' was heard as Galiazzi dropped suddenly to the ground, blood and brain matter exiting the back of his head.

Instantly and automatically, Rossini and De Falco drew their guns from their shoulder holsters, stood up and aimed at Sartori. "Police! Drop it! Do it now!" Rossini saw the gun drop and Sartori's hands go up over his head. They approached him cautiously, their guns pointed directly at him, but he made no attempt to move. He stood, hands high, his eyes downcast, his body slumped in defeat.

While De Falco handcuffed Sartori, Rossini pulled out his cell phone and dialed TPC headquarters. "Pick up Angelina Negretti and Rico Panello and get the police here with an ambulance…now!" he ordered.

Chapter 38

SHE SAT UP, the sheet wrapped around her as he stood the canvas against the wall. On it were the outlines of the painting that would follow, the curves of her form waiting for the brush strokes that would add the colors, bringing her likeness to life. She would be recreated by him.

She stood up and turned toward the bedroom, but he stopped her, his hands gently holding on to her upper arms. He noticed the bruises and felt the guilt; she had been hurt because of him and now he wouldn't ever leave her side. He cupped her chin in his hand and kissed her as she let go of the sheet and it dropped on the floor between them.

Now she pressed against him, her mouth hungry for his, the heat from her skin setting him on fire. He held her closer as they kissed, feeling the curvature of the small of her back and then the firm roundness of her buttocks.

He heard the imperceptible click of the doorknob and felt a knife of ice cut through his body. In his excitement when they'd arrived, he'd forgotten to lock it! He knew who was on the other side.

Shoving her away, he rushed toward the door to lock it as she instinctively grabbed the sheet off the floor and wrapped it around herself. The door flew open and he stomped in and grabbed Damiano. She'd never seen the intruder before, but knew who he was. It was the strong one who had made the bruises on her arms and now he was holding Damiano exactly as he had held her. Terror had her nailed to the spot where she stood, shaking and suddenly so cold, she could hardly breathe.

"Ah…Travani," Luca Bocchio said as he sauntered into the room. "Have I interrupted something?"

Before Travani could say a word, Bocchio pulled a gun out of his coat pocket and walked toward Noreen pointing the gun at her. "We meet again, Signorina, but this time, you do not wear the beautiful red dress. I liked it very much, but this…" He rubbed the fabric of the sheet between his finger and thumb. "…this will be more convenient, but we will get to that later."

He reached out and ran his left hand over the sheet as she clutched it tighter around her body. Only her shoulders were bare and that's where his hand rested next.

"You have lovely skin, my pet. Has Travani had you tonight? Do you have some left for me too?"

"Take your hands off of her, Bocchio!" Travani screamed, the rage coloring his face dark red. He tried breaking free from the bodyguard, but it was no use. Bruno had at least five inches of height and fifty pounds of muscle over him.

"I do not see that you have signed your name on her," Bocchio replied smugly. He was circling Noreen, looking at her exposed arms and back and running his left hand over the sheet as he walked around her, the gun still pointed at her. "Did I not warn you Signorina, to stay away from Travani? I thought I made myself perfectly clear."

Her mind was racing as she tried to think. She was taught to evaluate the situation, recognize the assets and liabilities and then form a plan. She was trying, but coming up with nothing. The bodyguard was too strong for Damiano. Her purse, with the gun inside, was lying on his bed in the other room where she'd undressed. If she tried to make a run for it, the fat man would surely shoot her or grab her before she reached it and then she knew what he'd do to her. If she made it to the bedroom, he'd take her there. If not, he'd drag her there. Either way, he'd get what he wanted and all she could think about was what Damiano would do to try to prevent that from happening. She knew he wouldn't survive the attempt. The fat man's right hand held both their fates.

She saw the gun come up to her face. "Tie them up, Bruno," he said and when she looked around, she saw the bodyguard remove a roll of tape from his jacket pocket. She knew it was the same tape he'd used on her the night before.

Bocchio circled behind her, his left arm wrapping around her in a choke hold like a piece of wood in a carpenter's vice. She was afraid he was going to choke her to death. Her mind was spinning, still weighing her options and she still had none. "Do not even think of resisting Travani or she will be but a memory to you," he warned, the gun now pressed against her temple.

The body guard taped Damiano's wrists behind his back, then put a piece of tape over his mouth, finishing the job by taping Damiano's ankles together. When he finished, he got the chair by the desk and shoved Damiano backwards into it.

"And now you, my pet," he said. The body guard slapped a piece of tape over her mouth. The force caused her lower lip to hit against her front teeth and she winced.

"My apologies," Bocchio said. "Bruno should not have been so rough with you." Then he smiled and the look on his face made her nauseated. "A time for playing rough is coming soon enough, as you will see."

Bruno tore another length of tape and bound her ankles together. When he grabbed her hands, she tried to pull away, still clutching the sheet tightly to her body. She wouldn't give either of them anything, not even a free look. If the creep wanted anything from her, he was going to have to take it and she didn't plan on making it easy for him.

"Bruno, watch what you are doing!" Bocchio growled angrily. "Do not expose the lady or cause her any embarrassment!" Obeying, the bodyguard carefully bound her wrists together without disturbing the death grip she had on the sheet. "In time, she will let go of the covering. I will see to that," Bocchio added and let go of the strangle hold he had on her.

The bodyguard left her then, as she clutched the sheet tighter to her trembling body. She looked at Damiano and if she was scared for herself, it was minor compared to her dread of what Bocchio or Bruno would do to him. She wanted to yell, to tell Bocchio that he could have her, that she would give herself willingly if he would only leave Damiano alone. But she couldn't yell. She wanted to cry, but she wouldn't let Bocchio see any weakness; she wouldn't give him the satisfaction.

She looked at Damiano and saw him shake his head ever so slightly. He was warning her not to do anything.

"And you, Travani. What shall I do with you?" Bocchio asked, walking to the chair. "Since the lovely lady did not heed my advice, you now owe another three hundred euro. That brings your total to two thousand if I am correct and I always am about such things. Also I am subtracting two days from the five you have left. I have been more than patient with you and feel this is fair. Is it not?"

He grinned at Damiano, who just glared back, his rage out of control. He tried to stand up. Bruno rushed over and slammed him back into the chair, almost tipping him over.

"Travani, calm down," The Teacher soothed. "I have done nothing to hurt you or your lovely lady, have I? I have not even left a mark on you. You are much too excitable. All of this…" he swept his hand around the room, "…is necessary for my protection. That is all. You have a very hot temper and it is my right to protect myself. That is reasonable, is it not?"

Bocchio sauntered back toward Noreen, turned and told the bodyguard, "Do not break anything. He needs to work so that he can repay me." Then he picked Noreen up in his arms, carried her into the bedroom and kicked the door shut with his foot.

ca

Vincenzo Sartori sat in the back of the police car as Rossini waited for the crime scene team and ambulance to arrive. He wouldn't touch Galiazzi's body yet, not until photographs had been taken and the scene swept and deemed free of evidence. The only thing he'd done was to check Galiazzi to make sure he was dead. It was a formality really. There was brain matter seeping from behind his head, mixed into a pool of blood that was now starting to clot. It was a lucky shot. The bullet had left a small hole almost directly between Galiazzi's eyes, but a much larger one in the back of his skull. The guy was killed instantly, but Rossini had to check.

He hadn't questioned Sartori either. There would be time for that at headquarters. He just hoped the police wouldn't get territorial and shut him out of the interview. He was police, but military, and this murder didn't fall under his jurisdiction; this case was local.

Sartori had said nothing; not one word. As De Falco had cuffed him, he'd hung his head and it didn't take a genius to realize that murder was something new for this guy. He looked totally submissive, like a dog that's been whipped by his master until he doesn't even bark any more.

"We found this, Inspector. It was in his coat pocket." He was handed a small notebook, the kind phone numbers were kept in. Rossini opened it. In contained letters and numbers, not many, but obviously information that Galiazzi didn't want known. It was in code: letters for initials and numbers for money. That was Rossini's experienced guess. The manner in which the information was listed told him the book was set up to record accounts that were due and accounts that were to be paid. These kinds of 'codes' were pretty common in the world of crime organizations.

He scanned the few pages there were and saw only three words among the letters and numbers: Allori, Memling and Vecellio. They were all listed in what he was pretty sure was the 'accounts receivable' list.

His heart skipped a beat. He knew these three were Renaissance masters and that all three of the current thefts from the Uffizi now under investigation involved these three artists. The lesser known forgeries were the *Madonna with the Symbols of the Passion of Christ* by Allessandro Allori and *Mater Dolorosa* by Hans Memling. Vecellio had painted *Flora.*

Next to Vecellio's name were the number 2 and the letter 'M.' It could only mean one thing: Galiazzi was indeed the middle-man they had been after and he was going to be paid two million euro for his part in the theft of *Flora.* Well, he wouldn't need the money now, Rossini thought, and he got into his car and headed to the police station.

Chapter 39

HE LAID HER gently on the bed, the sheet still wrapped around her, her hands still firmly clutching it to her chest. He'd put her down on top of her dress, the one she'd worn to dinner, and her bra and panties. As she lay there, she could feel them under her and she could feel her purse beneath the clothes. The hard bulk of her gun was pressing against her upper back and feeling it there so close made her want to cry; there was no way she could get at it without him knowing.

There were still no scenarios for getting out of this and she thought of something one of her instructors at the Academy had said. He taught self-defense and she remembered that she'd asked him what the best option was if an agent was ever in a position where there *were* no good options. His answer was concise and emotionless: "Whatever happens, take it and get over it as quickly as possible." Then he'd added: "If you come out with your life, spend the rest of it being grateful." At the time, she'd agreed with his wisdom. Now she wasn't so convinced. She still knew she was strong and could handle a lot, but not where Damiano was concerned. To lose him would be too much.

Bocchio was removing his coat and she knew what was coming. He sat on the bed next to her, his hand slowly searching the sheet for the edges. 'At least, he left his gun in the coat,' she thought.

"I thought I was very clear about telling you to stay away from Travani," he began softly. He'd found the edges now and was slowing uncovering her legs, his pupils dilating with excitement.

"You are American. I know this and so perhaps you do not understand how things are done in this country." He wasn't looking at her. He was looking at her legs, his hands feeling her skin the way Damiano had. That thought made her eyes fill, but she wouldn't let any tears fall. She wouldn't let him have that power over her.

"I could have you now. It would be delicious! You are very beautiful and it has been a long while for me." He was smiling at her, his hand working slowly up her thigh as he kept his voice low and soft. He unwrapped the tape from her ankles, pulling it off and dropping it on the floor. "You see how easy it would be?"

Her heart was pounding. She couldn't hold the tears back any longer. They were coming so heavy now that everything was blurry. She couldn't focus on anything, not even him, and for that she was thankful. She didn't want to see him or what he was about to do. She shut her eyes tightly and forced herself to be somewhere else, to float away to that landscape with the purple shadows that

Damiano had created. She would see herself there, hidden in the shadows.

"I will be watching you. I have my ways. Stay away from him. I will not tell you again." He pulled the sheet over her legs, got up and grabbing his coat, left the room.

She was so shocked, she couldn't move for several minutes. Her heart was pounding so hard, the bed shook in time with its rhythm. She took a deep breath, trying to ease her nausea.

There was muffled talking coming from the living room, but she couldn't make out what was being said. It was Bocchio; she knew that. His voice was low, just as it had been with her. She thought she heard Damiano, something of a muffled cry of pain several times and that terrified her, but she couldn't go to him…not until they were gone. Bocchio might change his mind and come back for her.

When she heard the entrance door slam shut, she threw her legs over the edge of the bed and then stood, momentarily dizzy, the nausea worse now. She was still clutching the sheet, but now held it with one hand as she bowed her head to her chest and pulled the tape off her mouth. She took a deep breath, the nausea subsiding.

Prying the door open all the way, she was relieved to see Damiano still in the chair and now looking at her. His expression shocked her. Even though she didn't see any bruises or blood on him, she knew the bodyguard had hurt him; pain was etched on his face and he was perspiring.

"Are you all right?" she asked, pulling the tape off his mouth. He nodded.

"Take the tape off my hands," he said.

She knelt down behind the chair. She had to drop the sheet. It was the only way to unwrap his wrists. She heard him moan and then noticed his left hand; his fingers were twisted at odd angles; they had all been dislocated.

Facing him now, she saw his eyes plead with her. She knelt down at his right side and held her wrists out to him. He was able to release her hands and then she removed the tape from around his chest and ankles, freeing him from the chair.

He stood immediately and threw his arms around her as she let herself cry out loud now.

"I am so sorry!" he said over and over again, holding on to her as if she would disappear before his eyes and he would never see her again. "Did he hurt you?" he asked at last.

She willed herself to get control and wiped her tears with her hands, his arms still firmly around her. "I'm okay," she said through the sobs that still racked her body. Bending over, he picked up the sheet and handed it to her.

"We have to get you to the hospital, Damiano," she pleaded as she covered herself.

"No! You do not understand! We cannot do that! We can do nothing about this!"

She couldn't comprehend what he was telling her. Couldn't do anything about being bound and gagged and held at gunpoint? Couldn't do anything about being molested and having his fingers dislocated?

"You're right. I don't understand! He held us at gunpoint! He assaulted me and look what he did to you! And you're telling me we can't go to the police? Someone tortured you and we're supposed to do nothing?" She was angry now; angry at him.

"This is Italy. It is different here. If we go to the police, we could get into even worse trouble. We have our own way of taking care of problems."

"What does that mean…that you're going after Bocchio yourself? Tell me, Damiano! Are you going to pay him back for what he did? Would you put your life in danger without even thinking about how I would feel if anything happened to you?"

He held her again, feeling her body shaking from nerves and fear. "If we pay him, he will leave us alone. That is all he wants…just his money. I will sell some paintings and pay him with the money. Everything will be all right. You will see. He will go back to his business and leave us alone."

She had nothing more to say to him. Maybe that's all they really needed to do. Bocchio hadn't raped her, although he could have very easily. Maybe all he did want was his money.

"I can give you the money. I have enough," she offered.

He smiled. "No, I cannot take it. I will sell my paintings. You will see. Everything will work out. Get dressed now, Noreen. Then you can help me. Please. Do this for me."

He gently pushed her toward the bedroom, still confused, but she did as he told her. She was in shock and it was best to follow his advice for now. There would be time to sort it all out. They were both alive…there would be time.

☙

Rossini was feeling better. The city police weren't bothered that he wanted to be present when Sartori was interviewed and even gave him a chance to ask questions.

Sartori unloaded his conscience and told the complete story. He was blackmailing Panello. Panello had crated the forgery of *Flora* the day before the flight and had hidden it in a false slot constructed in the van's container box. The false slot was unnoticeable. The real painting was loaded and after arriving at the airport, the forgery had been removed from the van and loaded into the plane. On the way back to the Uffizi, he and Panello had dropped Tavolaro at his sister's house and then dropped the real painting at Angelina's apartment. Then they'd driven back to the Uffizi. After his confession, the police let him know that Abdel Kadir was an undercover agent and that the entire affair was a sting operation. When Sartori heard that, he smiled.

As expected, he knew nothing about the person Galiazzi used to procure the canvas and paints or who did the forgery. He took pains to explain that he didn't want the trail to lead back to him, so he kept the contacts from knowing anything more than what was necessary to do their jobs. At one point in the questioning, it finally got through to him that he'd switched a forgery for a forgery and he actually laughed at the absurdity of it all. Rossini joined him.

The only thing going for Rossini now was the notebook found on Galiazzi's body; the initials and numbers in it his only connection to the person who had made the copy of the Titan. The best path to take now was to find out the name of the person who had delivered the canvas and paints to the forger. If that person was as naïve as Sartori, Rossini might have an easy time locating the forger. If not, if it was someone who knew how to cover his tracks, the TPC might never know who the artist was and could only assume he'd do another forgery as some point. They would have another shot at finding him, but the TPC and every gallery in Florence wanted him *this* time.

He smiled as he looked at the two copies of *Flora.* To the untrained eye, they were identical, but he could see the mastery of the one with the tiny cross in the bottom corner. It had life and soul, every bit as much as the original, and that's why he needed to find the forger who had created it.

He stepped into the interrogation room again, this time to listen to Angelina Negretti tell her story.

Chapter 40

"I CAN'T DO THIS, Damiano!" Her hands were cold and shaking. He wouldn't go to the hospital or to a doctor; they would ask too many questions, he said. He kept encouraging her, explaining that it was a simple thing to do.

"I will be all right. You will see," he said. "Just do as I showed you."

She bit her lower lip, not at all as confident as he was, but she knew it had to be done. She held his hand and closed her eyes for a second. Gripping the first finger, she did exactly as he had instructed and heard him cry out sharply as the joint popped back into place.

"I can't do this!" she repeated.

"Yes, you can. Look!" He held his hand up to her. "I heard it pop back into place." The finger looked normal. She was relieved until she realized she would have to inflict the same torture on him three more times before it was all over.

"Do the others. The pain is better as soon as the joint goes back into position." Knowing that helped her get through yanking the last three fingers back into place, although at one point, she thought she might faint. He hadn't told her that each subsequent relocation was more excruciating than the one before it. The pain from the procedure wore him down and it became more difficult to cope with it each time.

When she finished the last finger, perspiration was dripping down his forehead. His hand was sore, but he could move all the joints with much less pain, though they were stiff and swollen now.

She was an emotional wreck and he knew it. Her beautiful face was smeared with mascara. Her dress was wrinkled and her hair tangled wildly. He held her in a firm embrace and kissed her cheek, letting her cry until there was nothing left and she finally quieted down.

He sat with her on the sofa, his arm around her shoulder. "You have to tell me what happened," he said softly.

"I can't, Damiano!" She looked directly at him. His eyes were glassy and wet. She knew what he was thinking, knew it was worse than what Bocchio had actually done to her and so she had to tell him no matter how much she didn't want to relive it.

"He didn't rape me. I thought he was going to, but he didn't. He touched me, that's all. Then he told me that I should stay away from you…the same thing he told me the first time." She sniffed hard. "He just wanted to scare me. I don't think he could have raped me even if he had wanted to."

He held her close. "All of this is my fault, but he will pay for treating you that way."

"No, Damiano! He'll kill you! Promise me you won't do anything! Please!" He kissed her gently; her face was flushed and hot. "Take me back to my hotel. We can't let him see us together any more. He told me he would know if we were together."

"I cannot be away from you! I cannot live wondering if you are all right. You do not know him, Noreen but I saw it; he wants you. He will follow through. It is only a matter of time."

"He doesn't want me! If he did, he would have taken me by now. He's had two chances and he's done nothing. You said he just wants his money."

She was right. To stay with her would be more dangerous than leaving her alone, but he didn't want to take any chances.

"You must go back to America. Get out of Italy. Please do this for me!" he pleaded. He was holding her hands, squeezing them tightly knowing that Bocchio might rape her just out of spite and wondering why he hadn't yet.

"I can't go, Damiano. You say that we can't do anything…go to the police or report this. So what am I supposed to tell the Uffizi administration and Inspector Rossini? And what do I tell my superiors at the FBI when they want to know how my investigation went and why I came back early? I can't leave."

He was quiet for a moment, thinking about his options.

"I will take you back to your hotel, but you must call me every day, several times, and I will call you." It wasn't enough to satisfy him that she would be safe, but he could think of no other way to stay in contact with her. Bocchio could snatch her and take her anywhere at any time and Damiano would never be able to find her.

"Stay in the open, where there are many people," he instructed. "Do not let anyone into your room and do not go out after dark."

"Don't worry. I'll be careful." She smiled at him, trying to reassure him.

"Do you have a weapon?"

"Yes," she answered and then thought about how it hadn't done her any good either time she'd needed it. "It's late, Damiano. I want to go back to the hotel."

He nodded. They left his apartment, both of them with heightened awareness of everything around them, until they arrived at her hotel. He walked her up to her room, but she put her hand on his chest to stop him when he tried to come into the room with her.

"You have to go. I'll be okay now." She looked at him, trying to project as much intensity into her eyes as she could. "Promise me that you won't go after Bocchio."

"I promise," he lied and then kissed her, his mouth pressing firmly against hers, the memory of her beautiful, naked body relaxed and posed on his couch fresh in his mind. "I love you so much, my *Flora*!" he said and then turned and left.

ଓ

She decided not to wait for Rossini's call and was on her way to his office. She thought about telling him what had happed the night before, about Bocchio, Bruno and the assaults, but decided that Damiano was probably right when he told her she didn't understand how things were done in Italy. If he'd been so adamant about not going to the police, there was a good reason and she didn't want to do anything that would put him in danger. She would just have to trust him. Besides, she remembered what Rossini had said about street people not going to the police.

Rossini wasn't alone when he motioned her into his office. He introduced her to Mario De Falco and told her that De Falco was working the case with him.

De Falco looked about in his late twenties with black hair and large dark eyes. He had a neatly trimmed short beard that was as black as his hair. His skin was olive, but very dark and he could have passed for a man of Middle Eastern descent. As soon as she had the thought, Rossini told her that De Falco had posed as Abdel Kadir. She wanted to ask him if he was originally from the Middle East, but let it pass.

De Falco extended his hand to her and shook it warmly. "It is a pleasure to work with the FBI, Signorina. I have nothing but respect for you and your agency," he said and seemed genuine in his compliment, even though she knew he was checking her out.

"Marco is one of our best agents. I assigned him the task of following Sartori." Rossini motioned for her to take a chair and two men sat after she had gotten comfortable.

"How did it go? Was Sartori meeting with the man who helped in the theft?" She was hoping the investigation was far enough along that she could sign off. She wanted to get things worked out with Damiano.

"Yes, it was his contact. His name was Giorgio Galiazzi, an otherwise reputable art dealer with no known crime syndicate association, but unfortunately he is dead. Sartori shot him before we could intervene. We have Sartori in custody."

Noreen sat, too stunned to talk. This was the first time she'd ever worked an art crime case where murder had been part of the scenario. Things *were* different in Italy; different and more dangerous.

Rossini went on. "Our problem now is that Galiazzi is not here to tell us who his contacts were, the people he used to arrange the forgery. It is possible that he did not know the forger, that he had another person who contacted the artist, but it is also possible that he did that himself. For now, we do not know."

"So you have nothing?"

"We have a notebook. He kept his information in code; who his contacts were, how much they were to be paid and how much he was to receive for his part. We are very sure that he also was involved with the two previous thefts. The names of the artists who created the stolen paintings were also in the book."

"How much was he going to receive for *Flora*? Do you know?"

"Two million euro," Rossini said.

Noreen said nothing for a moment, the sum of twenty million euro flashing in her mind like a multi-faceted diamond under a bright light. "Can I see the notebook?" she asked at last.

"It is being examined by our forensics people. I will get you copies of the pages if you would like, but that may take a few days. Would that be acceptable?"

No, it wasn't acceptable, she thought. In all likelihood, he'd already copied the book and could easily make another copy for her. He was doing it again and she knew it. He was withholding information. She was convinced now that Rossini wanted to solve this case himself, that he didn't want some female from an outside agency getting the credit for solving the theft of *Flora.* If she wasn't sure before, his refusal to let her see the notebook clinched her suspicions, but there was nothing she could do but remind herself that it *was* his case after all. After what had happened the night before and now sure of how much she loved Damiano, she wasn't even sure she cared. He could have the credit if he wanted it; she wanted Damiano.

"Yes, if you could. I would like copies." She got up and extended her hand to both of them. She told them good-bye and to De Falco, she added that it had been a pleasure to meet him. She already liked him; *he* didn't seem territorial.

As she left the office and headed out the front of the building, De Falco came up behind her.

"Signorina, please wait," he said. She turned around as he continued. "If it would help, I may be able to get the copies for you by tomorrow or even today."

"That's very kind of you. Thank you." She was grateful, but suspicious. It was the way he was looking at her as though he'd really like to get to know her better.

"You must promise not to tell Inspector Rossini, yes?"

"Yes, of course. But why are you doing this for me?"

"The Inspector is from the old school. He does not believe that women should be police officers. But me? I have no trouble with that. I am more interested in getting the person who forged *Flora.*"

He seemed very sincere; he was relaxed and except for the desire she saw in his eyes, excited about art.

"Do you like the painting?" she asked.

"It is one of my favorites. When I have a day off, I go to the Uffizi and every time I go, I must see her! She would miss me if I did not visit." He smiled.

'Oh yeah,' she thought. 'He's pouring on the charm!' Noreen smiled too and told herself that there was no way she was going to give him the time of day! Not that he wasn't very handsome, which he was. She was in over her head right now with Damiano and what had happened with Alex and the last thing she needed was another man to complicate her life.

"Thank you again," she said, pulling her business card out of her purse. She didn't want him to have her number, but she did want that copy. "This is my cell number. Please call me when you have the copy."

He took the card, nodded and said good-bye.

"Before you leave, Inspector De Falco, may I ask you a personal question?"

"*Sì,* ask whatever you wish."

"What is your ethnic background, if you don't mind my asking?"

"I do not mind at all, Signorina. My father is Italian and my mother is Portuguese. You thought I was from the Middle East, yes?" She nodded. "I have been told that before," he said and smiled.

She smiled back at him. "Thank you again. I hope to hear from you soon."

She walked out into the street and headed back toward the Uffizi. She couldn't decide what more she could do with regard to her job here. The entire theft had been a sting operation from the beginning, Flora was never missing, Galiazzi was dead, Sartori in custody and Rico Panello too for all she knew and now it seemed as though the only investigating left to do was to decode Galiazzi's notebook and then arrest the persons whose names were in it. She hated to admit it, but it might be time to get to work writing her report.

Her immediate supervisor at Art Crimes had given her ten days in Florence and she still had four left; plenty of time to submit her report, visit the Uffizi as a civilian and maybe take in the Palazzo Pitti and the Galleria dell' Academia.

As good as those options sounded, being unable to be with Damiano would take all the pleasure out of doing them. To darken her mood even further, she was still worried he would try to get revenge for what Bocchio had done to her and worried about where he would get the money to pay him. She didn't want to think about Damiano picking pockets or whatever else he might try to get some cash. He told her he was going to sell his paintings, but he only seemed to have three and he'd said the one of his mother was special to him.

She didn't want to think about starting her report. She needed a diversion so she headed to the Uffizi.

Chapter 41

BECAUSE OF THE hours he'd spent working in the middle of the night, the painting was almost finished. It had not been tiring…he loved painting her. His passion for creating her was like a drug, keeping his energy boundless.

He was having a hard time keeping his mind on what he was doing today though, but he needed to get lost in his art for a while. He had some touch-up to do on the background and there was still the matter of adding some highlights, but he was pleased with what he had. She was almost finished. She was beautiful…as always. He put more highlights in the flowers she held.

Looking at his watch, he decided to call Noreen. He'd been worried all morning, trying to be patient for her call, but he hadn't gotten one. He dialed the number and waited, relieved when he heard her voice.

"Are you all right?"

"Yes, Damiano. I'm fine. I'm sorry I didn't call sooner. I had a meeting with the TPC. How are you? How's your hand?"

"Swollen and bruised, but better. I want to see you so much!"

"I know. I feel the same way."

"I am going to sell my paintings. I should make enough to pay Bocchio, and then we can be together."

"Where will you sell them?"

"Where you saw me doing the chalk of *Flora.* I always have good luck there."

For an instant, she wanted to see him so much she thought about meeting him there, but rejected the idea; somehow Bocchio would find out and she knew he would take her for sure.

"Will you call me and let me know if they sold?" she asked.

"Yes and even if they do not sell, I will call you. I love you. Remember that," he said softly.

"I will. I love you too." She heard the phone go dead.

She strolled into the Piazzale degli Uffizi and saw Giulio at his usual place. He was posing with a Japanese woman, her face broad with a smile as her husband held the camera out in front of himself and snapped the shot. He took another and the woman rushed over to look at the preview screen. She smiled broadly, then chattered away in Japanese. Her husband threw some euro into the money box. Giulio had resumed his motionless pose and waited until the euro hit the box before he bowed slowly to the couple, then stood still once again.

"Noreen! I am happy to see you!" he said, coming down from his perch. He looked at his watch. "You know exactly what time I take my break! Tortino's?"

She smiled and nodded. If the truth were told, his breaks seemed to arrive every time she did and not ever at exactly the same time. It pleased her though to know that he enjoyed spending time with her even if it was just to find out how her relationship with Damiano was proceeding. She didn't know what she would say about last night.

On the way to the café, she told him she'd gone out on a dinner date again and that they had both had a good time. Giulio seemed very pleased to hear that. Was she getting those corners smoothed out, he wanted to know? She nodded and decided that if anyone should tell him about Bocchio, Bruno and last night, it should be Damiano. She didn't want to upset Giulio; she just wanted some pleasant conversation and a strong cup of espresso.

As they sat enjoying the espresso and sunshine, Rossini and De Falco walked by. She wasn't going to engage them, but Rossini saw her and the two men approach their table. Rossini seemed amused to see her drinking espresso with Michelangelo, but he said nothing about it.

It was a short hello. They were on their way to inform the curator about what had happened, Rossini told her. He said nothing more, nodded at Giulio and then said 'good-bye.'

"They are police, no?" Giulio asked as he watched them walk away and enter the Uffizi.

"They are police, yes." she replied.

"Something is wrong?" Giulio eyes were boring through her. She didn't need to tell him about Sartori. She was sure the news would be out on the street before Rossini left the gallery. There didn't seem to be any point in going over it with Giulio.

"We're just making some headway in our investigation, that's all."

"No, Noreen. I am talking about you. I see your face. The sunshine is gone from it and a cloud has covered you. Tell me what is wrong. If my son has caused this, you should tell me."

She smiled. "You are a very good man, Giulio, and a good father. It's nothing, really. Damiano has been a perfect gentleman."

It was hard not to tell him the entire story, but the last thing she wanted to do was to tattle on Damiano; she wasn't sure if Giulio knew about Bocchio.

Giulio seemed to relax and finished his coffee. "I must get back to work. Perhaps the three of us can have dinner tonight?"

She was caught off-guard. "I'm sorry. I have a report to work on and it's going to take quite a while," she lied. Well, she thought, it was just a partial lie, but she couldn't tell him that she and Damiano had to remain apart.

He seemed satisfied, gave her 'air kisses' and stood looking at her. "We will have dinner another time then," he said and left.

She was finishing up her espresso, lost in thought, when De Falco approached her. Rossini was nowhere to be seen.

"Signorina, may I sit?" he asked. She nodded and he took the chair, moved it closer to her and then sat down.

"You will excuse me if I tell you that you are a bright flower out here among the drab buildings of Florence!"

'Oh, great,' she thought. 'He's coming on to me.' She smiled, sipped her espresso and didn't say anything.

"I want you to know that I will have those copies for you before the end of the day. May I bring them to your hotel or perhaps you will join me later for dinner?"

He was staring, unwilling to break eye contact with her. She didn't want to say or do anything that would prevent her from getting those copies, but she definitely didn't want to encourage him. She also had no plans to be alone with him.

"I have a big report that is due tonight. My superiors at the FBI are expecting it. I can come by your office tomorrow to pick up the copies."

"A beautiful woman such as yourself should not have to work so hard, not in such a romantic city as Florence. Can you not put the report off…just for tonight?"

'Talk about expressive eyes,' she thought. His were gorgeous and pretty darned expressive. The way he was coming at her, if she shut him down she might not ever get those copies. But what did it matter ? Her promotion was in the garbage now and she was pretty sure her career with the FBI was too. If she still had a job when she got back, she wasn't sure she even wanted it anymore.

"Sorry, I have to work on that report."

He got the idea, got up and said, "I will meet you here at twelve-thirty with the copies. Maybe you will have lunch with me?"

"That would be nice. Thank you." She looked at her watch; it was eleven-thirty.

He was still trying, but as long as she got the copies, she'd let him buy her lunch. Dessert though, would *not* be on the menu!

ଓ

She walked across the Piazza della Signoria, taking her time to admire the statues in the Loggia dei Lanzi, an arched, raised patio of sorts capping the west wing of the Uffizi. It was the perfect venue for displaying some well-known statues, including Giambologna's *Rape of a Sabine* and Cellini's *Perseus and Medusa. Rape of a Sabine* was a powerful work of marble, but its theme wasn't sitting too well with her and so she and headed up the street behind the statue of Cosimo I.

She wouldn't get too close, but she wanted to see if Damiano was there. She wondered if he had paintings other than the three he had shown her. She was pretty sure he wouldn't sell the portrait of his mother; he had seemed very attached to it. Could he get enough to pay Bocchio if the landscape and the *Venus* sold or did he have other paintings that he hadn't shown her?

When she passed a bank, she knew immediately what she would do. If Damiano wouldn't take the money from her, she'd make sure he got it some other way. Taking out her credit card, she handed it to the teller and got the amount in a cash advance, not even caring about the exchange rate.

Keeping an eye out for Bocchio or his bodyguard, she saw him immediately. He had all three paintings displayed on easels and was chalking on the street, drawing the *Madonna della Seggiola,* or *Madonna of the Chair*, by Rafael. She could only see part of what he was doing. A crowd of people were standing around him, intent and excited watching him. What she could see of the drawing was beautiful, but if he only had the three paintings, none of them had sold. She checked her watch: it was twelve-fifteen and she had to go.

De Falco was waiting at the same table, a cup of espresso in front of him, when she got back to the cafe. Getting up as she approached the table, he handed her a sheet of paper, his smile wide and way too eager.

"For you," he said and added, "I have taken the liberty of ordering our lunch."

He might look like a man from the Middle East, but he was all Italian as far as Noreen was concerned: he worked fast and she wasn't referring to the paperwork. She smiled politely, thanked him for the copies and sat down. There would be time later to go over the paper and try to decipher the code, so she stuffed it into her purse without looking at it; she needed to keep her eyes on him! He was moving way too fast and it had her on edge. The last thing she needed was to be accosted by another Italian man.

The lunch was delicious and Mario had behaved himself, though the sparkle in his eyes was disconcerting at best. She'd played him just right though and she knew at this point, he would do just about anything for the chance to see her again. This was not the way she ever operated, but she needed to get the two thousand euro to Damiano somehow and if she had to use Mario De Falco to do it, she would.

"Mario, I wonder if you would do a favor for me," she began.

"For you, anything!"

"Earlier I saw a painting I would like to have. I don't speak Italian at all, so could you purchase it for me?"

It took him less than two seconds to agree and they walked back to where Damiano was still working on the *Madonna*, all three paintings still on the easels. Fortunately, there were even more people on the street now, most of them milling around watching Damiano and she held back, using the crowd as a blind so that he couldn't see her.

She told Mario that she wanted the portrait of the woman and handed him the money.

"This is too much money! I will get a much better price for you!" he gushed, holding her hand and giving most of the money back to her. She noticed he was a bit hesitant to let go of her hand.

"No, don't do that," she insisted, handing the euros back to him. Now it was time for a good lie. "I have looked all over Florence for a particular painting, one that would go perfectly in a place I have picked out for it in my home. That painting of the woman is beautiful and I would like to have it. It is perfect. I love the street artists. They work hard for whatever they earn. I want the artist to have this money. Please give him all of it and say nothing about me…" she instructed and then sweetened the deal…"and I will have dinner with you tonight."

He didn't even hesitate, although his eyes practically popped out of his head when she mentioned dinner. She gave him a come-on look and he turned and shoved his way through the crowd toward Damiano. She saw him take the painting and then hand the money to Damiano, who looked stunned for a long moment, but then smiled. She could tell he was thanking De Falco profusely.

She turned her back, staying behind the crowds so that she was sure that as De Falco walked back to her, Damiano would not see her. She hurried De Falco back toward Tortino's.

"Thank you for doing that," she said, admiring the painting again. "This is so beautiful!"

"You are too generous, Signorina! I could have purchased it for you for much less," he said. "He was asking twelve hundred euro and I know I could have gotten it for a thousand." He was smiling and she knew exactly what he was thinking: she might be 'generous' where he was concerned after their dinner together.

"Shall we meet here? The food is very good," she suggested.

"If that is what you want." His face was positively glowing in expectation. "Will six o'clock be good for you?"

"That's fine."

He gave her very slow kisses to each cheek and she could tell he was enjoying her perfume as he did so. She would have to be very careful with this guy tonight or was that a cold she felt coming on…?

Chapter 42

IT WAS HIM! She had always known it. It had always been at the back of her mind, but she had refused to bring it forward and look at it. She had known the possibility could exist the first time she'd watched him chalking on the street, the first time she'd seen him blend the chalk between Flora's breasts, but she'd dreamed of him making love to her like that and so she'd put the possibility away.

When she'd seen his perfect copy of the *Venus of Urbino*, it had cemented his guilt into her knowing. The flesh tones of her skin were perfect, maybe even better than Titan's. Even though the canvas was new and that affected the overall 'feel' of the painting, his execution of *Venus* was amazing; it had the 'soul' of the original.

He was going to paint her picture; he was going to love her as he applied the paint to the canvas and brought her face and body into being. She would be the woman he made love to, the one he desired and 'spoke' to. They would share the same intimate moment that she saw when he drew *Flora*. He would stroke his fingers between her breasts, recreating her and she would be filled with him.

Now, holding the portrait of Carlotta in her hands, she knew it was him. The same imperfection, his 'signature', was there in the left-hand corner, just as it was on the fake *Flora*: a miniscule cross.

She was utterly empty inside. Her world had just collapsed around her and she was so empty she couldn't even cry. Her promotion was gone and probably her job too. Alex was gone and now she knew that Damiano had taken part in a major art theft and if discovered, he would go to prison and her heart would go with him. There would be nothing left but the crushing pain of his absence and the excruciating emptiness she felt at this moment, magnified hundreds of times.

As she sat on the bed in her hotel room, her only thought was: should she turn him in? The more she considered her options, the more depressed she became.

Her phone was ringing, the muffled chime coming from inside her purse. She knew it was him and answered it on the fifth ring. She didn't have a chance to say 'hello.'

"I have the money! I sold a painting!" She could imagine his beautiful smile, spreading from ear to ear and it took every bit of control she had not to start crying. She had already decided that she wouldn't say anything to him about what she knew until after he'd paid Bocchio.

"I'm so relieved," she said, trying to sound innocent.

"Bocchio is meeting me at my apartment in thirty minutes. Come over now, please! You can hide in the bedroom. I will pay him and then we can be together. I cannot be away from you any longer! Please do this! I need to be with you!"

She needed him too. She needed to feel him close to her, to feel his lips on hers, to fill herself with him before… She ended the thought. She didn't want to consider anything beyond being with him now.

"I'll be right there," she said. She put her phone into her purse and saw her gun. Pulling it out, she checked it. It was loaded and the safety on, just as always. She took the safety off. This time, she would be sure to keep it where she could get at it quickly…at least until Bocchio was paid off and gone for good.

As soon as she came into his living room, he wrapped her in his arms and wouldn't let her go. He kissed her long and hard and she knew then that whatever desire he'd felt in his love affair with Flora was now directed at her and right now, it was all she wanted.

"He will be here soon. You must hide," he said.

He walked with her into the bedroom. "Stay here. When he comes, I will pay him and then it will be all over." He kissed her again and left the room, closing the door behind him.

Laying her purse on the bed, she sat down. The tension was pressing in on her, making the room seem small and confining. How was she going to tell him that she knew he had forged *Flora*? What would he say? Could she even tell him at all?

Then she remembered the copy of the notebook De Falco had given her. She opened her purse, found it and unfolding it, saw the initials D.T. next to the name Vecellio.

She might have been able to lie to herself that somehow Damiano was innocent before this, but not now; she had the proof. Her hands were shaking badly as she searched her purse for some tissues, but she found nothing. She walked into the bathroom and grabbing some toilet paper, wiped her eyes.

She jumped when she heard a door bang open and slam against the wall behind it. Damiano was yelling in Italian. Terrified, she rushed to the bed to get her purse and the gun inside, but it was too late. Bocchio was in the room already, the barrel of his gun pointing at her chest. He grabbed her by the hair and put her in a choke hold again. then dragged her into the living room. Bruno had Damiano in a choke hold too.

"Where is my money, Travani?" Bocchio was snarling.

"In my pocket! All of it is in my pocket!" Damiano was having a hard time getting the words out.

Bocchio nodded at Bruno and the bodyguard stuck his hand into Damiano's front pocket. He pulled out the money and smiled.

Bocchio pressed his nose into Noreen's hair, smelling her. "I know who you are," he said into her ear. "It is too bad that Travani dragged you into this. Your presence has created a situation that must be resolved and I am afraid it will not go well for you or him, but do not be disappointed. Before this is over, I *will* have you." His arm tightened around her neck and she wondered if he was going to strangle her right then.

Damiano was struggling. He was trying to get out of the choke hold, but couldn't break free. Bocchio now had the gun aimed at directly at him.

"The lovely lady complicates our arrangement, Travani," Bocchio went on. "You see, I have people who I must answer to and they will not be pleased to know that she is with the police. Did you know that? Did you know that she is here investigating the theft of the very painting that you forged for Galiazzi? I told you he was dangerous and now see what you have done because you would not listen to me."

He turned his attention back to Noreen. "He should never have involved you in his business, but his mistake will add to my pleasure. He will watch us. Do you not think that is a fitting punishment for what he has done to you?"

She weighed her options; they weren't good, but she had to do something. She knew her time was up and so was Damiano's.

She tightened every muscle in her body and jammed her right elbow into Bocchio's upper body as hard as she could. The gun discharged and fell to the floor as Bocchio lost his hold on her and doubled over in pain, the wind knocked out of him so badly that he was gasping for air. She grabbed the gun off the floor and backed away from him as he coughed, saliva running out of his mouth. He was panting now and she hoped she'd broken all of his ribs. It would serve him right.

She looked at Damiano. Bruno was stunned, standing with a dazed look on his face. She turned the gun on him. He released Damiano, who fell to the floor, and it was then that she saw the blood on Bruno's shirt. Shock covered his face as he pulled it up and saw the bullet hole in his abdomen. Putting his hand over the area, he bolted for the door and was gone. Keeping Bocchio covered now, she backed toward Damiano.

"Are you all right?" she asked him. Bocchio's breathing was worse now and he had dropped to the floor. He was sitting there coughing and trying to take a deep breath, pain etching his repulsive face and his black cloak crumpled, but splayed out behind him like the broken wing of a bat.

"Damiano, answer me!" She glanced behind her when he didn't answer. He was sitting on the floor, leaning against the couch. There was blood on the front of his shirt.

"My phone is there," he said, cocking his head in the direction of the end table. "Give me the gun and the phone and then tie him up." For a moment the shock was so great, she couldn't think. Her hands were shaking so badly she thought she might drop the gun.

"Do it now, Noreen!" he shouted at her. She got the phone and handed it and the gun to him. "Now check his pockets."

Bocchio was holding himself, his arms wrapped around his abdomen. He wasn't breathing well at all, but Noreen didn't care. He could damn well stop breathing and she would be happy and if he didn't, she might take it upon herself to see that he did. Her fear of him was gone now as she checked his coat pockets, bringing out the roll of tape he'd used on her before. While she was searching him, she heard Damiano calling the police.

Bocchio could put up no resistance and she took great pleasure in taping his hands behind his back and then taping his ankles together, tugging the tape as hard as she could. It was so tight that she heard him moan, but she didn't care. She left him covered in his own spittle, still gasping for air, and hurried back to Damiano.

Tears were running down her face now. Damiano was pale, the area of blood on his shirt quickly getting larger. He was holding his left hand over it.

"Let me see," she told him. Pulling up his shirt, she saw that the bullet had entered his upper left abdomen. She put her hand behind him, feeling his back for an exit wound. When she withdrew her hand, it was covered in sticky, warm blood. She pulled the shirt back down. Putting her hand on the wound, she held pressure on it, the blood from the shirt oozing up between her fingers.

He stroked her face with his right hand. "I'm sorry, Flora," he said, his voice weaker now.

"Don't talk. The ambulance will be here soon."

"I have to tell you…" He sucked in a quick breath as his face contorted in pain.

"Shhh…there will be time for talking later; lots of time. Just be quiet now."

"I must tell you…I forged *Flora*…I made her go away. I was going to tell you after I paid Bocchio. I was going to go to the police. Tell Papa…please. Tell him I am sorry."

"*Flora* isn't gone, Damiano. She's safe. You'll see her again," she said. "The ambulance is coming. You'll be okay. I won't leave you, so don't you leave me!"

She wrapped her free arm around his back and held him as close as she could. "Don't you dare leave *Flora*," she whispered.

Epilogue

"THIS JUST CAME for you. UPS delivered it to IA. Guess they thought it was for me."

She smiled at him as he set the package down carefully on her desk, realizing that he was easier to look at today than he ever had been before. The blue dress shirt brought out the color of his eyes and he was wearing the necktie she'd gotten him for Christmas. It was a Giorgio Armani. It was very expensive and very like him: bold and beautiful. "It's from Italy," he added.

"I can see that," she replied, smiling demurely. The box was large, about thirty-five inches square and three inches thick. It was covered with Italian stamps and a customs label. She read it, her eyes getting glassy. Under 'contents' it said 'painting.'

"Is it from him?" Alex asked.

"Yeah, it's from Giulio," she answered. She got into the top drawer of her desk and pulled out a pair of scissors. She opened them and used one blade to cut through the tape that secured the end. Reaching in, she felt foam wrapping, grabbed it and pulled it out. An envelope was taped to the foam. It had her name on it.

"Read it to me," he said.

She cleared her throat, trying to push back the tears while she held the note. She remembered Giulio's expression when he found out what had happened and all she could do was to hold on to him, their grief too profound for words. In the days that followed, the only comfort she could give him was to promise she would come back and visit often. It was the only comfort she had too.

Her hands were shaking as she read:

My dearest Noreen,

I must again give you my sincere thanks for the painting of my Carlotta. As I told you, I did not know that Damiano had made that painting, but when I saw it, I knew that he was going to honor his promise to start working on his art instead of stealing to make his living. I knew this because of the cross in the corner. He put it on all his paintings to remind him about how his mama prayed for him.

In cleaning out his apartment, I found a letter that he had written to her. Yes, she was gone, but writing to her I think, was his way of making a promise to himself and to her memory.

He told her that he would try to become the man she always wanted him to be. He told her that he had met his Flora and that she had asked him why he stole when he could be using the gift that God gave him. I think maybe you were his Flora, no? Maybe you remember saying that to him? You see? I knew when I saw you that you could help him. I knew because it was in your eyes…the compassion and the love.

There were not many paintings when I cleared out his apartment, but I did find this one that I am sending you. I know he meant for you to have it. So I send it to you and tell you that it happened just as my Carlotta had prayed. She did not know those years that she prayed for him, that God would send you to make him into the man she could be proud of. But I know this and so I thank you for that. I thank you for the love you gave him and for caring about him, for being his inspiration and his Flora.

As always, my best regards and love,

Giulio

P.S. And I thank you for your pleasant company at Tortino's each time I took my break. Do not stay away from Florence too long. 'Michelangelo' misses you very much!

He wrapped his arms around her. "Go ahead and let it all out, Baby. It's okay," he said, seeing her eyes full of tears. He kissed her forehead and held her closer, feeling the grief washing over her as she cried.

"I loved him so much," she said, "and I miss him."

It felt good to have Alex's arms around her, to know that he was totally committed to her and loved her. If it hadn't been for him, she didn't know if she could have survived Damiano's death. When she'd returned home, she'd called him and had told him what had happened. He had supported her, had never even hinted at 'I told you so' and had never shown her any hostility about her relationship with Damiano. Even in the midst of the affair, he had only wanted her to be happy, even if that meant she chose to stay in Italy with Damiano for the rest of her life.

She reached for the box of tissues on her desk and pulled one out; she'd been through a lot of boxes the last several months. "I'm okay now, Alex. Thanks."

"Anytime," he replied. "You know I only want to get my hands on you and you're so willing to give me a reason!"

She smiled. His timing was perfect when to came to making her feel better.

"By the way, could you remove your holster when I hug you? I'm getting a bruise on my chest," he teased.

That remark made her laugh. Since she'd come back from Italy ten months ago, she'd taken to wearing her gun in a shoulder holster. He knew about her encounters with the loan shark Bocchio and his bodyguard and so he understood why, even though the chances of her needing it here were very slim.

She wiped the last of the tears and blew her nose. "Thanks for putting up with my crying spells. Rachel keeps telling me it's the normal grieving process, but that doesn't make it go away."

"She's right though, you know. Give yourself time. You loved him and you will always love him, but someday the crying will go away and you'll remember only the good times. Now unwrap that, okay? I'm anxious to see what it is."

She had wanted to keep Damiano's forgery of *Flora,* the one with the cross, but it was considered police evidence and was off-limits. She was told it would eventually be destroyed. She couldn't have the legitimate copy; it belonged to the gallery and was in their collection.

They would hang it when the real *Flora* was out for cleaning or on loan.

The painting he'd started when she'd posed for him would never be finished. It was only a shaky pencil sketch and even someone who knew her would never have been able to identify her as the model. She was happy knowing that considering her state of undress at the time he drew it.

When she left Italy, Sartori, Panello and Angelina were all in jail with charges pending against them. Bocchio too was taken to jail after two days in the hospital with broken ribs and a punctured lung, but was released even though Noreen had filed assault charges. Rossini told her that The Teacher had powerful friends, hinting at organized crime. Bruno had disappeared for a short time, but Rossini had told her that he'd eventually turned up at a hospital with a bullet lodged in his abdomen. The shot that had hit Damiano had gone through and hit Bruno. He was in custody and would be charged too.

The original *Flora* was back in the Titan Room at the Uffizi and 'Michelangelo' was back in the courtyard, doing what he loved to do.

She pulled the foam padding off and gasped. She was holding *Flora* in her hands, but not Titan's *Flora*! It was an exact, flawless copy of the original, but with *her* face and body!

"Wow! *That is beautiful!*" Alex exclaimed, putting his arm around her. "He *was* good! You weren't kidding! Of course, he was working with a gorgeous model and that had to help." He kissed her cheek.

She couldn't say anything. She was looking at a miracle…a piece of canvas and some paint…but at that moment, all the passion that she had so wanted from Damiano, the same passion she'd seen as he'd chalked *Flora* on the street, she now held in her hands.

He loved *Flora* and poured his love for her into this painting. It had the same soul as the one he had copied, the same sensuality and the same great love in it that she had felt from him. She saw again the amazing and wonderful gift that God had given him. As she held it, she saw herself as she had wanted to be: *his Flora*…the woman he had an affair with.

She held it up closer to her face, checking the left bottom corner and saw it: the cross in honor of Carlotta. His mother would have been happy, she thought, knowing that her son had admitted his guilt and had determined to turn his life around.

She wiped just a single tear out of her eye and then placed the painting back into the box. She remembered how he had stroked the chalk as he blended it between Flora's breasts and how he had dropped the canvas when he'd seen her naked. She smiled at that thought.

"You see," Alex said. "The tears will fade with time and the only thing left will be smiles. Come here, Baby."

She kissed him passionately, her arms wrapped around his neck. "Can we go to Florence this summer and visit Giulio?"

"Just tell me when and I'll make reservations."

"I love you, Alex Channing," she said.

"I love you too, Mrs. Channing, but we'd better get back to work. The FBI frowns on fraternization between its employees!"

About the Author

Cheryle Fisher was born in Oakland, California and raised in Spokane, Washington. After high school, she attended nursing school and worked in the medical field. She and her husband Doug, a chef and culinary educator, met in a high school art class and have happily put up with each other for forty-six years. They currently reside in Spokane with their spoiled cat, Marcello. Cheryle believes that every good gift comes from God. THE AFFAIR WITH FLORA is her third published novel.

41576847R00202

Made in the USA
Charleston, SC
01 May 2015